I0761449

The Curious Case of the Poisoned Professor

Also available by Lucy Connelly

THE SCOTTISH ISLES MYSTERIES

Death on a Scottish Train

Death at a Scottish Christmas

Death at a Scottish Wedding

An American in Scotland

THE MERCY McCARTHY MYSTERIES

Death at Inishmore Castle

Death by the Book

An Irish Bookshop Murder

The Curious Case of the Poisoned Professor

A WELSH VILLAGE MYSTERY

Lucy Connelly

NEW YORK

Books should be disposed of and recycled according to local requirements. All paper materials used are FSC compliant.

Published in the United States by Crooked Lane Books, an imprint of The Quick Brown Fox & Company LLC.

Library of Congress Catalog-in-Publication data available upon request.

ISBN (hardcover): 979-8-89242-407-3
ISBN (ebook): 979-8-89242-408-0

Cover design by Olivia Holmes

Printed in the United States.

www.crookedlanebooks.com

Crooked Lane Books
34 West 27th St., 10th Floor
New York, NY 10001

First Edition: February 2026

The authorized representative in the EU for product safety and compliance is eucomply OÜPärnu mnt 139b-14, 11317 Tallinn, Estonia, hello@eucompliancepartner.com, +33757690241

10 9 8 7 6 5 4 3 2 1

Tara Gavin, thank you for everything.

Chapter One

As the train jolted to a halt, I pried open my eyes and was met with a sight that defied my expectations of Wales in early January. A verdant forest enveloped the train station in the university town of Dillynaidd, where my new job was set to commence in less than two weeks. I had deciphered the Welsh translation of the town's name when I'd been here years ago. It meant beauty, and that was still true. I'd also add idyllic, and so very different from the place I'd called home for the last fifteen years.

There wasn't a skyscraper in sight, and most of the buildings here on the main street of town were far older than any in America. Age only added to the lovely charm of the place.

My breath caught in my chest, and it wasn't from the bone-chilling cold. Dillynaidd, where I'd gone to university for undergrad decades ago, was the one place that had always felt like home for my wandering soul. And while I'd been back for visits a few times through the years, this time I planned to stay for good. Or at least the year, depending on how my new job at the university went.

But first, Gwen, you have to get off the train.

And you're going to be a few miles away from your best friend for the first time in decades.

I reminded myself to be grateful even though my near future was a bit scary. This was a big life change, and I'd promised myself to take each day as it came. Otherwise, the world would close in around me and be too overwhelming. The anxiety I'd had as a teen had returned during the last few months. And I had no idea why. I'd spent the early part of my adult life chasing after dangerous news stories. Then this sudden life change had come about and, boom, all those old fears came back.

After exiting the train, I glanced up at the signs and smiled. Everything was in Welsh, which I didn't know very well, even though I'd lived here four years. But I understood enough to know the arrows led to the small station.

It was cold and damp, which seemed at odds with the station's lush greenery. There on the platform was a young man with a sign that read DR. GWEN GRIFFITH. He waved as if he knew who I was.

"Bore da, Dr. Griffith. I'm Ellis, your teaching assistant. We spoke on the phone." He was dressed in a heavy sweater and jeans. His hair and round spectacles made me think of a Black Daniel Radcliffe, the actor from the Harry Potter films. He was adorable and looked like he'd sounded on the phone.

I remembered the Welsh I'd learned years ago. *Bore da* meant good morning. Ellis had contacted me a few days ago, and we'd had a lovely chat. He was enthusiastic about the plans to level up—his words—the journalism department at the university. He'd also been very kind.

"Hi, Ellis. It's nice to meet you in person." He shook my hand and then took my bags from the porter. "I can carry those," I said.

"Oh, it's no bother. We've been looking forward to your arrival," he said enthusiastically. "The whole department is excited to have you join us." He sounded like he meant it. While we'd only spoken on the phone a few times, I respected his great love for journalism. He reminded me of a younger me.

"Thanks. I wasn't expecting to be met at the station."

"Right. The dean wanted to make sure your transition into our town was as easy as possible," he said.

"That's kind of both of you. I'm sorry you had to bother, though. It's very early in the morning." I'd been flying for seventeen hours, first on a plane from Texas to New York, then on another to Heathrow before the last leg to Cardiff. Then I'd taken a three-and-a-half-hour train ride from Cardiff to Aberystwyth, where I'd switched to the locomotive that brought me here to the north coast, and my watch said it was barely seven AM in Wales.

I desperately needed sleep and a shower.

"Aye, I'm an early riser. It's not a bother. The dean wanted to make sure you had a proper welcome. She has planned a party for this evening to introduce you to the department."

I flinched. I wasn't much of a party person, and the dean, Carolyn Montgomery, knew that. We'd been friends since we were in college. She knew better than anyone that small talk was not my forte. That is, unless I was on the hunt for a story. When it was part of the job, I could talk to anyone, and I had when I was a young investigative reporter.

The world of academia was new to me. I'd spent the last ten years running one of the largest newspapers in Texas, and I'd been good at it. But papers were in a cost-cutting phase, and it didn't matter how great someone might be at their job. If another body could do it cheaper, it was a no-brainer for the corporate culture that had taken over free speech.

The last time I'd been anywhere near a university was when I went for my doctorate at Columbia in my twenties. But this was my new world, and I would make it work. I followed Ellis through the station, which wasn't much more than a small cottage, with a ticket window at the end of the big room and several wooden benches.

Outside, his car was a tiny green box, and he had to do a bit of finagling to get my huge bags in the back of it. I'd packed everything I thought I might need until my belongings arrived from across the pond.

While he struggled with the bags, waving me off when I tried to help, I glanced up and down the cobbled street. It was something out of a storybook, one of those fairy-tale ones with villages that didn't look quite real. I was delighted that it appeared nothing had changed. Past the village and down the hill was the sea, with a horizon that never failed to make me breathless. I'd spent a great deal of time on the beach, sometimes wrapped in layers of cozy blankets, watching the waves.

"This is Main Street," Ellis said as I put my seat belt on. "You'll find our town quite walkable. The university is on the hill at the top of the street." Carolyn must not have told him I'd lived here years ago. I didn't bother to share. A refresher about the town was welcome.

The stone buildings were mixed in with painted ones. They reminded me of the medieval towns I'd encountered while traveling across England. The buildings were quaint and beautiful, unlike where I'd lived in Dallas, which had been a sea of high-rises and concrete.

The beauty of the place was beyond that of anywhere I'd lived. It was like something out of a picture postcard or Norman Rockwell painting.

I should have done this years ago.

But I'd been too busy with my career to ever think about quitting it all to teach at a university. It wasn't lost on me that coming back to Wales was a full-circle moment. At least here I would have a say in the future of journalism by preparing students for a new frontier.

"Things happen for a reason," Carolyn had said when I'd told her I'd lost my job in Dallas. As I glanced at the town and the tightness in my chest went away, I agreed with her. This was the perfect time in my life to make big changes, whether I wanted to or not.

Across from the train station was a greengrocer, and next to that was a bookshop painted a deep navy. I wondered if the same gentleman, Mr. Morgan, still owned it. I'd thought him so old back then, but he'd probably been the same age I am now.

I smiled. Funny how that didn't seem so ancient these days.

A brass sign hung over the door: MORGAN'S BOOK NOOK.

At least that hasn't changed. Mr. Morgan was a kind man who always had time to chat about books.

The shops were so quaint, and many had been here when I'd gone to university. I couldn't wait to revisit some of my favorites.

"Everything is so pretty," I said.

"I sometimes forget to look around, as I always have my head in a book or I'm thinking about a story. But it is a fair town."

"Have you done all of your studies here?"

"Yes, and stayed for my graduate studies. It's one of the best schools for journalism and will be even better now that you're here. We're all very excited. By *we*, I mean the students. You're all anyone can talk about."

"Oh, that's kind of you. But you don't have to butter me up, Ellis."

He frowned. "Butter you up?"

I laughed. "Texas phrase I picked up. Compliments aren't necessary."

"Well, it's true. Dr. Montgomery says you're going to bring a realism to the department we've never had before. And that's something we've needed. Very few of the professors on the journalism side have practical experience. They are academics. Nothing wrong with that, mind you."

I smiled. "I get it. But I hope she hasn't built me up too much. From what I've seen, you have a great journalism department. I'm just here to help make it separate from the literature side of things."

"Yes, but I did some researching, and you have more practical experience than all the other professors combined. You were a war correspondent and were there during the riots in Greece."

I laughed.

"What?"

"In my world, those things happened a million years ago when I was a young reporter. But good for you for doing some research about your new boss."

He smiled.

We'd gone only a few blocks when Elis pulled off the side of the road in front of what looked like a French château. The sign above the double doors said *Afon House*.

"This is you," he said.

I glanced down the street to the station and laughed. "I could have walked."

"Aye, but it's raining. The dean didn't want you to get wet on your first day here. There's plenty of time for that. You'll soon get used to our weather." He was out of the back of the car before I could loosen my seat belt.

The weather was the one thing I wasn't looking forward to. I remembered that those lush plants meant lots of rain, and this time of year, that came with a bone-chilling cold. Some areas of Wales had their own microclimate. I'd always been cold when I lived here before. But I would take the frigid weather over the Texas heat any day.

"Let me help you with those," I said.

"No. I have them. Can you catch the door?"

The right side of the huge double doors wasn't locked, and I opened it to find a grand entry with a chandelier and marble floors.

I'm definitely not in Texas anymore. My one-bedroom apartment had a great view of downtown Dallas, but it hadn't been opulent. I'd sold my sofa, chair, television, and bed. The only things being shipped over were clothes, my books, art, and a few antiques I'd picked up on my travels.

On the far right of the entry, a man who reminded me of Santa Claus bustled around an ornate wooden desk. "Dr. Griffith, I'm Paul, the housemaster. We are so happy you are here."

I had no idea what a housemaster was. "Hi, Paul, please call me Gwen."

He looked at Ellis, and they laughed.

"I'm missing out on a joke," I said as I glanced between them.

"Not at all. We are just a wee bit more formal here than you might be used to," Paul said. He handed Ellis a set of keys. "Do you need help with the bags?"

"I've got them," Ellis said.

"You are well in hand with Ellis, but I'm here to help," Paul said. "Anything from grocery delivery and cleaning services to building maintenance. You let me know, and I'll make sure it is handled for you."

"I . . . uh, thanks," I said. I'd been raised by a single mom who was a lawyer and worked all the time to put a roof over our heads. I'd learned to take care of my own needs long ago.

It had been two years since she died, but she would have loved this place. We had been able to travel a great deal during vacations. Mom had wanted to open my eyes to what was going on in the world outside our bubble and believed in experiences over things. She'd been supportive of my going into journalism. She considered it a noble profession, but she'd just made partner when I entered university here, and she'd never been able to come visit.

I missed her. She had been my last surviving family member. I was an orphan, which was why the newspaper had become my family. Unfortunately, the powers that be hadn't been as loyal as I had been.

"This is the faculty house for the journalism and literature department," Ellis said. "Your rooms are on the first floor." He proceeded up the stairs to the left with my bags. I remembered then that the first floor in the UK was usually up some stairs. There didn't seem to be an elevator, but I needed the exercise. I'd been sitting behind a desk for much too long.

At the top of the stairs was a hallway. "Your rooms are here," he said. Then he pulled out the key, which was an old-fashioned brass one with a dragon head. The key was enormous, and I wouldn't be losing that in my bag. I followed him through the door and then stopped.

Even with the grayness outside, the floor-to-ceiling windows let in tons of light. To the left was a tiny kitchen with a marble breakfast bar, which opened to the living area. The furnishings were cozy—an L-shaped couch and leather club chairs around a fireplace in the center of the far wall.

"Would you like these in your bedroom?" Ellis blushed a bit when he said it.

I shook my head. "You can leave them there."

He nodded, then handed me a key ring. "The key to your rooms is the dragon one. The other, gold one with the university crest at the top is for your office. When you're ready to go to the university, you can give me a call." He handed me a thick envelope that he pulled from his jacket pocket. "Right. My number and other contacts are here, as is a map of the town and university. Across the street is the Murder of Crows Pub, which has excellent food and pints. There is also a list of stores and other restaurants, not that we have many. Is there anything I can do for you before I go?"

"No, thank you. I am grateful you came to the station. I'm sure I could have found my way, though. I need you to know I'm no diva. As my assistant, I'll need your help grading papers and keeping attendance. But you don't need to run errands for me."

He laughed. "It's no bother. I wanted the chance to meet you before you were swarmed with well-wishers and questions. Like I said, I read up on you. I've never met a Pulitzer Prize–winning journalist before."

I laughed. "That was years ago when I wasn't much older than you, Ellis. When you were researching, did you happen to notice I'd gone to university here?"

His eyes went wide, and he shook his head. "I thought you went to Columbia," he said. "And here I've been giving you a tour of the town."

I shrugged. "It's all right. I did my undergrad work here. I've been back to visit over the years to see the dean"—she happened to be my best friend, Carolyn—"but it has been a few years. I didn't mind the refresher. Perhaps this could be a teachable moment." I smiled.

"How's that?" he asked curiously.

"When doing research on a subject, always do a deep dive into the past," I said. "Many times you'll be able to make connections to what is going on in the present, and it will give you context for the piece you're working on."

"Brilliant," he said. "I'm already learning from the best."

I chuckled. "I don't know about that, but I do appreciate your help today." I was dead on my feet and very much wanted to find the bed and bath, probably in that order. "Is there anything else you think I should know before you go?"

He seemed to take the hint and stepped toward the door. "You'll find most of our staff are the good sort," he said. "Are you sure there isn't anything I can do? The dean made sure the household staff filled the refrigerator for you. They come by to clean twice a week. All of that is in the information package I just gave you. Again, if you need anything, just text or call my number; it's in those pages."

"I'm good. Thank you again for your help," I said as I closed the door behind him.

Dragging my bags along with me, I went down the hallway off the living area. There was a small study with a desk and bookshelves on every wall except the one with the floor-to-ceiling window that looked out onto Main Street. I fell in love with the cozy space. I had a feeling I'd be spending a great deal of time in there. Everything was painted white, including the desk, making the room feel bigger than it was. Deep-green velvet curtains hung just below the fancy moldings. I'd never lived anywhere with this kind of grandeur.

At the end of the hall was a bedroom decorated in the Georgian style—again, much fancier than anything I was used to, with ornate fixtures on the dark wood. The marble bathroom had a tub, for which I was grateful. I preferred a hot bath to relax. Everything I'd known about Wales, with its cozy homes, was quite different from this apartment. When my art and books arrived, they would fit well in the space.

"This will definitely do," I said as I sat on the edge of the bed and glanced out the window. I hadn't been sure what to expect when Carolyn said they had accommodations for me, but this was much nicer than anything I could have imagined.

It was as if I'd stepped into a different world, not just a new country. But I'd promised myself to give it all a try. Worst case, I could return home and try to find a new job. Not that anyone in journalism was hiring a woman of a certain age.

And I'm that age.

I blew out a breath. No. I needed to make this new world work. I hadn't been ready to retire when it was forced on me, but I had a chance to make a new life for myself here in Wales.

I took a deep breath. "Right, then. I'll take a bath and get some sleep, and when I wake up, I'll be ready to take on this new world."

* * *

I woke up with a start. It took me a minute to remember where I was. I checked my watch; it was two PM. I laughed. I'd been more tired than I thought.

After brushing my teeth and throwing on jeans and a sweater, I heard my stomach grumble. I checked the small fridge. There were eggs and some deli meats. In one of the cabinets, I found a loaf of brown bread. I made an egg sandwich, which I ate while staring at the pub across the street. I'd spent a great deal of time there as an undergrad. I wondered if it had changed much.

I'd have to check it out, as I wasn't much of a cook. And it would be nice to have food so close.

In Texas, if it couldn't be delivered, I didn't eat. Egg sandwiches were about as far as my culinary skills went.

My watch buzzed with a text from Carolyn.

Don't forget. Party at six tonight. I can't wait to see you.

Ugh. While I was excited to see my friend, I wasn't as happy to do so at a party.

Right after her text came, another one dinged on my wrist.

This is Ellis. The dean asked me to pick you up for the party tonight. I'll be there at 5:45.

I started to text back that it wasn't necessary, but I was a coward. At least I wouldn't be going to the party alone if Ellis was there.

* * *

Later that night, as promised, Ellis pulled up in front of the apartment building. I'd steamed my black suit and white blouse enough in the bathroom to remove most of the wrinkles. I paired them with my low-heeled boots, as snow had started falling while I was getting ready. And while it wasn't very party-like, my black puffer coat I'd bought before I left was warm.

"Nos da, Dr. Griffith."

"Nos da," I said.

That was *good evening* in Welsh. It was one of the few phrases I remembered. When perusing the language app before the trip, trying to revive my memory, I'd figured those sayings would at least get me through the next couple of days. Carolyn had promised that everyone at the university spoke English but had reminded me that many older villagers preferred using Welsh.

"Hi, Ellis, you really can call me Gwen. We'll be working together, so there is no reason to be so formal."

He laughed. "I do not think I can," he said. "Like the housemaster says, you'll find that though we are in the north of Wales, things are a bit more formal at the university. But I could call you Professor if you prefer."

He opened the door of the car for me, and I climbed in.

I smiled. "That will work. So, who all will be there tonight?"

"It's a mix of the literature and journalism departments," he said. "Though some of the professors are still on break. They will not be back until a few days before classes begin. So it is a small crew. Most of them are nice, maybe, and I'm not the only one who thinks so, but steer clear of Dr. Rice. She is not as friendly as the rest. I should not have said that, but she's mean."

I laughed. "Oh, no, I appreciate the honesty. What makes her mean?"

"I'm fairly certain she was born that way." He smiled. "She is one of those people who is impossible to please. Everyone who takes her classes understands that they just have to get through them.

"But where you are concerned, I think she was expecting your job as head of the journalism department. At least that was the rumor before the announcement that you'd be taking over as the chair."

"Oh?" That was surprising. From what Carolyn had said, she hadn't had anyone else in mind for the position. In fact, she'd begged me to take it on because there hadn't been anyone else willing.

Had she lied to me to get me here? That wasn't like her.

A few minutes later, Ellis pulled off the main drag into a neighborhood with several grand houses, and then into the circular drive of a beautiful Georgian one.

"Is this Carolyn's house?" When I'd visited before, she'd lived in a town house a few blocks away from Main Street.

She'd become the dean a few years ago, and I'd had no idea it came with this sort of upgrade.

"Aye," he said. "It's the dean's home. It is quite grand."

I followed him to the front door, which swung open as we reached it.

"You're here," Carolyn screeched, and then grabbed me up into a face-smushing hug.

"Hi," I said softly. I wrapped my arms around her and squeezed back. She was the closest person I had to someone who felt like family.

Then she held me out by the shoulders. "How is it you never age? Not an ounce since I saw you last. Did you bring your Dorian Gray picture to store in the attic?"

I laughed. She hadn't changed at all.

"It's good to see you too. And while my face may not show it, I feel my age in my bones, I promise."

"Come in out of the snow. It's always cold here, as you remember. But you'll get used to it. They say it's a mild climate, but what they mean is it's mild for polar bears."

She wore a green dress with long sleeves and a string of pearls around her neck. There was a streak of gray framing her face that only added to her elegance.

"You haven't aged either," I said. "I do like the gray."

"Do you?"

"You would still give Kerry Washington a run for her money!" I laughed.

"You're only saying that because you know she's my favorite actress, but I love you for it. Anyway, I gave up coloring my hair a few years ago. Just too much upkeep. And I think it makes me look more like the dean of college."

"Which you are," I said. "Congratulations, by the way."

"Thank you. I'm still getting used to the workload and this house. It's enormous. Henry keeps getting lost trying to find the kitchen."

Henry was her beloved husband. He was a retired astrophysicist who taught part-time at the university.

"How is he?"

"He's Henry," she said, as if that explained everything. He'd always been kind to me, which I appreciated. From her stories, I'd learned he was the epitome of the absent-minded professor. He would never remember to eat and to teach his classes if she weren't there to tell him. She liked to complain about him, but it was more than obvious she loved him dearly. And he absolutely adored her. I'd always envied their relationship, as I'd never been lucky in that department.

"Come on and meet the crew."

She led us into a room just off the entry that had an enormous fireplace, where a group of about nine people had gathered.

They all turned to stare when we entered.

"Everyone, this is the talented Dr. Gwen Griffiths. Gwen, this is everyone."

Some in the crowd gave me a curious stare, while others waved and smiled.

"Not everyone is back from our winter break, and I thought you might like this first outing to be kept small. I didn't forget you don't like crowds, but I wanted you to have a few friendly faces on campus."

A man near the bar cart turned, and I recognized Henry. "Ah, here she is," he said, crossing the room. He kissed me on the cheek. "You are all this one can talk about these days." He pointed to his wife. "Did you have a good flight? Are you settling in?"

"Pause, luv, so she can answer you," Carolyn said sweetly.

"Quite right. Words tend to tumble from my brain," he said.

"It's good to see you," I said. "And yes, everything is better than I could have imagined. Though I must admit I slept most of the day away. I'll have to explore the town tomorrow."

"You were on planes and trains for a very long time," Henry said. "That is understandable. It's quite a journey to our fair town. Would you like a drink?"

I glanced around. Several people held wineglasses. "Wine is fine," I said.

He went back to the bar cart, and Ellis followed him.

Carolyn led me closer to the group gathered by the fireplace. "This is our main faculty and support services for the journalism department," she said. "Meet your new boss, gang."

Like that wasn't embarrassing, especially given that at least one of these people had wanted the job. Something I would be talking to Carolyn about soon.

She made introductions, and because I'm me, I instantly forgot the names. It was a terrible trait for a reporter, which was why I always had some sort of recorder or notebook when I did interviews.

I nodded and shook hands. Everyone was polite—even Dr. Rice, the one Ellis had warned me about.

Dressed in a black dress with her red hair in a tight bun, she narrowed her eyes when she reached out to shake my hand, and her smile wasn't as friendly as the others'. I preferred making my own judgments about people rather than relying on hearsay, but I had a feeling Ellis hadn't been wrong about the woman.

"Now, this is Gladys." Carolyn put her arm around an older woman and squeezed. "She is the executive administrator of the department and keeps everything running smoothly. We couldn't do anything without her."

"There she goes bragging—just trying to keep on my good side, mind you." The older woman smiled as she took my hand. She wore cat-eye glasses and was dressed head to toe in red, from the giant bow in her white hair to the bright boots on her feet. "We have heard wonderful things about you, Dr. Griffith, and we are excited to have you as head of the department. Quite a feather in our cap."

I didn't miss the sneer on Dr. Rice's face, but it was gone as quickly as it came. I didn't blame her. I'd be upset if some outsider came in and took a job I had my eye on.

Well, it *had* happened to me. The paper had brought in a managing editor half my age at half the price and then asked me politely to retire.

At the time, I was devastated. I'd given the paper my life. I'd never married or had children—my children were the columnists and reporters who worked for me. And then, in one week, all of it was gone. Half the staff and I were out on the street so the paper could survive and live another day.

In the end, all those hours of overtime and stress hadn't mattered to those in charge of the paper's bottom line. It had been a tough lesson for me to learn, though I should have seen it coming. Few papers in America had survived the many layoffs and downward turn in print readership. Everyone's focus was online. I'd thought I'd been good about helping the paper make the transition, but it hadn't been enough.

When Carolyn heard the news, she was on the phone the next day, begging me to come to Wales and set up a more formal journalism curriculum for the university. She'd brought it up every so often over the previous few years, but I'd loved my job too much to ever think about leaving.

I'd sent my résumé out the same week I retired to several newspapers and online publications, and I'd had no takers. My prospects of finding a new position dwindled quickly. The newspaper industry was hurting, and even with everything moving online, there was no place for me.

In a bit of a panic over my future, I said yes to Carolyn. She was my best friend, and she needed help with the department, since the former chair had planned to retire at the end of the fall term. I didn't believe in woo-woo universe stuff, but the opportunity seemed too good to pass up.

It had taken two months to work out the paperwork and sell my apartment, but the days had flown by.

"Are you okay?" the man next to me asked.

What was his name? He was handsome in a sophisticated Pierce Brosnan kind of way. "Dr. Davies, right?"

"I'm surprised you remembered after being introduced to all of us at once." I was surprised as well. But he was extremely handsome. "And please, call me Rhys."

"Rhys. I was in my head for a bit. I wasn't expecting all of this, and it's been a wild twenty-four hours."

He smiled, and I must admit there was a tiny flutter in my chest. I wasn't sure when that had happened before. "You'll soon settle in. Carolyn is quite the administrator. Life at the university has improved greatly since she took over as dean."

Carolyn had always been a force to be reckoned with, and I wasn't surprised she'd used her power to make things better for everyone involved. It was the kind of person she was.

"You have been friends for a long time, right?"

I nodded. "We were undergrads here together." And even though we had never lived near each other after school, we always visited on holidays and stayed in touch. It had been a few years since we'd seen one another. I tended to work through holidays.

A lot of good that did me.

"I was wondering what you thought of our fair town. It is quite a bit smaller than Dallas."

This time I laughed. "That isn't such a bad thing. I only lived a few blocks from work because of the traffic. I won't miss that or the heat. Have you always lived in Wales?"

"I grew up in Cardiff, and I went to boarding school in London and studied at Oxford, so no. But I came back as soon as I could. I love it here in the North."

"I'd forgotten how beautiful it is here. I can't wait to see more and refamiliarize myself with the town and people."

"Well, I'm sure you will settle in soon. I emailed over my curriculum in case you had notes you might want to include before classes begin."

I had an email already. Was that in the paperwork Ellis had given me?

"I'll take a look. I'm sure whatever you're doing is great." What had he said he taught? I racked my brain. Oh. Yes. Ethics and the history of journalism. He didn't look like an ethics professor, more like a guy who taught romantic languages or something.

But what did I know?

My journalistic spidey-sense kicked in, and I turned to find Dr. Rice staring at me again from across the room.

Rhys seemed to notice where I was looking.

"For the most part, we are an easygoing group. We are happy to help you adjust."

"For the most part?"

"Right. It is not for me to say, but steer clear of Dr. Rice. I cannot believe I said that out loud. But you seem a decent sort. She is . . ."

"Different. You aren't the only one who has mentioned her," I whispered.

He chuckled. "*Different* is a good word for her. I'd say her ambitions sometimes get the best of her. You are lucky to have Ellis as your TA. He is the best. I worked with him the last few years."

"Oh no. I've stolen your TA?"

He laughed. "Nothing of the sort. He applied for the job, and Carolyn hired him for you. I gave him a glowing reference."

"That is kind of you."

"He's a good kid. You'll see. He's highly intelligent and well informed. He's excited to learn everything he can from you."

"Well, thank you."

"You are welcome. If you need anything, please let me know. We live in the same building. I'm on your floor at the end of the hall."

"Oh?" I had a handsome new neighbor.

And I'm his boss.

It didn't matter. Even if he had any sort of interest in me, I wasn't one for relationships. I'd had my fair share through the years, but I'd always been married to my work, and that probably wouldn't change.

I'd be more than busy with my new position.

"Most of the single faculty in the department live there, as there is a housing shortage and it takes ages to get permission to build in Dillynaidd. Dr. Rice lives there as well, on the second floor. And everyone else up there is on holiday."

"Let's go to dinner," Carolyn interrupted. She motioned for us to follow her into a formal dining room set up like a five-star restaurant. Several wineglasses were on the table. It was going to be a much longer night than I'd expected.

Ellis was there, pulling out a chair for me. I'd been positioned between him and Rhys, for which I was grateful.

But it was impossible not to feel the harsh stares from across the table. Dr. Rice didn't like me, and I didn't need to speak to her to understand just how much she wanted me gone.

The first course was a tasty vegetable soup, and I hadn't realized how hungry I was. My food and sleep schedules were off.

"So, was it difficult being fired at your age?" Dr. Rice shot across the table. "I mean, word is you have a Pulitzer. Why would they let you go if you were any good? And what makes you think you can be a good professor, let alone the head of the department, without any experience in teaching?"

"Alice," Carolyn hissed. "That is inappropriate, and you know it."

The room went silent.

I dabbed my face with a napkin and then leveled a stare at Dr. Rice. I'd dealt with the Alices of the world my whole life. After being a reporter and then a columnist before I was ever an editor, I'd had to learn how to deal with all kinds of people. Journalism was a cutthroat business, and my skin was tougher than most people's.

"I wasn't fired," I said, and then I smiled. I didn't bother to explain. I took another bite of my soup.

I owed this woman nothing. Yes, maybe she'd expected to fill the position, but Carolyn hadn't chosen her, and the reasons were becoming quite obvious.

"I don't suppose you are a fan of football?" Rhys asked.

I smiled at him as a way of thanking him for changing the subject.

"I wasn't until I watched the reality series about Wrexham. I've become a fan of that team. Though I still don't know much about the game."

He laughed. "Those Yanks did a great job of reviving the team and interest in the game. I have to give it to them."

The daggers continued to fly my way from the other side of the table. I could feel Dr. Rice's eyes on me, but I ignored her. I'd have to find a way to work with her, but that would come with time.

The only way to deal with bullies was to refuse to give them power. And I was a pro at that.

Later, after dinner, Alice Rice cornered me.

"Are you going to make sweeping changes in the department?"

"I don't see why. Is there a particular reason? Do you need help with your classes?" I kept my voice even, but I couldn't keep my eyebrows from rising. It was her tone that rubbed me the wrong way.

"I have a set curriculum that works. I do not plan to make any changes."

"I see. Well, I'd appreciate it if you emailed your class notes to me. I'll take a look and let you know if I feel we need to update anything."

"Are you saying you know more about teaching than I do? I have more than a decade of experience."

Carolyn caught my eye across the room and started to head over. I gave a short shake of my head.

"Teaching, no. Practical experience, perhaps. And make no mistake, Carolyn has given me goals she wants me to meet for the department. I will do everything in my power to make certain we reach those goals. Now, if you'll excuse me."

Her eyes went wide. If she'd been a cartoon character, steam would have come from her ears.

I walked away. Like I said, I'd dealt with my fair share of bullies, and I was no pushover.

* * *

I could barely keep my eyes open when Ellis dropped me off at my building. We'd been the first to leave, but after the food and wine, my body had just given up.

A few inches of snow covered the sidewalk.

"I'm sorry, Professor, about Dr. Rice," he said. "She can be a bit much."

I laughed, and his eyes widened in surprise.

"I'm made of tougher stuff than most," I said. "It comes with the territory of being a journalist for so many years. If you want to be a good reporter, you can't allow other people's opinions to bother you. That's their business. Yours is to get to the heart of the story, whatever that might be."

"I think I have a problem with wanting people to like me."

I chuckled. "It is human nature. But you'll have to thicken that skin if you want to survive in the world of journalism. We have to look at every situation objectively, and we can't worry about if people like us."

"That's great advice," he said.

"All I ask is that you keep an open mind. I think we will work well together, Ellis."

"We will, Professor."

"I'll see you later." I jumped out of the car and headed inside. It was snowing and frigid.

"Noswaith dda, Dr. Griffith." Paul greeted me from the desk.

I stopped, trying to remember what that one meant. Maybe, in context, *good evening.*

"Hi again. Do they give you any time off, or are you a permanent fixture at that desk?"

He laughed. "The night manager will be here soon. We switch out depending on our schedules. Just so you know, the doors to the front are locked at midnight, but you need only hit the buzzer and one of us will let you in."

"Thank you," I said, and then yawned. The combination of wine at dinner mixed with jet lag had me more relaxed than I'd been in ages. "Good night, Paul." I said as I trudged upstairs.

Once I was inside, I flipped on the lights by the front door, then sat down on the comfy couch to take off my boots. I leaned back, and I must have dozed off.

Something banged against my front door. It was so loud it made me jump.

"What was that?"

I glanced at my watch, and it was after eleven.

There was no peephole, so I cracked the door a bit to see who it was.

"Dr. Rice?" What was she doing here? I opened the door wider. The last thing I wanted was a confrontation with the woman. And how rude to go banging on my door so late at night. "Look, whatever this is about, certainly it can wait until morning."

It was important to set boundaries, especially with bullies.

"I have something I need to—" Her eyes rolled back, and she pitched forward simultaneously.

I awkwardly caught her before we both hit the ground. I landed on my bottom with her on top of me. "I . . . uh, Dr. Rice, I need you to move so I can get up."

She was dead weight. I turned her head, and her eyes were wide open but vacant. I lifted my fingers to check her neck, but she had no pulse.

Oh. My. I used all my strength to carefully push her off me.

She wasn't responsive. I kept yelling at her like that might revive her, but nothing worked.

"Dr. Rice? Help!" I yelled. I tried to remember my CPR training from years ago. "Help!" I screamed again. Footsteps came running down the hall, and then Rhys was at the door.

"What's going on?" he asked. He stared down at us with wide eyes. I would have done the same. No one was more surprised than I was by this sudden turn of events.

"Something is wrong with her," I said. "I can't find a pulse. Call an ambulance."

While he made the call, I took my jacket off and put it beneath her head.

"Tell me what I can do to help," Rhys said. He knelt on the other side of her.

I checked for a pulse again, but there wasn't one. "Do you know how to do chest compressions?"

He shook his head. "Show me."

I did. "You keep doing what I showed you; I'm going to try mouth-to-mouth." While he pressed several times above her rib cage, I worked to blow air into her mouth. A minute into it, she still had no pulse. That said, we didn't stop until the emergency staff arrived and took over.

We stood watching as they tried to bring her back to life, but it was too late.

Dr. Rice was dead.

Chapter Two

I had no idea what time it was as I sat across the table from Detective Gareth Jones in my dining room. He wore a cable-knit sweater and jeans and didn't look like any policeman I'd ever seen before. But maybe that was how they dressed here. If I weren't so exhausted, I might have thought he was quite handsome. Annoying, but good looking. I'd been answering his questions for a while, and all I wanted to do was go to bed.

I leaned my chin on my hand. Even though I was upset, I could have fallen asleep on the spot. After everything that had happened in the last few hours, my body had given up and I'd discovered a new level of tired.

"And how long had you known Dr. Rice?" he asked.

"A few hours? I think. What time is it?" I glanced down at my fitness watch, which was dead. I'd forgotten to charge it.

"And when did you first meet?"

"At a party tonight," I said. "My friend Carolyn threw it so I could get to know some of the staff and faculty before the term begins. But I didn't speak much to Dr. Rice."

He cocked his head and stared at me with disbelief. "Then why had she come to your door in the middle of the night?"

I shrugged. "I'm not trying to be a jerk, but your guess is as good as mine. When I opened the door, she said she had something to tell me. Or I assume that's what she meant. Then she fell on top of me, and I started administering CPR. Did I do something wrong?"

"Did you?" he asked. I'd dealt with enough police officers to know when they were asking leading questions. I'd been on the crime beat for years before I ever became an editor.

"I meant with the CPR. I had to take a class at my old job, but it's been a few years. We administered chest compressions, and I tried to blow air into her lungs. Rhys was there helping me." I searched my brain. Had I forgotten a step? I glanced around to see if the other professor was still there, but he wasn't. He'd been sitting on my couch for a long time.

"You said she had something to tell you?"

I nodded. "But then, before she could say anything more, her eyes rolled back in her head, and as I've said many times, she landed on top of me. I'm not sure what else I can tell you."

"You said you were at a party. Did anything happen?"

I put a hand over my mouth to stifle my yawn. "I'm not sure what you mean."

"Did you have an argument?"

I shook my head. "Why would we argue? At dinner she asked about me being fired. I said I wasn't fired. After dinner, she came up to me and asked if I planned on making sweeping changes to the department. I told her I was reviewing everything, and I walked away. I didn't speak to her after that. Well, until she showed up at the door."

"And you have no idea why she was here?"

"No." I sighed. "Rhys said she lives upstairs. Maybe she came by to apologize for being so rude or to carry on the conversation I cut short at dinner. Since she didn't get a chance to explain, there isn't much more I can tell you. Can you tell me what happened? Did she have a heart attack?"

"Why would you ask that?" He cocked his head.

"If someone you didn't know died in your doorway so suddenly, wouldn't you be curious as to how it happened?"

He nodded. "We'll know more once the reports come in. For now, we are treating it as a suspicious death."

He stared at me.

I sighed again. "Do I need a lawyer or barrister, or whatever you have in Wales?" I couldn't remember. It had been years since I'd lived here, and since I'd never been in trouble, I didn't have a clue about the judicial system—aside from the occasional news story about someone's sheep gone missing, which was pretty much the biggest crime that happened in this small university town.

"Only if you've done something wrong," he said. Yes, he was good looking, but also beyond annoying with his insinuations.

"Okay. Well, if that's all, I'd like to go to bed." I started to stand.

"Can't."

I stared wide-eyed at him. "And why not? I've told you everything. I didn't know her, and I have no idea why she was here. It's been a very long day, and I'm tired. I've only been in the country for about twenty-four hours; there's not much more I can do for you."

"Your flat is a possible crime scene. My techs will need a minimum of twenty-four hours to clear it." He waved a hand toward several officers.

I sat back down. "And what am I supposed to do for a place to stay?"

"You're coming with me," Carolyn said as she bustled through the door. "Detective"—she nodded toward him—"I hear you've been harassing our newest professor."

He smirked. "Only trying to find out what happened," he said. "I have questions for you as well."

"Which can wait until a decent hour tomorrow, and with the university's solicitor in attendance. Whatever is happening here is done."

I blinked. My friend had always been a force of nature, especially when making her dreams come true, but I'd never seen her like this.

"I'm going to take one of your female officers, pack a bag for my friend, and you are going to exit until we leave."

He opened his mouth, but she waved a hand at him.

"And please know, at a decent hour today, I will make certain your boss and the mayor are aware of your behavior. This poor woman does not deserve your pesky questions."

"Pesky questions?" he repeated.

"Do we understand one another?" She raised her eyebrows.

He glanced from her to me. Then he nodded and made a quick exit.

"When did you become such a bada—"

She held up a finger. "Let's get out of here. Officer Rene, please come with me to pack a bag for my friend."

The redheaded officer turned toward her. "Yes, ma'am."

I cringed and then held up my hand.

"Is something wrong?" Carolyn asked.

"Well, I never actually unpacked. I just took out what I needed to wear tonight. Unpacking was on my list for tomorrow."

"Well, that will make things easy."

"Uh, ma'am, I'm afraid the cases will have to stay until the techs go over them," the officer said. "But I'm sure we can put together a few things for your friend."

Did they really think I'd killed a woman I didn't know? This was surreal and like some kind of bad dream. My stay in Wales wasn't off to a very good start.

A few minutes later, the officer and Carolyn came back with a paper grocery bag full of my clothes.

"I could have done that," I said.

"Yes, of course," Carolyn said. "But from your pale skin and red-rimmed eyes, I'd say you're in shock. You need a cuppa and a good sleep. Come on, luv."

I stood on wobbly legs. She wasn't wrong; I was a mess. She put the jacket I'd thrown on my couch back around my shoulders.

A black SUV waited for us, and Henry was at the wheel. "I was about to call in the cavalry," he said. "Are you okay? Horrible business."

"I think so. I don't understand what happened. One minute she was banging on my door, the next second she fell on top of me. She's dead. I can't believe she's dead. Like, how did that even happen?"

"Bad business," Henry said. "I'm glad Rhys called us. He said the police were harassing you."

After pulling on my seat belt, I stuck my hands in my pockets. I was so cold my teeth chattered. "Rhys called you?"

"Yes," Carolyn said as she grabbed something out of the back of the SUV. Then she was beside me, tossing a nice wool blanket around me. "You shouldn't have been speaking to the police without a solicitor."

"I don't have anything to be guilty about. I was just trying to help out." My teeth chattered again.

"Maybe we should take her to A&E," Carolyn said. "She's definitely in shock."

"No. Please. No hospitals." I had never been a fan. "Tea and bed sound really good."

She sucked air through her teeth. "Okay, but if you aren't feeling better later, we're going to call our doctor."

"Thanks. Was she ill? Do you know if she had anything wrong with her?"

"Not as far as I know," Caroyln said. "She's always been a bit cold, and if she wasn't tenured probably would have been tossed out years ago. Her students hated her. But there was nothing I could do about it."

"She was jealous you gave me the job."

My friend pursed her lips. "I couldn't, in good conscious, give her any more power. She would have made everyone miserable. And she was old-school in her teaching methods. She hasn't worked in the real world for more than twenty years. There was no question you were much better suited for the job."

"So you gave the job to someone with no teaching experience."

"That isn't true. Look at all the cub reporters you brought up through the ranks over the years. I read the stories. I've always followed your career. Everyone you've worked with always thanks you for believing in them. That was the kind of leader and instructor I wanted."

She put her arms around me and squeezed. "I'm so sorry for all this bother. And before you ask, I have no idea what she was doing at your door so late at night. I did say a few words to her after what she said at dinner. Maybe she'd come to apologize. After all, you were her new boss."

Snow hit the windshield. It blurred the scenery before the wipers slashed across the windows.

"I tried to do CPR."

"Of course you did. I talked to one of the officers when I came in; they said you were quite heroic."

I frowned. "You seem to know the police force fairly well."

She smiled. "As you well know, university students aren't always perfect. It's my job to smooth things over. So I'm familiar with everyone we need to deal with at the station. Also, more than a few of the officers went to university here."

"I don't understand why the detective was so suspicious. I kept telling him I'd barely met Dr. Rice, but he didn't seem to believe me."

She smiled. "He's a good detective, and thorough. But he's a stickler for going by the book. We've had a few run-ins with him, but he is a fair man. You don't need to worry."

"It's like when you're driving and there's a police car following you and even though you did nothing wrong, you still feel guilty."

She and Henry laughed.

"I'm so sorry about all of this," she said. "This is not how I wanted your time with us to begin. It's all so stressful. Alice wasn't the kindest human being, but it's still sad she is gone. And so sudden."

"Do you think someone did try to hurt her? I mean, like you said, she didn't have many friends."

She wrapped the blanket tighter around me. "We'll have to see what the autopsy says. From the suddenness of it all, it sounds like she had a heart attack. I feel guilty in a way, because perhaps my decisions led to her stress. That said, I wouldn't have changed my mind. I did what was best for the department."

"Whatever happened, it is not your fault," Henry said from the driver's seat. "And do not forget she made your life difficult as well."

"She did?" I asked.

Carolyn nodded. "Always second-guessing and questioning. More than once she's gone over my head to the president of the university. Luckily, Marge is a dear friend and always has my back. She was the one who brought me on as dean.

"Back then, Alice felt like she'd been looked over again. She could never seem to take responsibility for her attitude and behavior. She liked to blame others. And I shouldn't be speaking ill of the dead. But I just want it to be clear to you that no matter what happened tonight, none of it was your fault."

We pulled up in front of their huge mansion. "It's hard to imagine you here," I said. "I mean, well deserved, but it's a far cry from our one-bedroom dorm with bunk beds during university."

She and Henry laughed. "We've lived here for two years, and I still sometimes get lost," he said.

"It is rather grand for the likes of us but came with the job," Caroyln said. "It does come in handy for the events we have to throw all year long. And we're both so busy; having a staff at the house is a wonderful bonus. I never have liked housework."

"I don't blame you. It's not my favorite either."

"Well, luckily, your flat comes with cleaners as well."

They ushered me inside and showed me to a room on the second floor. Henry insisted on carrying the grocery bag full of my things and set it on the end of the bed.

"Thank you," I said.

"Not at all," he said. "We'll leave you to it. Get some rest. It's the best thing for a shock like you've had."

"Thanks for coming to get me," I said.

"Never a question about that." He left.

"I packed pajamas for you," Carolyn said. "You get settled in, and I'll get us a cuppa."

"You don't have to do that. I can come down to the kitchen."

"No, no. You settle in, and I'll be back in a few minutes. Oh, first, let me do this." She picked up a small remote from the fireplace mantel and clicked it. A fire roared to life, and I was drawn to it. Even though it was electric, it gave off warmth.

She gave me a quick hug and then left.

The room was decorated in various shades of green silks, and a velvety bedspread covered the mattress of the king-size four-poster. The walls were toile and had pictures of dogs running through gardens. It was a sweet room, and elegant at the same time.

I shivered as I stripped off my clothes and put on the flannel pajamas Carolyn had packed for me. Then I found my furry slippers in the shape of bears and put them on. I sat on the wing-backed chair nearest the fireplace. The events of my day spun through my head like an out-of-control roller coaster, and I couldn't shake the cold in my bones.

So much had happened in the last twenty-four hours, and I couldn't quite wrap my mind around it. I sat back in the chair and closed my eyes.

I'd watched a woman die. Then the police had tried to act like it was my fault. Maybe it was all a sign. One that screamed *You shouldn't have come here.*

But I refused to give in to those feelings. Yes, it had been crazy, but things happened.

That and my reporter brain couldn't quite let go of the facts as I knew them. A woman who wasn't liked by very many had died in my arms.

The question was, had someone killed her, or had it been natural causes?

I discovered that I needed to know the truth for my own sanity.

Chapter Three

I woke up late the next day and made my way down to the kitchen, following the scent of coffee. I found Carolyn and Henry at the breakfast bar, eating, in the enormous navy-and-brass kitchen. Like the rest of the house, it was something out of a magazine. I had a hard time reconciling the fact that my used-to-be-bohemian friend lived in a place like this.

"Good morning," I said, and my voice squeaked a bit.

"How are you feeling," Carolyn asked.

"Much better, but still like last night was some weird nightmare. Have you heard anything?"

She shook her head. "Let me get you some breakfast."

I waved her away. "Just point me toward the coffee; I can figure it out for myself. Finish eating."

She pointed to the coffee bar, which blissfully had an espresso machine. It was like the one I'd had in my apartment back home, so I soon had a steaming cup. That first sip was always so welcome. It was as if my brain joined the rest of me and woke up.

Carolyn moved around the kitchen behind me. When I turned, she handed me a plate full of eggs and sausages. "Eat," she said. She had that look I remembered, and there would be no arguing with her.

I'd just sat down when her cell rang. She frowned but answered.

"Yes," she said. "I'll let her know. Thank you."

She turned toward me. "That was the detective. Your apartment has been cleared. But I think you should stay with us for a while. I don't like that you've had such a rough beginning, and I don't want you to be scared off."

I put a hand on her shoulder. "Carolyn, I'm a seasoned journalist who has covered everything from wars to dog shows; this isn't going to scare me away. It's strange, I'll grant you that. And absolutely not something I will soon forget, but it hasn't scared me away. I'm much more frightened about facing your students in class."

She smiled. "You needn't worry about the latter. When we made the announcement at the end of last term, you created quite the buzz. The students—and staff—are excited to have you."

"Except for Dr. Rice," I said. "I wonder if the detective still thinks I had something to do with her death."

She rolled her eyes. "Of course you didn't. It is tragic what happened, but I'm betting it was a heart attack. She was always high-strung and put undue stress on herself and others."

"Do you know why she showed up on my doorstep last night? She said she had something to tell me before she passed out."

"I'm certain it was to cause trouble," Henry said.

"Darling, you shouldn't speak ill of the dead."

"Well, she caused you so much angst over the years. While I wouldn't wish death on anyone, I'm glad you no longer have to deal with that thorn in your side."

"Henry. Really."

He shrugged. He'd always been one to speak his mind, and that hadn't changed.

"Since my place is clear, could I ask for a ride back to my apartment? I'd like to get unpacked today."

"Are you sure you don't want to stay with us a bit longer? I can even find you another place to live if you think it might be too disturbing."

"No, I'll be fine," I said. At least I hoped I would.

"I can drive you," Henry said. "I need to do some errands in town."

Carolyn smiled. "By errands, he means a run to the bookstore. It's his favorite place outside his study."

He grinned. "She isn't wrong. But this time I'm going to check to see if the order for the new textbooks came in for the class I'm teaching."

"Oh? And what's that?" I asked.

"Well, the title is a bit on the nose, but it is *A History of Astrophysics*."

"That sounds like something I might be interested in reading as well," I said.

"For the last twenty years, I've been focused on teaching the latest changes in the field, but now that my friend Gilbert retired, I'm taking over some of his classes." He sounded as excited as Henry could be. He picked up his plate and then rinsed it off before putting it in the dishwasher. "I like the idea of giving context to the work."

I stood. "I don't want to make you wait."

Carolyn laughed. "Finish your meal. He'll do twenty more things before he's ready to leave and then forget that he was going to the bookstore. I'll remind him in a bit." Then she added, "But I need you to tell me you're really okay. I was so worried about you last night."

"I promise I am. Is it strange what happened? Yes. Am I still a bit weirded out by the situation? Who wouldn't be? But I'm fine. And yes, before you ask, I'm still excited that I came. Though I wasn't lying about facing the students for the first time."

"Well, if it helps, you can do some practice before the term begins. I've looked over the notes you sent me, and the curriculum is dead-on. It's exactly the kind of fresh take I've been wanting for our students."

"Oh, that reminds me. Am I the one who approves the other professors' curriculum? A few of them mentioned it last night."

"Yes. I want to avoid any sort of duplication in the classes, and again, I want a new take on what's happening in the world of journalism. At the same time, I'd like some of those old-fashioned ideas, like ethics, to be a big part of what we do here."

I nodded. "I couldn't agree more."

* * *

An hour later, Henry dropped me off in front of my building.

"Let us know if you need anything or if it's too strange to stay in your flat. You are always welcome at ours," he said.

"Thanks." I grabbed my bag of clothes and headed inside.

"Morning, Professor," Paul said. "Nasty business last night. Are you feeling okay today?"

"I am." I glanced up the stairs.

"Would you like me to go up with you? I'm sure it was a fright with everything that happened."

As a cub reporter, I'd dealt with death and murder cases all the time. Not that this was murder; Dr. Rice might have died from natural causes. But I'd never been actively involved in a case. And certainly no one had ever died in my home.

Well, it was barely home. I'd been in town only a short time.

"I'll be fine," I said. "But thank you for the offer."

I took the stairs slowly and half expected to see crime scene tape on my door when I arrived on the first floor. But there wasn't any.

I pulled the funny key from my pocket and unlocked the door. Everything appeared as it had the day before. There was no fingerprint dust or any of the things I'd expected. It appeared as though someone had cleaned quite thoroughly after the police left.

I put my clothes away and finally unpacked, the mundane activity giving my brain a chance to catch up. I wasn't sure if it was shock or jet lag, but I felt foggy and as if I were in some sort of surreal dream—or nightmare.

This was not at all how I'd expected to begin my life here in Dillynaidd. My mind whirled with the events from the night before, and I had to take some deep breaths and focus on the task at hand.

The police had a handle on things, and I had to trust they would figure out what had happened to the poor professor.

When I'd finished unpacking, my stomach grumbled. I glanced out the window at the pub across the street. Maybe what I needed was a good meal and some strong coffee.

After throwing on my jacket, I headed over.

It was a bit early for lunch, and there weren't many customers inside the Murder of Crows Pub. Inside, the stone walls and dark-green decor made me think more of a hunting lodge than a pub. There were cozy booths and tables strewn about, and the bar had several stools. Not much had changed since I'd been here years ago.

While there weren't many people, the ones who were here turned and stared at me. There was no one behind the bar, but I sat down just the same.

A woman came out, and it took me a moment to realize I recognized her. "Catrin, is that you?" I asked. She had brown hair up in a bun, but I'd remember those piercing blue eyes anywhere.

She cocked her head. "It's me," she said. "And you would be?"

"I'm Gwen Griffith," I said. "I lived here years ago when I was going to the university."

She made a face. "Gwennie? Is that really you? Where have you been? I read about you coming back in the paper, but you don't look like the picture. I didn't realize it was you."

I laughed as she peppered me with questions. "I've been all over the world, most recently Texas working as an executive editor at a newspaper," I said. "I can't explain the picture. It may have been an old one used for press releases. And now I'm here to teach and run the journalism department."

She tapped the side of her forehead with her finger. "You always were a smart one, but so kind. I remember."

"How have you been?" I asked.

"Do you remember Arnall, who used to tend the bar?"

Vaguely. I nodded.

"We married years ago and bought the pub from his da. We've been running the place for the last fifteen years or so."

"It looks the same and is still so cozy. I always loved it here."

"Well, thank you. What can I get you?"

"Do you still have coffee that would wake the dead?"

She laughed. They were known for it, as many university students came here for a fix.

"We do. Though most of the students head to the new coffee shop down the way."

"Nothing could ever work as well as yours for waking up my brain," I said. "And I'm so hungry. Whatever you have available would be great."

"Welsh breakfast coming up."

I hadn't touched the one Carolyn had made me. I'd just moved my eggs around on my plate.

I struggled to remember what a Welsh breakfast entailed, but my stomach growled again. Whatever she brought out, I'd eat it.

A few minutes later she came out with a platter of eggs, laverbread, seaweed puree, tomatoes, baked beans, cockles, and sausage. I'd forgotten about the cockles at breakfast. They tasted a bit like scallops but were milder.

"Did you hear about the trouble across the street? Bad business," she said.

The pub had always been a hub for gossip even all those years ago.

"Oh?" I acted surprised. No way I'd share that it happened at my place.

"One of the professors from the university, she wasn't so well liked around here. I wouldn't be surprised if someone killed her. Though from what I hear, it was some sort of allergic reaction."

That was a surprise to me.

She waved a hand. "Listen to me, speaking ill of the dead."

"I heard she wasn't the nicest person." I didn't mention I'd experienced that firsthand. I was curious about her reputation in the town.

"You heard right. Again, I shouldn't say. But when you are so mean to everyone around you, it's bound to come back on you. Makes you believe in karma, right?"

I nodded. "Was there anyone that might have wanted to, um, hurt her?"

"Ha," she said loudly. "Sorry again. She was one of those who never had a kind word for anyone. She kept insulting our regulars, and Arnall tried to bar her from the pub at one point. She sicced a barrister on him. A piece of work, that one."

She sounded like it.

"Did she have an argument with anyone in particular?"

Catrin stared at me with a strange look on her face.

"It's not about gossip," I said, covering. "It's more my reporter's brain being curious about her. I was going to be her boss, and for some reason I feel responsible in a way."

"Oh, luv, you don't need to worry about that. No one would blame you if you did kill her."

They might if they found out she'd died at the door of my home.

"But to answer your question, it would be easier to say who she hasn't offended. Like I said, she was a piece of work, that one. No one liked her, and that is not an exaggeration."

Someone came in behind me and sat at a table. Catrin walked over to the table and took their order.

Interesting news about Dr. Rice. It seemed she had made many enemies.

I only hoped the gossip train didn't find out exactly where she'd died. I would never hear the end of it. I remembered how it was in this small town. Most people were kind and extremely friendly, but they were also cautious when it came to outsiders.

And I was definitely that.

* * *

I was so full when I left the pub that I decided to head down to the bookstore. I passed the bakery and coffee shop Catrin had mentioned. I was partial to straight black coffee. I'd probably be sticking with the pub's version, but I did notice there was a small crowd inside.

The bakery gave off a heavenly smell. If I hadn't just eaten my weight in food, I might have been tempted to go inside.

A light mist fell, and I pulled my hood up on my jacket. When I'd lived here years ago, I'd never minded the gloomy weather. I found it conducive for staying inside by a fire and studying.

After dealing with the Texas heat for so many years, I welcomed these cooler temps, even if it was consistently damp.

My phone buzzed in my pocket.

It was a text from Ellis. *When would you like to go to the university?* he asked.

I typed back *Around one this afternoon.* That would give me time to peruse the bookstore and finish settling in at home.

He sent a thumbs-up emoji.

I smiled.

When I opened the bookstore door, a bell tinkled above. I glanced up. It was the same brass bell that had been there when I'd been a student years ago. No one was behind the counter.

"Bore da." A female voice came from the back of the store.

"Good morning," I said.

"Ah, a Yank. I'll be with you in a bit. Feel free to browse."

I smiled. The store was two floors tall. If it was set up the same way as when I'd lived here, the textbooks for the university would be upstairs. Fiction and nonfiction would be on the first floor.

I'd come in to see if I could find a few novels to read at night while I waited for my library of books to be delivered, and I wanted to see if the journalism texts I'd ordered for my classes had arrived. While they also came in e-book form to save trees, I preferred paper textbooks. They were easier to highlight and annotate.

I was looking for some Welsh authors, and I did a quick search on my phone.

I'd found the first one, *The Matter of Wales: Epic Views of a Small Country*, by Jan Morris, when the woman from the back came down the aisle where I'd been standing.

"Oh, it's you," she said. She wore a jade sweater with jeans and boots. "Welcome."

I glanced behind me to see if someone else was standing there. I didn't know her. "Hi," I said. "Have we met before?"

She smiled. "Oh. No. They had your picture in the paper. I've been looking forward to meeting you." She stuck out her hand. "I'm Rhian Morgan."

"I'm Gwen Griffith. It's nice to meet you." I shook her hand. I was curious about what kind of story the paper had run about me, but it seemed egotistical to ask. "I've always loved this store. Is Mr. Morgan still the owner? I loved talking about books with him when I was studying at the university."

"He was my granddad. He passed a few years ago and left this beauty to me." She waved a hand around. "I spent most of my summers here and have been helping out since I was a kid. I can't imagine doing anything else."

"I'm so very sorry for your loss."

"Thank you. He was one of the good ones. I miss him every day."

I nodded. "He was so kind and intelligent. He used to let me study in the small loft behind the shelves on the second floor."

She smiled. "I spent a great deal of time there as well when I visited. I've turned it into a reading nook for kids."

"I love that. This place has always been magical to me. While I didn't have a lot of extra reading time when I was at uni, your granddad always suggested something that I couldn't put down."

"I see you are studying our wee country." She pointed to the book in my hand.

"Just trying to reacquaint myself," I said. "If you have other suggestions, I'd love to hear about them."

She took me around the store, and we chatted about how the town had barely changed since I'd been here twenty years ago.

"I can probably get the list at my office when I go in, but would you by chance have ordered the textbooks for Dr. Rice's classes?"

"Oh, now, that was a bad business. I wonder if she died of natural causes or meanness."

I raised my eyebrows.

She threw a hand over her mouth. "I can't believe I said that out loud. You must think me terrible."

I shook my head. "I've heard the rumors. I only met her once, but I can see why you might say something like that. So, did you know her well?"

She shrugged. "I have to admit she was a good customer. Most of the professors use digital textbooks, which they order through us. But she always preferred paper."

Dr. Rice and I had that in common. While I used both forms to read, I preferred the smell and feel of paper copies. That said, I offered my students a choice, as the digital formats were slightly cheaper.

"Was she as rude to you as she was everyone else? I mean, at least from the stories I've heard."

"Not so much rude as cold," she said. "Grandpa used to say she was a cold fish. And he never spoke ill of anyone. Do you think she was murdered? That's the rumor."

"I barely knew her," I said. "I don't have any idea." At least that much was true.

"Will you be taking over her classes?"

I blew out a breath. "I haven't sorted that yet. I would imagine the other professors and I will have to divide them up. I'm heading into my office later on today for the first time."

I didn't want to admit that I hadn't really looked at anything work related. I had a lot of catching up to do when it came to my new position at the university. The last few weeks had been crazy with packing, shipping, and saying goodbye to my old life.

"I'm curious," I said.

"About?"

"Did Dr. Rice ever come to the bookstore with anyone else? I wondered if she had family," I said. "I want to send my condolences." That last part was true, but I was also curious about her. She lived in my building and didn't seem to have a spouse, but I didn't know for sure.

My reporter brain needed facts in order to make sense of the situation.

"Not that I know of," she said. "She seemed lonely. I once asked if she wanted to join one of our book clubs. She gave me a wicked look I will never forget. Speaking of which, we have a new book club starting on Saturdays. It is for singles, and I would love for you to come. It will be a fun way for you to meet people in town. At least think about it." She put a flyer into my paper shopping bag with the books I'd bought.

I smiled. "Thank you," I said.

"You know, for all her faults, I always thought it was interesting the kind of books she bought."

"What do you mean?"

"She purchased a great deal of romance, fantasy, and the occult. She just never seemed the type to me for any of those." Rhian laughed.

"What's funny?"

"My grandfather would use that old cliché about not judging a book by its cover or by what a person reads."

That was interesting. Was Dr. Rice a secret romantic who liked the occult?

Was she in a relationship?

I had so many questions, and I needed answers.

Chapter Four

Promptly at one in the afternoon, Ellis waited for me outside my apartment—or flat, as they called them here.

"Afternoon, Professor," he said as he opened the car door. "How are you? I'm so sorry about the troubles."

I smiled. "Hi, Ellis, it was . . . a crazy night. I'm sure there are all sorts of rumors among the staff. Have you heard anything?"

"Uh . . ."

"You can tell me."

He pulled out onto the road. "I'm a reporter. I deal with facts, but yes, Professor, there are rumors."

"Tell me," I said.

"Everyone says she died in your flat, and that you killed her."

I half laughed, half coughed. "Wait. What?"

"Don't feel bad about it. Most of them think you did us all a favor."

"Wow. I knew she wasn't well liked, but that's just wrong."

He grinned. "You have no idea what she put everyone through."

"I'm starting to get an idea," I said. "How about you? What were your thoughts about Dr. Rice?"

"I had to take her classes. We all do. She is one of those professors you try to survive. She makes life harder. I've never understood that. When my gran passed, I had to miss a test. She wouldn't allow me to take it at a later date. I went over her head to the dean, and she forced Dr. Rice to let me do it. But she made my life hell after that."

I blew out a breath. "I don't understand people like Dr. Rice. Especially when it comes to teaching. I was tough on my reporters because the news business is fast paced and brutal. But in a supportive way." At least I'd hoped so. "But I was never intentionally cruel or mean."

"She was both," he said. "Luckily, she was the only one in the department. Everyone did their best to avoid her."

"It's an odd question to ask, but do you know if she had a romantic partner? Did you ever see her with anyone?" I was curious about her love of romance.

He laughed. And then his eyes went wide. "Sorry. No, Professor. I never saw her with anyone. She seemed to have a crush on Dr. Davies, but he avoided her like the rest of us."

My neighbor? Rhys? That was interesting. He lived just down the hall. If something was wrong, why had she come to me? It would have made more sense for her to go to someone she knew, like Rhys.

Because there was something she wanted me to know. Unfortunately, she'd never had a chance to tell me what that was.

"What else can you tell me about her? Other than no one liked her?"

He blew out a breath. "I'm afraid not much. Like I said, most of us avoided her. She had tenure, so we thought that was why the former chairman put up with her. I sometimes pulled reports at the end of the semester for him. He insisted on doing surveys with the students about the professors."

"That's actually a great way of keeping track of how the faculty is being received," I said. I'd be doing the same. I'd done that with my staff rather than the standard employee reports.

"She always had the lowest marks out of all the professors. But he kept her on. I sometimes wondered if she had some sort of blackmail hanging over him."

"Ellis?"

He seemed to realize what he'd said. "Sorry. I shouldn't have said that out loud. But it wasn't just her unpleasant nature. The students didn't feel like they learned anything from her outdated curriculum. She refused to use textbooks that weren't from the nineties or before that. I'd never seen someone so resistant to change."

His words made me think the dead professor was stuck in the past.

"She taught English and journalism classes?"

"Yes. Until you came along, the departments have always been combined, and many in the faculty taught both subjects."

The fields were so different, but I remembered what my friend Carolyn had told me when she'd been insisting I come to Wales. She wanted to divide the departments and create a new journalism hub. She and I had talked about big plans for making the university a go-to for digital, broadcast, and print journalism. If I were honest with myself, it was the first time I'd been this excited in a long time.

I liked the idea of creating a hub that helped to create journalists with integrity in an ever-changing world where that word wasn't always synonymous with the job.

"There's not liking someone and maybe wanting to kill them," I said out loud. Though I'd been more talking to myself than Ellis.

"Do you really think someone killed the professor? I thought it was just rumors."

"Oh, I didn't mean to say that out loud. I've just been wondering what happened. It was so sudden. And she seemed surprised before she died."

"Do you mind me asking exactly what happened?"

I'd told the police more than once, but I appreciated Ellis's curious mind.

"If I do, can you keep it to yourself? I don't want to add to the rumor mill. And we really should wait and see what the medical examiner, or whoever it is in Wales, has to say."

"We do have a medical examiner, though usually it is a local doctor who looks into cause of death. I have sources there, if you would like me to use them."

I turned to face him. He'd stopped at a corner and smiled.

"A good journalist cultivates sources everywhere," he said. "As the advisory editor of the university newspaper, I've done my best to do exactly that."

"I knew I liked you, Ellis."

He grinned wider. "So I'm guessing you'd like me to check with those sources?"

"That is a good guess. It's more out of curiosity. One minute she was standing, and the next she was on my floor. I have no idea why she was there so late at night. I'd just met her at the party."

"She had been staring you down," he said. "And she hadn't been very nice. We were all dying to know what she said to you after dinner."

"You noticed that?"

He nodded. "It was hard not to notice. We all knew she wasn't happy about you taking the top spot, but it wasn't your fault. I couldn't believe when she called you out in front of everyone. I thought Dr. Montgomery was going to kill her on the spot."

He seemed to realize what he'd said. "That was a bad choice of words. But she was quite obviously angry with Dr. Rice."

I shrugged. "Part of our business is learning to navigate all kinds of people. If you want to be a good reporter and editor, you have to be able to get your sources to believe in you. And you have to adapt to different situations as you climb the ladder in our chosen career. Though I feel like you know all this. From what I've seen so far, you're on the right track."

"This is going to be great," he said.

"What do you mean?"

"I feel like I'm already learning so much from you."

I laughed. "Stick with me, kid. I'll teach you everything I know."

"I plan on it," he said seriously.

"I do feel bad about taking you away from Dr. Davies."

"Oh, don't. He's grand, don't get me wrong. I enjoyed working for him. But I begged the dean to let me be your assistant. And Dr. Davies is the kind of man who wants the best for everyone. He is excited for me."

"That's good to know."

He pulled through the gates, which were never closed, and onto the main road going through the university grounds. I hadn't been here in twenty-odd years. The old stone buildings hadn't changed, and as we drove through the campus, I remembered several of the building names, even though they were in Welsh.

Parking was set away from the buildings, so we had a bit of a hike as we headed for the building that housed the English and journalism departments. Unlike at many American universities, the classes here were small. Sometimes they were held in the offices of the professors. Others were in slightly larger classrooms.

The cold wind whipped around us, and the skies were dark gray.

"Snow is coming, again," Ellis said beside me. "We're in for it the next few days."

I had no idea. I realized I hadn't read any news or watched anything since I'd arrived the day before. For someone who was a news junkie, that was very unlike me.

I was curious about what had been written about Dr. Rice's death. Had it made the news already? I planned to do a bit of searching once I was settled.

I'd spent a great deal of time in the old building where my offices would be, and once again that familiarity settled around me when we went through the heavy wooden doors that had withstood the test of time—and students—since the 1700s.

While the stone walls protected us from the winds, it was still quite chilly inside. That I had forgotten. We used to have to bundle up to go to class, even in the fall and spring. These old buildings never seemed to warm up.

We followed the sign on the wall that pointed to the journalism department.

Ellis pushed through another pair of wooden doors. These weren't quite as thick as the ones at the front of the building.

Gladys was at her computer to the right, and there was another desk across from her.

"That's me, there." Ellis pointed to the empty desk. "You met Gladys last night."

"Good to see you," I said.

She smiled as she rose from her chair. Then she grabbed a vase full of purple and white flowers. "I brought a little something to cheer up your office," she said. "And to make up for what happened with Dr. Rice. I heard she died right in front of you."

I sighed. Small towns and gossip. Well, I wouldn't be adding to the rumors.

"Thank you, the flowers are beautiful."

She seemed disappointed that I didn't comment on the professor's death.

"You're welcome," she said.

I used the key Ellis had given me that first day and opened the door to my office. It seemed like all the keys in Wales were old-fashioned and another part of the charm of the place.

In Dallas I used a key card in the elevator to get to my office and into my apartment.

The first thing that hit me when I opened the door was that it was huge. There was a fireplace with a conference table in front of it. My desk was centered in the room, and there were arched floor-to-ceiling windows on the far wall. Since I'd always worked in the newsroom, I'd never had this sort of old-world luxury in my offices.

I could get used to this.

Floor-to-ceiling bookshelves and cabinets in a dark wood occupied the other walls. It was all so beautiful and elegant.

Then I noticed the pile of folders on the right side of the desk.

Time to get to work.

Ellis and Gladys had followed me inside.

"We didn't want to pile on the work, but we've organized by priority what we need you to sign off on," Gladys said. "The professors on your team have sent in their syllabi and curricula for their classes, both in email and paper form. We weren't sure about your preference. Those need to be approved so they can move forward and send the syllabi to students."

Since this was my first time in this kind of position, I would have to trust the professors to know what was best, but I did intend to oversee their plans so we didn't duplicate efforts. That was something Carolyn had told me she was worried about. The retired head of the department had "let them run wild," as my friend put it, referring to the professors. She wanted the classes streamlined and to have a clear delineation between the journalism and English departments. That I could do.

"We also have the surveys of the various professors from last semester," Gladys added. "Even the tenured instructors are surveyed by the students. And Dr. Montgomery said to tell you she already has some adjunct professor candidates to fill the position left by Dr. Rice. She'll be sending over a list later today."

It had been a strange couple of days and my mind could only handle one thing at a time, but that seemed rather quick to fill Dr. Rice's position. "Okay, thank you."

Even though Carolyn wanted to separate the departments, the chairman—me—was still over literature and journalism classes. This was a test semester, and if things went the way we hoped, she would be hiring a new chairman to head the literature department.

"If you need help with anything, let us know," Ellis said. "I'll be just outside the door."

"Thanks," I said.

"Oh, but first, let me show you how to sign in to the server," Ellis said. He pointed to the desktop computer. "You'll be able to log in here, and on your laptop." He showed me how to do it and even used my username and password. "Don't worry about security. You can change both once you are in."

"Thanks."

After he and Gladys left, I took a deep breath and sat down in the big leather executive chair.

The information the professors had sent in was pretty straightforward and even gave me an idea about some changes I could make in my curriculum. I made a few notes and then emailed my approvals. It was a good way for me to introduce myself to those who hadn't gotten back from their holiday break.

I'd almost finished the first pile when there was a knock on the door.

"Come in," I said.

Ellis opened thc door. "There is a Detective Gareth Jones here to see you," he whispered.

I wondered how he'd tracked me down here. Though I supposed if I wasn't at my apartment, this was a good bet.

"Show him in," I said. I stood to greet him. The man had been ruthless with his questions, but I understood he had a job to do. When I'd been a reporter, a good relationship with those in the police department had been a necessity.

"Detective," I said. Once again, he wore a cable-knit sweater, this one in a dark green, and jeans. His dark hair looked a bit more mussed than it had the night before, and a curl curved over his eye.

"Doctor, thank you for seeing me."

I waved to the leather chairs in front of my desk. "Please, have a seat. How can I help you?"

"I have a few follow-up questions for you," he said.

"Okay."

He stood there, and I realized he was waiting for me to take a seat. So I sat.

He crossed his legs and then flipped open his notebook.

"I understand you have only been in town a short time," he said. "But you lived here before." I was fairly certain I'd made that clear, but I'd been jet-lagged, so maybe not.

"Yes, I did my undergrad studies here. And I arrived yesterday."

"Right." He wrote something down in his notebook.

"And you said the first time you met Dr. Rice was at the party thrown by Dean Montgomery."

"Yes."

"And there was an altercation between you and the victim?"

"An altercation? I'm not sure what you mean by that."

He flipped a couple of pages. "She said something about you being fired from your last job at the party you were attending."

I shook my head. "She was misinformed, and I told her so. It was in no way an altercation. From what I understand, and this is directly from the dean, Dr. Rice was not happy that she was passed over for a promotion. But that had nothing to do with me. I was offered a job, and I took it."

"May I ask why? Our fair town is a far beat from Texas."

I nodded. "I'd taken early retirement," I said. It was either that or being laid off. I decided I was ready for a big life change. As you know by now, Carolyn and I have been friends since we were in university here. I'm fairly certain we discussed this already."

"Yes. I'm going over the facts. The big questions are why Dr. Rice showed up at your place so late and died suddenly."

I blew out a breath. "I am wondering the same thing, Detective. I have no idea why she was there. I opened the door. She said she wanted to tell me something, and then she hit the floor. I have nothing else to share with you. I didn't know anything about her. I've heard she could be difficult, but that is all rumor from other people.

"I didn't have a chance to work with her. Maybe she thought about what she said and came to apologize that night, but I don't think we'll ever know. Do you have a cause of death? I know it's a bit soon, yet I can't help but be curious."

"In an ongoing investigation, we do not share that information," he said.

I frowned. "I don't remember the laws here, but once it's filed by the medical examiner, wouldn't it become public knowledge?"

He sighed. "We do not have a cause yet, but we are viewing this as a suspicious death. You mentioned you've heard rumors. Would you want to share those?"

I shrugged. "You and I both deal with facts, Detective. Rumor and innuendo do not have a place in an investigation."

He pointed his pen at me. "Agreed. But I wondered if in your dealings you've come across someone who was upset with the victim."

I didn't want to say everyone she'd ever talked to, because I didn't know if that was true.

"As we've stated, I'm the new kid here. I wish I could help you, but I cannot."

"Had she sent you any emails or letters?" He motioned toward the piles of files on my desk.

I held up a file folder. "I had her curriculum, but that's it. No letters or emails." For which I was grateful.

"We would like permission to look in her office," he said.

"Am I the person who can give that to you? Don't you need some kind of warrant?"

"We were hoping you would be more cooperative."

What did he mean by that? "I believe I am. I'm not telling you no, I just don't know the rules of the university. Hold on. I need to make a quick call."

I pulled my cell out and called Carolyn. She answered on the second ring.

"How's the office?"

"It's great, and more beautiful than I could ever have imagined."

"I knew you'd love it."

"Listen, I have the detective in charge of Dr. Rice's case here. He's asked to look in her office."

"Why is he coming to you with that?" she asked. "And does he have a warrant?"

I had a feeling he could hear her, as the eyebrows went up on his handsome mug.

"I don't believe he has a warrant, and I think he came to me as the head of the department."

"Right. I don't think there's a problem, but someone has to be there as they go through things. There may be class notes, et cetera, that the incoming professor might need right away. I'd have you send him to me, but I'm a few towns away right now. We're lunching with Henry's aunt. Do you mind taking charge?"

"No problem. I don't know how he'll feel about it, but I'll let him know what you said."

"Thanks, and sorry he is harassing you. At least he's being thorough. We all want to know what happened."

"There is that."

I hung up. "Okay, so the dean says she has no problem with you going through the professor's things as long as I'm there. She's worried about you taking notes her replacement might need. And she asked if you had a warrant, but I think if you're willing to work with me on the notes and let me oversee your search or even help, she'd appreciate that."

He cocked his head. "I'm shorthanded at the moment, so fine."

I glanced down at my desk to hide my smile.

As we headed out to get the keys from Gladys, I hoped we'd find something that might lead to a clue. And maybe I would get to know more about the grumpy Dr. Rice.

I couldn't help but wonder if someone had tried to kill her.

Chapter Five

Gladys was curious when I asked her for the keys and directions to Dr. Rice's office, which was just across the hallway from my office.

"I am happy to help," she offered. "If you tell me what you're looking for, perhaps I can direct you. I have been working with her for years. I know where all the bodies are buried." She seemed to realize what she'd said. "So to speak," she added.

"It's an ongoing investigation," the detective said. "And I appreciate that you want to help, but I'd like to keep the intrusion into the office to a minimum. Dr. Griffith has offered to help."

She stared at me and then opened and closed her mouth. "I . . . fine," she said. It was obvious she wasn't happy about the situation. I was certain she was just curious. I certainly was.

Then she handed him a key ring. The key to Dr. Rice's office had a mouse at the top. I wondered how much it would cost to replace these special keys if they were lost.

Before unlocking the door, the detective gave me a pair of gloves.

"Try not to touch anything, but if you do, please use these."

"Got it. Is there anything in particular we're looking for?"

He opened the door. The office was half the size of mine but still bigger than any I'd worked in during my life at newspapers. Bookshelves lined the walls, and a huge desk was centered in the space. A small round table with a few chairs stood in the corner. Her desk surprised me. While the rest of the room was neat and organized, piles of file folders, manuscripts, and scraps of paper were scattered over the surface.

After shutting the door behind him, the detective frowned as he stared down at the piles of paper.

"Change of plans," he said.

I didn't even know there was a plan. "Okay."

"Can you sort through the paper? I'm looking for anything that might appear as a threat. I'm going to try and access her email. Our techs were able to get into her laptop last night. It was in her flat. My hope is she used the same passwords. Most people do."

"So I hear." I'd been a journalist for so long that my go-to was encrypted files, but Dr. Rice had been a professor at a university in Wales. We came from different worlds.

He sat down in her chair and pushed the piles of paper across the desk at me. "Like I said, anything that appears to be a threat, put it in a stack."

"Got it," I said.

Most of the papers were student tests and essays. Some had been marked up; others appeared to be rough drafts. I made two piles of dissertations. Given what I'd heard about Dr. Rice, I wondered if it might be a good idea for me or another professor to go through all the dissertations. Everyone had told me she was a bit overzealous when it came to grading, and from what I saw of her notes, which were less than kind, I had to agree.

I had a feeling Gladys would know where the students were in their studies and such. I'd work with her on finding new advisers to take over.

There were some papers from the previous semester. The grading was tough, but I'd had professors like her here. One had retired years ago, but getting a B in his class was considered impressive.

Even though I was supposed to be looking for something specific, I learned a great deal glancing through Dr. Rice's notes. She wasn't wrong in most cases, but there were better, more constructive ways to say things.

The detective's fingers clicked on the keyboard.

"Are you having more luck than me?" I asked. "Most of what I found is to do with students."

"I'm in her email," he said, as if he were distracted.

"Anything interesting?"

"Unfortunately. I'll need my team to trace some IPs. She has several emails from two different people that escalate."

He frowned and glanced up at me.

He'd been thinking out loud. I did the same thing, and it seemed to dawn on him that he was talking to me.

"Please keep that quiet."

"I can keep a secret," I said. "You don't need to worry. But do they work at the university? Are they people we should be wary of in some way?"

"No. They are persons outside of the university," he said.

That only made me more curious. "Okay. But you seem to be approaching this as a suspicious death. You mentioned earlier that the ME, or whomever you use in Wales, didn't have a report yet. I'm curious why it seems you're going the extra mile to investigate Dr. Rice's life. I mean, I gave her mouth-to-mouth; do I need to worry?"

I hadn't thought about that until just that moment. But what if she'd been ill with something? Or had ingested some sort of toxin?

"You are fine. The whites of her eyes were discolored," he said. "That's all I'll say for now. Did you notice anything unusual about her that night? You mentioned that she just collapsed, but did she have some sort of seizure beforehand?"

"No. Not at all. It was like I said. She had something to tell me, and then she just fell forward on top of me. I tried to keep us both from hitting the floor, but the weight of her took me down. And then I couldn't find a pulse. It was instant, whatever happened." I shuddered. "So, if you think it might have been poison, is there a chance I could have ingested some of it?"

"Like I said, early days. But I checked with our local doctor, and you should be fine."

"That's not very comforting."

"Whatever happened, it appears that she may have been receiving small doses over time. At least from what we know so far."

"So you do know more than you've been saying. And how awful that someone might have been poisoning her over a long period."

"Again, I need you to keep that to yourself."

"I will. Like I said before, I can keep a secret. I protected my sources when I worked as a reporter. It's the same sort of thing."

"Good," he said.

"I didn't know her well, but she seems to have made more than one enemy during her time here."

"We aren't lacking for suspects, it is true," he said.

"Since she might have been poisoned over some length of time, am I off your list?" I smiled like it was a joke.

"Again, early days." But he smiled back.

I snorted. "Is it okay if I take these dissertations back to my office? Other than some rather grumpy notes, I don't think you'll find much."

"I'll need a list of students' names," he said.

"Wouldn't most of them still be on holidays?"

His eyebrows went up.

"I mean, if you're narrowing down suspects. Many of them wouldn't be in town, right? I'd be looking at staff, faculty, her neighbors and any girlfriends or boyfriends she might have. Everyone I've talked to, which is basically my assistant and a few folks around town, said she was persnickety everywhere she went."

"Persnickety?"

"Old American word meaning fussy and picky about things. But as we've discussed, that is hearsay."

I waited a moment.

"Did you find anything out of order in her apartment? I'm fairly certain she came from there and not straight from the party."

He frowned. "Why would say that?"

"Well, at the party, she'd been wearing a pair of black kitten heels. It was chilly outside, and I thought her choice of footwear was odd. I wore boots."

"Okay?"

"When she came to my door, she was in a pair of booties that looked like Uggs. So she must have gone home to change her footwear. Maybe she ingested the poison in her apartment? I mean, we all ate the same things at the party, and no one else became ill or died."

I made a face.

"Sorry, I'm just talking off the top of my head. Maybe there was a box of chocolates or tea in her house that was poisoned."

He grinned. I had to admit he had a nice smile. "We've taken everything for testing," he said. He seemed to be watching me carefully. "You seem to know a lot about crime procedures and poisonings."

I sighed. "Another reminder I started out as a crime reporter. And I'm quite fond of all sorts of mysteries and thrillers when it comes to books and television series." I read everything, to be honest, but I preferred a good murder mystery.

"Her desk drawers seemed to be locked," he said.

I checked the key fob Gladys had given us. There were a couple of smaller ones on there.

"Maybe one of these will work." I walked around to the other side of the desk. The scent of sandalwood hit me, and I realized it was Detective Jones's cologne. It was quite pleasant.

I tried the first key, but it didn't work. Then I tried another one, and it did. He took it from me and opened the other drawers. There were office supplies in one, but in the bottom drawer on the right side was a bottle of Penderyn, which was a famous whiskey in Wales.

"Well, she had good taste in drink," he said. But he took the bottle out with his gloves and put it in a large plastic bag. "I'm bagging this for the team. They'll be through here soon when they finish her flat."

So that was where his team was.

"Do you want help going through her file cabinets?" I asked. "I could flag anything that isn't student related. A lot of these papers are just test scores. They must be available electronically as well; otherwise, why wouldn't she give them back to the students?"

Once again, I'd been thinking out loud to myself.

"Go ahead," he said. "If you see anything that might help our investigation, flag it with one of these." He handed me a roll of evidence tabs. "And put it in a stack on top of the cabinet."

"Right." It felt good to be helping in some way. When Dr. Rice had fallen at my doorstep, I'd tried to administer aid, but ever since I'd been feeling a bit helpless. As I went through the drawers, I found student files, but also some ideas for classes she'd thought would benefit the university. I also found some of her surveys from students and employee reports.

"Wow," I said.

"Did you find something?" the detective asked.

I shook my head. "I found some of the reports compiled from the student surveys and her personnel files from the dean. The rumors I heard were right. If she hadn't been tenured, her days would have been numbered."

"Put them in the stack for us to box for evidence," he said.

After a bit more searching, I found a file that was nothing but copies of some sort of logbook. There were accounts and numbers. The file was named *Home*, so I figured it must have been some of her banking information. Still, when the detective wasn't looking, I took a couple of photos with my phone.

Right as I was doing that, there was a knock on the door. I jumped, dropping my phone into a file drawer. After I quickly picked it up and stuck it in my pocket, I opened the door. Gladys stood there with a tray full of tea and small cookies, or biscuits, as they called them here.

"You're working hard, and I thought you might want a cuppa," she said, smiling.

She glanced around the room curiously.

"Thank you," Detective Jones said. "If you don't mind, set it on the table there."

I thought it a bit odd that he would take tea in the middle of a crime scene, but what did I know?

"You didn't have to do this," I said to Gladys, but I took one of the cups of tea she poured and added a bit of sugar. I hadn't quite taken up putting milk in my tea. I preferred coffee but had learned to love tea when I'd lived here a couple of decades ago.

"Is there anything I can help you with?" Gladys asked. She stared at the pile of folders on the desk.

"We have it in hand," the detective said. His phone rang, and he answered it. "Right. Yes, we're at the university. Bring evidence boxes; I won't have enough in my car."

"Thank you for the tea," I whispered. "It was very kind of you to think of us."

She nodded, but I caught her shifting her gaze to the files on top of the cabinet. "I'm good with organizing," she said.

"The detective has a system," I said. "And it sounds like his team is on the way. Maybe you could show them where we are when they arrive?"

"Oh, yes. Of course." She gave me an absent smile. "Did he explain why he needed to rummage through Dr. Rice's things?"

She was looking for gossip, that much was evident.

"He's just being thorough. I'm sure he'll want to interview you as well."

"But I thought she died of a heart attack." Gladys frowned. "That was what I heard. She was always getting herself worked up over things. I'm not surprised."

"Again, I believe the police are just being thorough."

"You were there; do you think it was a heart attack?" Gladys was determined to get information. I didn't blame her. I would probably be curious as well.

"It was sudden," I said. "I don't know any more than that."

"But you tried to save her. I heard that from Dr. Davies when he was in earlier. He said you were quite heroic."

"Uh . . ." I stared at the detective, who had hung up his phone. "I tried to administer CPR, but I'm afraid it didn't help."

"Well, deary, you tried. And you didn't even know her. Bad business all around. No one blames you."

"Um. Thanks."

"My team will be here in ten minutes," the detective said. "Professor, we could use any personnel files you might have related to the victim. Unless you need me to get that warrant."

"I'm sure it will be fine, but I need to call the dean again."

"Seems a lot of fuss for a heart attack," Gladys said.

"They are doing their due diligence," I said. "When someone dies suddenly, there is almost always some sort of investigation." I remembered that from my crime reporting days.

"The professor is correct," Detective Jones said.

"Well, if you have more people coming, I suppose I should turn the kettle back on," Gladys said.

"You don't have to do that," he said.

"It's no bother. Least I can do, as you and your crew keep our wee town safe."

She toddled off toward the offices.

"If you don't mind, I'll take the pile I made that I need to go through with the staff, and I'll call the dean. I'm sure she will be happy for you to take whatever you need. She said as much before."

He nodded. "Thank you for your help, Professor."

"You're welcome. I'll let you know what she says."

I went out and through the offices and then put the pile of papers on my desk. I quickly called my friend.

"Is everything okay?" Carolyn asked.

"Yes. Sorry to bother you again. They do want to take some of the personnel files and such. And her computer. I wanted to double-check that it's okay, or do you want them to get a warrant?"

She blew out a breath over the phone. "I'm sorry you're having to deal with this. I should have been there."

"No. Don't worry about it. I just want to make certain I'm not overstepping by allowing the police to take whatever they want."

"While I'd normally say something like we need to protect the privacy of our students, Detective Jones would only get the warrants. I see no reason to hold him up."

"Okay, great."

"I will ask that they give us some sort of accounting of all the files and items they take," she said.

"That makes sense. I'll let him know."

By the time I was off the phone, his team had arrived. They were busy boxing things that we'd already taken out of the cabinets.

"I spoke with the dean," I said.

Detective Jones turned toward me. "And?"

"She has no problem with you taking what you need but asked two things: one, that the student files be protected, and two, that you make a complete list of every file you boxed, so that there is some sort of accounting."

"That's reasonable," he said. "We have to make a list for the evidence log, which I'm happy to share."

"Great. Do you need my help with anything else?"

"No. We'll take it from here. Oh, and we won't be taking the computer. My staff has copied the hard drive."

"Okay, great." I waved goodbye.

When I returned to my office, Gladys was there. She handed me a file folder.

"The dean called with that list of adjunct professors we've used in the past to help take over some of Dr. Rice's classes. Only the ones that were journalism specific. She's handling the literature ones, so you needn't worry about those.

"Also, Professor Davies mentioned that he was happy to cover some of the classes if you needed him to."

"Thank you, Gladys, for staying on top of everything. I'm very grateful for you."

Her cheeks grew rosy, and she smiled. "It's my job, Professor."

"If you want, I can go through and tell you which professors the students like the best," Ellis said behind me. He'd been so quiet, I'd forgotten he was there.

"Thank you."

"It doesn't have to be decided today," Gladys said. "I'm sure you're exhausted."

"I'm good. If I have all this sorted, I'll be able to rest easier. Besides, I want to give whomever we hire as much time as possible to prepare."

"Good on you," she said.

"Ellis, I'll take you up on your offer, though."

But my mind was on the police across the hall. Was the detective right? Had Dr. Rice been poisoned? And if so, when?

If the crime had taken place over a period of time, was the poison in her apartment? Perhaps in something she ate on a regular basis? I shivered. Paranoid, I glanced up at Ellis and Gladys.

They stared back with smiles. But could I trust them?

Great. Now everyone who was close to her was a suspect.

Chapter Six

After Ellis dropped me at the apartment, I decided to go across the street to the pub. Even after Gladys's tea and biscuits, I was starving. My stomach and schedule were off-kilter.

When I walked in, the place was full, and everyone seemed to turn my way. Then there was a hush across the pub. I'd never felt more uncomfortable. I almost turned around and walked out, but my stomach won that battle. And this was my new town; I wouldn't be a coward.

There was one stool left at the bar. After putting my coat on one of the racks by the door, I went and sat down.

The pub was still quiet when Catrin came out of the kitchen and frowned. "You lot, stop trying to scare the poor professor," she said. "Don't pay attention to them, a bunch of busybodies," she said loudly.

A few people laughed, and the conversations resumed.

I sat between two elderly gents, who looked like they'd just stepped off a ship with their long, white beards and thick sweaters. Those sweaters seemed popular among the males in Dillynaidd.

Each of them nodded toward me. "Evening," one of them said.

"Evening. What do you recommend for a starving professor?"

They laughed. "Can't go wrong with the stew," the man on my right said.

"And a piece of Catrin's cake. We keep telling her she needs to open a bakery."

She laughed from across the bar. "And I keep telling them this pub is enough for any ten people to run. We also have a perfectly lovely bakery down the road. Now, can I start you off with a pint?"

"Yes, please. Whatever you have on tap. And the stew sounds lovely."

She smiled.

"And the cake," I added.

"So how do you like our town?" the man on my left said. "Heard you were caught up in that business with the snooty professor."

"Uh . . ."

"Leave her alone," Catrin says. "She doesn't need to be interrogated by you lot. She's only been in town a couple of days. Dr. Rice barely knew the professor and Gwennie's an old friend, so leave her alone."

"Heard she died on your doorstep," the man continued without missing a beat.

Catrin rolled her eyes.

Yep. Small towns. In Dallas, if someone died on your doorstep, it probably wouldn't even make the news. And no one else in my building would have paid attention. In fact, they probably would have just stepped over the body.

That wasn't a joke.

But in Dillynaidd it was probably the most exciting, albeit terrible, thing that had happened in ages.

"Leave her alone, I said. Or I'll be showing ya the door," Catrin warned them.

The man shrugged. "Just being friendly."

"Nosy, more like it," Catrin said on the way back to the kitchen.

"It's okay," I said. "I would be curious as well. Unfortunately, Detective Jones told me to keep my mouth shut. Even if I wanted to, I can't say anything. He kept repeating something about an ongoing investigation." Best to blame it on the police. That way I didn't appear unwilling or rude.

"Ah, our boy Gareth is good at his job. Best grandson a man ever had," the man on my right said.

"Oh, so you're related to the detective?"

He held his head high. "I am. He was named after me, ya know. Gareth Jones Senior," he said, pointing a thumb at himself.

"You sound very proud."

"Couldn't be prouder," the other man said. "Talks about him all the time. Never shuts up."

"Don't mind Cecil, he's just jealous."

Cecil blew a raspberry and then sipped his beer. "No one calls me Cecil but that old coot. I'm known as the Captain."

It was all I could do not to belly laugh. It was funny seeing an older man act like a child who didn't get his way.

"Well, I haven't known your grandson long, but he appears quite capable and thorough."

"He is."

"You mentioned you knew the professor," I said.

He made a face. "Did I?"

"I believe your friend called her snooty?"

"A reputation that one had, and it wasn't good. Some folks have a way of upsetting everyone around them. And she was exactly that. Didn't have to know her well to hear about her reputation."

"It's sad, though, her passing, right?" I asked.

He shrugged. "She never had a kind word, mind you. Never made a friend for as long as she was here, as far as I know. Despised. That's the word."

Wow. I hadn't expected him to be so open about it, but I wasn't surprised. Dr. Rice didn't appear to have left any friends behind. At least none that I had found so far.

"Do you know why she was that way?"

"Like I said, didn't know her well," he said. "Only by reputation. Saw her here a few times, but she was alone. People like that usually are."

While I didn't disagree, I felt a bit sad for Dr. Rice. It was one thing to not be liked but quite another to be so alone.

"So she didn't have a boyfriend who joined her for meals?"

"Not that I ever saw. But ask Catrin, or Arnall; they would know better than I."

I'd already spoken to Catrin.

"Now, I hear you came from Texas," the older Gareth said. "Do they have oil wells like on the telly?"

I laughed. "They do in West Texas. But most of the wells near where I was located were natural gas."

"Does everyone wear a cowboy hat?" his friend Cecil asked.

"Some do," I said.

They peppered me with questions until Catrin came back from the kitchen with my stew. "Leave the poor woman alone, you gossipy hens. Let her eat her meal."

"I don't mind," I said.

"Oh, these two will run you ragged with the questions and then tell the rest of the town every word, with a few stories added on."

"Hey, not fair," Gareth said.

"Lies," Cecil added.

Then they both laughed, as did Catrin.

Her husband, Arnall, came out of the kitchen with a huge tray of food. While there was a bit of gray at his temples, I remembered him from when he was the bartender here.

"Ah, it's Gwen," he said as he passed behind his wife with the tray. "You made it back to us."

"I did. I can't believe you remembered me."

"That one is good with faces," Catrin says. "Never forgets one."

Arnall delivered the plates of food on his tray and then came back. He put an arm around his wife and kissed her cheek.

"This one tells me you're back in town to teach."

"I am," I said. "You two haven't changed."

"Ah, we're a bit older and wiser, but my wife never ages."

She waved her bar towel at him and rolled her eyes.

"Bad business across the street. Heard you were caught up in it," he said.

"Uh . . ." I wasn't sure what to say.

"Rumor is you tried to save her life," he said. "Good on you. She was prickly, that one. Always had to have her meals a special way. Not once did she eat something the way it came."

"I'd forgotten that," Catrin said. "You're right. Still sad. We don't have many deaths in town—well, except for old age."

She waved a hand at the men seated next to me.

"Hey, now. Mind who you're calling old," Gareth Senior said.

Everyone laughed.

"When you finish your food, I'll introduce you around," Catrin said. "Our regulars, minus these two, are a lovely crowd."

* * *

A half hour later, she did exactly that. Taking me from one table to the next, she introduced me as the new chairman of the journalism department. People acted impressed, and many asked questions. I could see the curiosity in their eyes, and I wondered how many of them thought I'd killed Dr. Rice.

It didn't look good that she'd died so quickly after meeting me. And even though the police were being thorough and looking for files, I still felt like I had a big target on my back.

As I grabbed my coat, Catrin came over to me. "I hope you had fun tonight."

"I did. Thank you for introducing me around."

"We can be a bit standoffish with strangers, but I remembered how lovely you were back in the day. I want you to feel at home."

"That is kind of you."

"There's something else, since you seemed curious about Alice Rice."

"Oh?"

"Before she died, she was in here with a gentleman who seemed to be a friend."

"Was it Dr. Davies?"

She laughed. "No, it wasn't Mr. Handsome, which is what most of the students call him. I'd never seen this bloke before. He had a cap on the whole time, but his hair was gray. And he carried a pipe around but didn't actually smoke it. I thought that was odd.

"Anyway, I forgot all about it until just now when I was introducing you around. Dr. Rice wasn't friendly like you.

Whenever we delivered food or drink to her table that night, she couldn't wait for us to leave. We were curious about the man."

"Was there anything else that stuck out about him?"

"No, other than he was Welsh. I heard him say a few words in our language."

"Thanks," I said. "Oh, do you by chance have security cameras in the pub?"

She frowned. "No. We've never needed them. Why?"

"Oh, I was just thinking that if you had a picture or film of the man, it might help the police."

"I didn't think about that. We could give them a description. I'll have Arnall call Detective Jones."

"Good idea. See you later."

She waved goodbye.

The day had been a long one, and after my second pint, I was ready to go to bed.

When I arrived at the lobby of my apartment, I thought it odd that no one was at the front desk.

I made my way up the stairs and was unlocking my front door when I heard someone coming down from the floor above.

"I'm telling you I looked, but I didn't find it. And the police have been through it all more than once. It isn't there." That was the housemaster Paul's voice.

I stepped through my door but kept it open a crack.

"No. I'm telling you I've looked as well as anyone. And if the police found it, you'd be knowing, right?"

What was he talking about?

Chapter Seven

After changing clothes and washing my face, I fell into bed. The last few days had been exhausting, and my mind whirred with so many ideas. Why had Paul been going through Dr. Rice's place? Well, at least that was what I assumed. She was the only one on that floor who hadn't gone away for the holidays.

Though he could have been in one of the other flats. There was no way for me to know. But his behavior was suspicious. Had he rifled through my things when I was gone?

Paranoid? Perhaps. But it all seemed so odd. Even though Paul had been nothing but kind, I wasn't sure who I could trust in my new environment. And yes, I understood that made me paranoid.

While I'd known many people who were disliked by others, the ones who spoke about Dr. Rice were vehement about it. The older gentlemen in the pub seemed to be right about her not having a single friend in town.

Though I didn't know if that was true. She had been at the pub with a stranger. I was dying to know who that was.

While I had been tough on my team at the paper, we were also friends. And I'd made many friends through the years all over the world. It wasn't a brag; I just couldn't imagine being so disliked. Well, I could now. But it made me sad for Dr. Rice that she seemed so short on friends. She had to have been so lonely.

I sat down on the edge of my bed. The weight of the last couple of days had me curling up on my bed in the fetal position. I needed to look through the things I'd taken pictures of on my phone when I was in her office, but I was too tired to move.

* * *

The next morning, I woke up on top of the comforter, freezing. I'd had a strange dream about sneaking into Dr. Rice's apartment and looking for clues.

Clues for what? As far as I knew, she'd died of a heart attack like everyone said. At least that was what the police at the scene had thought.

But in my dream, the handsome detective had brought up the discoloration in her eyes. Had he been right about the poison? My dumb dream made me want to search her apartment, but I had a feeling the detective would give me a big fat no if I asked.

I mean, if the police and Paul had searched, what did I think I'd find?

If that was really where Paul had been. I had no proof, just suspicion.

After a shower and a change of clothes, I decided to head out for food.

When I opened the door to my flat, I jumped a bit. Rhys stood on the other side with his hand raised.

He smiled, and my stomach did a dive down to my toes and back up again. I had no idea what that was about.

"Hi," I said.

"Didn't meant to scare you."

I shook my head. "You didn't. I was just surprised to see you there."

"I was going to gently knock to see if you might want to join me on my daily walk to the bakery for breakfast and some coffee."

I'd been headed to the Murder of Crows Pub, but I'd been wanting to check out the new bakery. "That sounds great."

I locked my door and then walked toward the steps with him.

"After your fright, I wanted to check on you," he said.

"Thanks. All things considered, I'm fine. I spent a great deal of time yesterday helping Detective Jones go through her office. It was an odd way to get to know someone, though."

He frowned. "The detective?"

I laughed. "No, Dr. Rice. The detective likes to keep things close to the vest. I was going through some of her files looking for anything that might help them. I did come across some dissertations. If you're open to it, I'd like to work with you and Gladys to make sure everything is properly processed for the students."

"I'm happy to help however I can," he said as we climbed down the steps.

"Morning, Professors," Paul said cheerfully from behind the desk.

"How are you?" I asked.

"Good, good. Storms coming in, so my knees are acting up. Might want to put your caps on; it's windy out there."

"Thanks," I said.

As Rhys opened the door, the wind blew in, and the door would have slammed against the wall if he hadn't caught it. The heavy door couldn't have been easy to hold on to, which meant he was strong.

"Oh. My," I said as we stepped outside. I put my cap and gloves on and pulled my collar up. Even though it wasn't raining or snowing, the air was damp, and it was quite gray outside.

"Luckily, the bakery is only a half block away," Rhys said against the wind. Then he took my hand and put it in the crook of his arm. "We'll keep each other up," he said.

I laughed. He was right, the sidewalks were a bit slick. But I'd remembered from the last time I'd lived here to always wear shoes and boots with a good rubber sole.

It was a chilly walk, but when he opened the door to the bakery, which was in one of the old stone buildings on Main Street, the warmth of the place and the scent of bread made my shoulders drop a few inches.

The name of the bakery, Bakestone, was on the front window in gold filigree.

"This smells like heaven," I said.

He laughed. "I quite agree. It's definitely worth the short walk."

"I don't remember this being here when I lived here during college."

We moved into the line near the door. It was one of those places where I wanted to eat the air, it smelled so good.

"I believe it was in a different location a few blocks off Main Street, nearer the university up the hill."

"Oh, right. I remember it was the same name."

"Yes," he said. "They still have the smaller location there for students and staff at the university, but they opened this one up a few years ago."

"I only visited the old location a few times," I said. I'd been on a tight budget back then. I ate at the university because those meals were already paid for, and if I splurged on something, it was usually novels at the bookstore. "They had amazing Welsh cakes."

"That hasn't changed," he said as we moved up in line. "Nor has their coffee. It is the best in town."

"Good to know. So you're not a tea drinker?"

"I like both," he said. "But I need my coffee in the morning."

"I'm the same way," I laughed.

Behind the counter, which was rich with baked goods in glass cases, was a huge window looking into the kitchen. I watched one of the bakers making the Welsh cakes. They were sort of like a scone, but flatter and cooked on the griddle. I remembered learning long ago that the cakes had first been made for the coal miners, because they would hold up in the weather and made a good snack.

Funny how the scent of something could bring back so many memories. I'd loved living here. Even though my nose was usually in a book, my friend Carolyn would drag me out for trips to the pub and the bakery, and I'd made some great friends along the way.

In many ways, this place felt like the closest thing I had to home. When Carolyn had mentioned coming to work here, I'd thought she was crazy, mostly because I'd never taught before and she'd recommended me for a position I wasn't sure about. But I'd taken the leap because coming back to Dillynaidd felt right.

After we picked up our order, we walked over to a table near the large window.

"I've been wanting to check on you," he said.

"What do you mean?"

We sat down.

"After the other night. You were quite valiant in your attempt to save Alice's life. I was more than impressed by your efforts. It couldn't have been easy on you with everything that happened."

"It has been . . . I guess *weird* is the best word for it. Almost surreal. I know it happened, but it feels like it was someone else that night and not me."

"I don't know much about psychology, but I would imagine that is your brain trying to protect you from the shock."

I nodded. "You may be right. Can I ask you something?"

He seemed surprised by the question. "Of course."

I took a deep breath. "It seems as though she wasn't very well liked, and I remember you mentioning something to that effect at the party. Did she have any friends at all that you know of? I haven't found a single person who would say something nice about her."

He sighed. "I'm afraid she was not an easy person to like. You're right, I tried to warn you that night at the party."

"Ellis tried to tell me as well, but I thought perhaps she was just jealous that I took the position she wanted. Do you feel that way? Like you were passed over?"

He laughed. "No. I'm not one for politics, and in your position, you'll have to deal with that quite a bit. I love teaching, and I'm grateful to have tenure. But I have no ambition to be an administrator. Does that make me sound like a lazy sort? I'm not."

"Not at all. I admire that you love teaching so much. I think part of the reason Carolyn hired me is because of the editorial management position I held. Wrangling reporters and columnists and deciding every day what stories make it into the paper was like herding gerbils. She promised that the chairperson position would be much easier."

He laughed again. "Herding gerbils. I'd heard of cats."

"Gerbils fits reporters better. Everyone is always going at their own speed and direction. I have another question."

"I'm all yours." He gave me a charming smile.

"While they haven't said exactly, I think the police believe there was foul play." I whispered the last bit because the bakery had quieted down, much like the pub the evening before. I had a feeling the other people in line were listening to our conversation.

Again, if I'd been in Dallas, no one would have cared. But here it appeared complete strangers held on to your every word.

"Really?" He frowned. "She was prickly, but I can't imagine anyone wanting to kill her. She'd always been that way. I suppose I got along with her better than most, though it was a bit tough in the beginning. She kept asking me out. I didn't think it was a good idea to date someone I worked with, so I kept putting her off. And then, one day, I had to have a very honest conversation with her."

"Oh?"

He nodded. "I didn't want to hurt her feelings, but I told her that we would never be more than friends. It took her a few weeks to stop staring daggers at me, but then she seemed to accept what I'd said."

"Well, at least she had one friend. I've been feeling bad for her because no one seemed to like her much."

"That was her own fault. She never tried to make friends."

"I heard she was at the pub with a man not long ago. Do you maybe know who that was?"

He shook his head. "That surprises me. For privacy, like me, she usually dated outside of our town. There isn't a space here in Dillynaidd you can go to that you won't bump into students or faculty."

"I hadn't thought of that. I mean, not that I was thinking about dating. I'm focused on the job right now."

"Well, take it from me. If you want to keep your love life private, don't date anyone here in town."

We laughed. "Good to know."

"By the way, before you mentioned it, I did hear you were helping the police go through her office yesterday."

I grinned.

"What?" he asked.

"Nothing is a secret in this town. Let me guess, Gladys mentioned it?"

"She did when she called to see if I could help you out with some of the work you'd found. The woman may be a gossip, but she keeps us all going. And like I said, of course I'll help you."

"Thanks on that count. We'll have to notify the students when they come back about the changes."

"Again, you needn't worry. Gladys will take care of it. Like I said, a bit of a busybody, but she gets things done. Why do the police think there was foul play?"

I didn't want to add to the rumors, so I shrugged. "The detective is being cagey. Every time I ask, he says something like 'It's an ongoing investigation' and that they're looking at all possibilities until they get their cause of death."

That was the truth.

"Interesting. I'm sorry about Alice. Like I said, I was one of the few people she actually got along with. I can't imagine someone wanting to hurt her."

"There's something else," I said. Again, I lowered my voice.

He leaned in and nodded. "Tell me."

Here goes nothing. But I needed help with my plan, and my resources were limited.

"Last night when I was coming home, Paul, the housemaster, seemed to be coming down from her flat. He was talking about the fact that he couldn't find something and he didn't think the police did either."

His eyes went wide. "You think Paul killed her?"

"No. I'm not saying that. I'm just curious about what he might have been looking for in her flat. I found it odd that he would go in there and look for something without the police knowing."

"You're right, that is odd. Should you maybe tell the detective?" He appeared genuinely concerned. "Don't get me wrong—I can't imagine Paul having anything to do with Alice's death—but maybe the police should search again."

"Or I could," I whispered.

His eyebrows rose. "I don't understand. You want to go searching through her apartment? Why?"

"I don't want to cause Paul any problems. It could be I misunderstood the situation. Telling the detective that I suspected our housemaster of maybe looking for something in Alice's apartment seems lame. Especially without any proof. I just want to have a look around. Call it morbid curiosity. I tried to save her life, but I knew nothing about her. I've been through her office, but I'd like to go through her home. If I do find something, I'll let the police know."

"Why do I have a bad feeling that you want me to help you?" He was beyond charming, and I didn't think I imagined we had a connection of sorts—not that I would ever date someone I worked with or that I'd have time to even think of that sort of thing. And he'd stated he never dated anyone in town.

Oh. And I was his boss.

That didn't mean we couldn't be friends.

"Well, I do have an idea how I could make it happen, if you're willing to help me. And there will be zero chances of you getting into trouble. But don't feel any pressure to help out; I don't want you doing this because I'm technically your boss. You are quite free to say no."

He shook his head and laughed. "I would be happy to help. But you've known me a few days and you don't think I'm the kind of guy who might tell someone about your sneaking around?"

"I'm hoping not." I smiled. "Think of it as a game. I'm looking for pieces in the game, and if I find them, I promise to share them with you. You have to be even more curious than I am, since you knew her."

"You aren't wrong. But what if you get caught by the police?"

"Well, that's where you come in," I said.

He laughed heartily. "Circumventing law enforcement; this does sound fun. Okay, I'm in."

Chapter Eight

After we finished our breakfast (and I picked up a few more baked goods to take home), we headed back to our building. As expected, the jovial Paul was at the front desk. While we said hello—again—I glanced at the wall to see the key to Alice's apartment still hung on the board behind him.

That was the first part of the plan. I needed time to take the key, and that meant getting Paul away from the desk.

I stuck my hands in my pockets. "Oh no."

"What's wrong?" Rhys asked.

"I seem to have dropped my gloves along the way. They're the only pair I have until my boxes get here. I should go back and look for them . . . or I guess I could buy some more."

Rhys shook his head. "You're already freezing. I'll go look," he said.

"Let me grab my coat, and I'll help," Paul said.

"Oh, I hate for you to do that. He's right, it is freezing outside."

"It's part of my job to look after you all," Paul said kindly. He quickly grabbed his coat from the rack. "I'm sure we'll find them."

My mouth grew dry. I felt guilty about making them go out in the cold, but this was Rhys's idea. He had my gloves in his pocket and would find them about halfway down the block.

Meanwhile, I was to take the key so that I'd have it for later. The men headed out, and I waited thirty seconds before going behind the desk and taking the key. I stuffed it in my pocket. Then I moved a key from the bottom of the rack to fill its place, hoping that Paul wouldn't notice. The figurine at the top of Alice's key was a lion, and the one I replaced it with had a sheep's head. There was something funny about that.

If I hadn't been so nervous, I might have laughed. As it was, my bakery goods churned in my stomach. I never liked deceiving anyone, but I desperately needed to get into that apartment, if for no other reason than to understand Alice better. I felt I owed her something.

"Found them," Rhys said as they came back in. I sat on the stairs waiting. "They must have fallen out of your pocket when you put your scarf on."

"Thank you both," I said gratefully.

"You're going to need those," Paul said. "My missus put a special clip in my pocket so I don't lose mine. You should maybe try one of those."

"Your missus? I didn't know you were married," I said.

"You know my wife, Gladys," he said.

"Oh. I do. She's lovely. You both are."

His cheeks were pink from the weather, but they turned a darker shade.

"We do our best."

"Well, I've only known you both a few days, but even I understand this place and my department wouldn't be nearly as efficient without you. Thank you again for finding my gloves, and I'll look into that clip."

He waved us away when the phone rang at his desk.

Rhys and I headed upstairs.

"What time do you plan to go up?"

"Well, Ellis is coming to get me to head to the university—though I worry about him driving in this mess. So it will probably be much later tonight."

"Don't worry about Ellis. He's used to driving in all sorts of weather. Sounds good. I'm ready whenever you want. And thanks for approving my syllabi. I'm going to organize all of that today and put it up on my site."

"That is something I'll have to get used to," I said, "all the digital progress the university has made. It's one of the reasons I thought it odd that Dr. Rice graded paper tests."

He nodded. "She worried about students cheating if they worked on computers. No matter how much the last chairman tried to convince her there were ways to set things up so that didn't happen, she wouldn't listen. He eventually gave up trying to change her mind."

"She did seem very set in her ways."

"And she didn't care who she offended or if she made something more difficult," he said. His words were sharper than usual.

"Did she cause trouble for you, Rhys?"

He shook his head. "No, but I had to deal with several student complaints. I'm the student adviser and faculty liaison. If a student had a problem with a professor, they came to me. If I couldn't solve the situation on my own, then we escalated to the chairman and dean. The only times I couldn't handle things on my own were situations with Dr. Rice. She wouldn't bend, even when she was in the wrong."

"I know she had tenure, but I just don't understand why the university would put up with her. Are any of those students . . . um, would they have wanted to hurt her?"

"I would like to say no, but she's dead. And we have no idea what happened. If she was murdered like the police think, then everyone is a suspect."

Well, hopefully not everyone.

I smiled. "Thank you again for helping me," I whispered as we reached my door. "I'll just need you to be a lookout. Let's say eleven or so tonight?"

"I feel like an international spy." He laughed. "But maybe you'll find some insight that will help the police."

"Maybe. I promise I'm not usually so curious, but the police seem to think I had something to do with her death. The sooner I can prove that I didn't, the better."

"So you do believe it as well?"

"What do you mean?"

"That she died suspiciously."

I shrugged. "Like I said before, it's enough that the detective seems to think that's what happened. As long as they're treating it that way, yes. I just don't want my new start to be tainted by all this. It's important to me to have my life here be uncomplicated."

"I can understand that and will help however I can."

"You don't know me well, but I promise I had nothing to do with any of this. I just want to clear my name."

"I never thought you did," he said. "You only met her that night. It took most of us at least a few weeks to discover that, yes, she really was quite unpleasant. Though, honestly, if someone did hurt her, I would have thought one of her students. But most of them are at home for the holidays. Except for a few who may have stayed in the halls."

"Oh? Do you think any of her students are around? Not that I think they killed her. I'm just curious." The crime seemed to be a bit too sophisticated for a young person, but I knew I could be wrong.

"I'll check with the housemasters at the university. A few students who don't have anywhere to go during the holidays stay and spend it with the staff and remaining faculty. The dean threw them a party on Boxing Day."

"That sounds like Carolyn."

He nodded. "The students enjoyed it. Some live off campus, others in the halls. A few can't afford to travel home, and others prefer to stay and begin their studies for the next term."

"Did you go anywhere for the holidays?"

He shook his head. "I find it too crowded most places that are warm this time of year. I prefer a good fire and my books."

"That sounds like my kind of holiday."

He laughed.

My phone buzzed. It was Ellis.

"I have to go, but I'll see you tonight."

"I feel like I should say *roger that* or something clandestine."

This time we both laughed.

I waved goodbye and gathered my things for the office.

Was I really going to break into Alice's apartment?

Yes. Yes, I was.

* * *

I was nervous all afternoon, thinking about my plans for later that night. While I'd been good at talking to people to find the truth when I was younger, I'd never broken into a place to investigate.

I had once taken pictures of a file on a corrupt councilman's desk when he'd left our interview to go to the restroom. But that had been enough to make me nervous. I'd never done it again. Though those files had come in handy.

I didn't know what I thought I might find, but I had to try.

* * *

Later that evening, I was tired, but the key still burned in my pants pocket. I wanted to put off sneaking through Alice's apartment, but the longer I kept her key, the greater the chances of someone noticing.

At eleven, there was a soft knock on my door. I opened it to see Rhys standing there.

"You ready?" he whispered.

I nodded. He would be my alibi.

"Oh, hi. Come in," I said loudly in the hallway so that Paul would hear me down the stairwell.

I shut the door quickly.

"Is he at the front desk?"

"Yes. He's watching one of his favorite programs on the telly. I'd say you have a good forty-five minutes."

"Oh, I don't plan to be that long. I'm going to look in unlikely places, maybe check a vent or two, and then I'm out. I'm sure the police were thorough and there's nothing to find, but my mind won't let me rest until I check for myself. You'll keep a lookout? Stall him if he tries to come upstairs?"

"Consider it done."

I grinned, and so did he. He really was quite handsome.

I stepped into the hallway. Rhys stood there with the door cracked open so he could hear anyone coming up.

I'd taken off my shoes and donned fuzzy socks that allowed me to quietly walk up the stairs. My stomach was in my throat, my nerves so on edge that I kept forgetting to breathe. When I made it up to Alice's floor, I tried the key in the door.

It clicked so loudly I was certain everyone in the building heard it.

Rhys had mentioned that the two other flats on this floor were unoccupied during the holidays. The professors living there would be back in a few days; at least there was that. But every sound seemed to echo in the empty hallway.

I slipped inside Alice's flat and quietly shut the door. I used my phone's flashlight app, which worked surprisingly well in the dark space. The setup of her apartment was much like mine, but her walls were lined with books.

Everything on the shelves was organized by subject, and I was surprised to discover a huge section on Wales witches and the occult. That didn't seem like something the stuffy Alice might read. More than once at the party, I'd overheard her quote the classics, and yes, she'd come across just as pretentious as that made her sound. Though I'd learned long ago to never assume anything about anybody. People were full of surprises. And Rhian from the bookstore had said she did like a romance.

There was a rather well-worn copy of *The Witches of Wales*. I was curious and grabbed the book. I wouldn't keep it, but I had a feeling she might have made notes, since it looked so well read. I was hoping for some sort of insight into the woman. I slipped the book into the small backpack I'd brought with me. I was well aware I was taking things that didn't belong to me, but I'd convinced myself it was for the greater good.

I checked around her fireplace for any loose bricks or tiles. Maybe I'd read too many mysteries, but people often hid things around fireplaces. However, everything seemed in order. Except for the books, there wasn't a lot of anything in the apartment. Alice appeared to be a minimalist. There was nothing wrong with that, but it felt like her surroundings were as cold as she was.

I made my way to the closet in the bedroom. Most of the older apartments like this had very small closets, so there wasn't much to look through. There was a bigger wardrobe on the far wall. It was neatly organized by color. The professor had been fastidiously organized in that respect. Her life was as orderly as she was.

Even though the police had been through her place, nothing seemed out of sorts. They'd left my place equally clean. That wasn't always the case after a police search; I'd been to enough crime scenes to know that.

There was art on the wall, and most of it was either baroque or impressionist prints. Well, except for a few watercolors and acrylic art pieces, though not by anyone I'd heard of before. My guess was Alice had bought them at a student art show. The university had held one twice a year when I'd been here, and I'd heard Caroyln mention it through the years.

That said, I was disappointed to find nothing behind the paintings. Not even a safe.

I was about to give up when I accidentally knocked into a brass candlestick on a side table and it tumbled to the floor.

Crud.

I waited for a bit and then heard someone coming up the stairs. I glanced around the apartment, looking for a place to hide. The only place I would fit was under the bed.

I slid under, my feet bumping into a box hidden in the shadow of the headboard as I did.

"Did you hear anything?" Paul said to someone outside the door.

It was so quiet up here that I could hear everything happening down the hall.

"No," Rhys said. "It's been quiet tonight."

"I could have sworn I heard something," Paul said.

"I'm sure it was nothing."

Paul grumbled. "It was a banging sound."

"Well, you don't want to disrupt the crime scene. If someone is here," Rhys said loudly.

"True. I've misplaced the key. I'm sure I put it on the board."

"It's been windy; perhaps it blew off when the door opened. That's happened before. Let me grab my slippers, and I'll come down and help you look," Rhys said.

As they walked away, I scrambled out from under the bed, pulling the box with me.

I quickly took photos of the contents. What appeared to be some kind of logbook and a number of personal letters rested atop a bunch of knickknacks and a few coins. After snapping a bunch of pictures without really looking, I slid the box back under the bed. Then I locked the front door and hurried down the stairs and into my apartment.

Rhys knocked on my door. "Did you hear anything upstairs?" he asked loudly.

"No," I said. "I must have dozed off on the couch. Is everything okay?" I handed him the key, and he slipped it in his pocket.

He smiled. "Nothing to worry about. The key seems to be missing, though. Might be some kids playing a prank or something."

I put on my slippers by the door, then we headed downstairs.

"I cannot find the key," Paul said when we made it to the lobby. He was quite flustered, and I felt terrible for causing him so much distress.

What I'd found had hardly been worth his worry. The guilt multiplied within me. I felt sick with it. Poor man, and I'd done that to him.

I'm a terrible person.

"Here, let me look under the desk," Rhys said. "I know your back is bad."

"I can do it, Professor."

"I know you can, but no use possibly hurting yourself. Come out from there and let me look."

Rhys knelt behind the big wooden reception desk.

"Here, use the light on my phone," I added helpfully.

He took the phone from me. "Thanks. This will help."

We sounded like some awful stage play, but Paul didn't seem to notice. He was genuinely worried about the missing key.

"Wait, I think I feel something," Rhys said. "Is this the key?" He held it up.

"Oh, it is." Paul put a hand to his chest. "Thank you, Professor. It must have fallen and I didn't notice. Though I'm still calling the detective. He asked me to if anything strange happened."

I let out the breath I'd been holding. I'd worn my gloves so there wouldn't be fingerprints, but I prayed I hadn't left anything behind that would make the detective suspicious.

"It was just a noise," Rhys said, "and you were the only one who heard it. There is a storm outside. I'd hate if we bothered the police for no reason."

Paul frowned. "Right. But someone has been messing with my keys. They were out of order. I think I need to call them."

I also prayed Rhys wouldn't be upset with me for involving him in all of this. Some great detective I'd turned out to be, knocking something over my first time searching.

Even with all of that, I was curious about the box. The pictures probably weren't great, since I'd taken them in the dark, but I couldn't wait to take a look.

"You should do whatever makes you feel best," I said. "But is it possible the other night manager moved the keys?"

"It's possible," Paul said, "but I want to make sure kids haven't snuck in."

He picked up the phone. Rhys and I made our way upstairs and stood at my cracked door while we waited.

* * *

"We'll take a look, headmaster," Gareth said a few minutes later when he arrived. His voice carried up the stairwell.

Darn. I'd been hoping it would be one of his men who came to check things out. I had a feeling if I'd accidentally left anything amiss, he would know it was me. He was already suspicious.

I only hoped that, if questioned, Rhys would keep my secret. Rhys quickly made his way to his flat and waved before going into his apartment.

I listened at the door, but I couldn't hear anything.

I'd sat down on my couch and was about to pick up my phone when someone banged on the door.

I jumped. Dropped my phone on the floor and then quickly grabbed my robe from my room. I put it over my clothes. Then I mussed my hair.

There was another knock.

"Just a minute," I said.

I opened the door and blinked against the light in the hallway. I deserved an Oscar for this performance.

"What's wrong now?" I asked the detective.

He glanced from my head to my toes and smirked.

"Do you usually sleep in your clothes?" he asked suspiciously.

I glanced down to see my jeans poking out the bottom of my robe.

"Why do you care? I was cold, so I put my robe over my clothes, and I must have fallen asleep. What's going on? Why are you here?"

His eyes narrowed. "Did you hear a noise earlier?"

"Where?" I yawned. That was real. I was so tired, and all the adrenaline I'd been feeling had left my body. "I don't understand what you mean." Being sneaky had exhausted me.

"There were noises upstairs. Did you hear anyone pass by?"

I shook my head. That much was true. I'd been the one passing by. Again I prayed Rhys didn't share my secret. "Did you find out what happened to her?" I asked. "Was it natural causes?"

"You seem very curious," he said.

"Well, as I've mentioned many times, I'm a journalist. And also, the poor woman died right here on my doorstep. I tried to save her and I didn't know her, so of course I'm curious. Anyone would be."

"The case is still ongoing."

I sighed. "But in the office earlier, you intimated that there were suspicious circumstances. You would tell me if anyone tried to kill her, right? I mean, I thought of all the places in the world, I would be safe here, but I'm beginning to wonder. If something did happen to her, you seemed focused on me. And since I know I had nothing to do with it, it makes me wonder if I'm safe."

"I assure you, you're perfectly safe in our town," he said, but it was easy to see he was frustrated by the turn in the conversation.

"Still, I think everyone in town should know what's going on with the investigation. The school paper will want to run a story.

In fact, I'll run by the station with one of my students tomorrow. We'll do an interview. But I promise to call first to find the best time for you. We don't want to be an inconvenience."

He opened his mouth and then shut it. He frowned.

"And don't think you can circumvent the interview. We'll have to publish that the police continue to say 'No comment' but seem to be investigating as though the professor's death were a murder. Good night, Detective." I shut the door in his face.

My hands shook. I'd been so sure he was about to arrest me for breaking and entering. I had to remind myself there was no way he could know.

After turning on the electric fireplace, I sat down on my couch. At least my screen hadn't cracked when I dropped my phone.

I pulled up the pictures I'd taken. The flash had worked in the dark, but some of the photos were blurry because I'd been moving so fast. The letters I'd found seemed to be from a man to Alice, and there was a prison stamp on them. I'd only taken pictures of the first letter; I hadn't had time to open the others. But all of them had the same name: Alan.

Was this a lover or an ex? Was that why she seldom dated and had been so cranky?

I rolled my eyes. I reminded myself that in my profession, it was best if one didn't assume anything.

"Go by the facts," I said out loud as a reminder. I would research the name and the prison later. But Alan was in prison; the professor wouldn't have been the first woman to fall in love with someone behind bars.

The only other thing in the box had been a logbook, and I'd taken pictures of only a few of the pages. They consisted of lists of what looked like account names along with numbers that seemed to form some sort of code. I was no code breaker, but the book seemed like an odd thing for the professor to be hiding under her bed. And then I remembered the file I'd found in her office. I compared the pictures. The logs were similar, but the numbers by each account were different.

Could it have something to do with her death?

Well, that was a reach. I still wasn't sure if she'd been murdered, though of course the detective had let it slip that it appeared she'd been poisoned.

Had her friend Alan been released from jail and killed her? I remembered what Catrin had said about Alice being with a man she hadn't recognized in the pub a few nights ago.

If only the pub had cameras.

Then it hit me. Maybe there were cameras on the streets. CCTV was a big thing over here. There was a chance the couple might have been caught on camera that night.

But how did I bring that up to the detective without sounding suspicious?

Then my brain cells clicked, and I came up with a clever idea.

Chapter Nine

The next afternoon, Ellis and I showed up at the police station, which was just a few blocks up from my apartment, but the weather had turned once again, and snow fell heavily.

"I'm sorry for making you go out in this," I said.

Ellis shrugged. "Please, don't worry about the weather. My flat is small, and I'd rather be out of it than in it. And I'm used to the weather. Besides, as the advisory editor of the school newspaper, I should have already been on this story. Thank you for the suggestion."

"Don't beat yourself up about it. Were you the editor in undergrad?"

He nodded. "I was editor for two years, and when I graduated, the dean asked me to stay on in an advisory position. It counts toward my coursework hours, and I enjoy it. Though I haven't had a chance to write a story in several months. I think the last one was in the fall when I wrote about our attendance being higher than it had been in years.

"I directly related that to the hard work the dean has been doing during her time in the position."

That sounded like Caroyln. No matter where she was, she excelled. Her A-type personality wouldn't allow for any sort of failure. And yet she was one of the best friends I'd ever had and always thought of others. Those two traits didn't always go together.

Inside the station, which was in an old stone cottage, I was surprised to see a large fireplace in the lobby.

Ellis gave the desk sergeant our names, and she asked for us to take a seat.

"Detective Jones will be with you shortly," she said. She was young but had a kind face and a soft voice.

"It is unusual for a faculty member to oversee an interview," Ellis said. He wasn't being judgmental, just curious.

"I want to make sure he doesn't give you the same run-around he gives me," I said.

Ellis smiled. "Thanks for having my back."

"I won't interfere unless he tries to bully you."

"And why would I do that?" a deep baritone said from behind me.

The man is a ninja.

"Hello, Detective," I said before turning around. "You shouldn't sneak up on people like that."

"I wasn't sneaking. I've come to take Ellis back for our interview. I assure you I won't bully him. There is no need for you to be there."

"As his adviser, I'm here merely to observe his interview techniques. If I'm to craft the next wave of journalists with 'extreme integrity,' as the dean puts it, I need to be on the front lines. I promise you won't hear a word out of me."

"I doubt that," he said under his breath.

Ellis ducked his head as he smiled.

We followed the detective back to his office. First, we walked through the bullpen of other officers. There were far more than I'd expected. There were at least eight desks, though only half of them were occupied.

His office was just to the left. As he waved us inside, he shut the door behind us. "Please, have a seat."

As promised, I sat next to Ellis and didn't say a word.

"Thank you for seeing me," Ellis said politely. "Do you mind if I record you? It is best for us both, since you will be on the record."

"That's fine," the detective said.

Ellis pulled out his phone, which also held his list of questions. He'd showed it to me in the car before we'd left my place. He'd done a good job, but I'd given him an idea for a few more questions.

"Detective, can you tell me how Dr. Alice Rice died?"

Gareth glanced at me, then focused on Ellis. "She collapsed on the first floor of faculty housing. At present, it looks as though it was cardiac arrest."

"Right. And was it natural causes? Have you heard from the medical examiner or coroner?"

"Preliminary test results from the ME show that there may have been foul play involved."

Ellis's head popped up from his phone. "Oh? So, is it a suspicious death?"

"While it isn't our department policy to comment during an ongoing investigation, the ME's first reports will be made public later this afternoon. We are going forward as if it were a suspicious death."

Well, that was new. At least for him to admit it.

"I understand you won't comment, since it is an ongoing investigation, but do you have some leads?"

"Yes, we are following up on a few leads," the detective said. He glanced at me.

It was all I could do not to roll my eyes.

"Right. And is one of those suspects the man she was with at the pub? Were you able to find some photographic evidence of the man?"

Gareth's eyes widened, and he stared at me suspiciously.

I shrugged.

"Where did you hear that?" he asked. Then he wrote down something in his notebook.

"At the pub," Ellis said. "There was a rumor that she was with a stranger that night. I asked the owners, but they do not have security cameras. I wondered if you perhaps had caught the man on CCTV on one of the streets?"

Gareth cleared his throat and then frowned. "We're looking into it." He absolutely had not been. I knew he'd been surprised. And I felt like I'd been manipulative, but this was much better than me just coming out and asking. He would have thought I was up to something.

Well, you are.

"Is there anything else you can tell us about Dr. Rice that makes you believe someone tried to kill her?" Ellis asked.

"I never said that—only that we are examining the evidence and found reason to be suspicious. She still could have died from natural causes."

"Or self-harm?" Ellis asked.

The detective frowned. "Why would you say that?"

This time Ellis cleared his throat. "I've done a bit of digging. She was hospitalized when she was younger for depression."

That was news to me.

"Medical records are sealed; how would you know that?"

"It was in a newspaper article from years ago. When she was younger, her parents were killed in a car accident. She was sent to a hospital for several months before being released to her aunt's care. It was written up in a news article."

Well, that was also news to me. And so tragic. Was that why she'd been so cold and standoffish? If she'd lost her parents at an early age and then been sent to some institution, she likely had trust issues. I would.

"May I ask where you saw that article?"

Ellis nodded. "I found bits of it online. It was in her hometown newspaper—Crumby, which, as you know, is a few towns over. In 1999, her parents were killed. Her father had been accused of some sort of financial scheme, and they died in a car accident, but the police found it suspicious."

I wondered if that had something to do with the logbook I'd found under her bed. I hadn't dared take evidence from the scene, but I wanted a second look at the photos I'd taken. I also thought it would be a good idea for the police to take a look; it might help solve her murder. But how did I tell the detective to search her home better without giving myself up?

And who was the man in the pub? Had that been Alan?

I'd be doing more research on him later. Was he her boyfriend, or had he been involved in the financial scheme? That might explain the log entries. Or perhaps she'd been researching her parents' death and someone didn't like that. Maybe that was why he was in prison.

There were too many variables.

The problem was, I couldn't share any of this information with the detective. He would know I'd been snooping.

Ugh. That's what I got for trying to circumvent the law. But I didn't think he'd have let me take a look. How had they missed that box under the bed?

I eyed several file folders on the detective's desk. I desperately wanted to look into what he'd found, especially the ME's report. I faked a cough.

The two men stared at me.

"Are you all right, Professor?" Ellis asked.

"I could use some water," I said. And then coughed again.

The detective sighed. "I'll get you some."

He left his office.

"Ellis, do you mind stepping out for a minute?"

"What?"

"I need a private moment to pull my thoughts together." I didn't want to involve him in my plan.

"Uh. Okay." He stepped out and shut the door.

I knew it was wrong, and I was a big believer in ethics. But the detective wasn't telling us everything, and I knew I could help. I opened the files and took pictures, not bothering to look at the content.

"What are you doing out here?" The detective's voice outside the door startled me.

"She needed a moment," Ellis said.

"Oh, really?" I could hear the smirk in the detective's voice.

I closed everything and took a seat.

"Sorry," I said as the door to the office opened. "This has all been a lot, and I needed a moment to collect myself. It just really hit me that she died right in front of me and we have no clue why." That last part was the truth. Being here had brought everything into focus.

"Here." Gareth handed over some cups of water to me and Ellis.

A few minutes later, Ellis finished up his interview and thanked the detective for taking the time to see him.

But before we left, I had to ask. "Did you find anything about her parents in her apartment—or flat, as you call them?"

He frowned. "Why do you ask?"

"She seemed to be a bit of a tortured soul. People like that keep their secrets hidden. At least, that's been my experience. You seemed surprised when Ellis mentioned her past. I would have thought you'd have found photos or something."

He eyed me suspiciously. He did that a lot.

"My team was thorough, but I may go back and search," he said.

I wanted to scream *Look under the bed.*

But I just nodded and followed Ellis out.

"Good job," I said as we climbed into his tiny car.

"I was fine until the snooping."

I laughed. "Sorry about that. And here I am trying to make sure our ethics are beyond reproach, but he hasn't been sharing all he knows."

"He's a nice guy," Ellis said. "I've talked to him a few times," he said. "He seemed on edge around you."

"Oh? I hadn't noticed." I smiled. "Probably because he knows I hold him to a high standard. How about I treat you to lunch at the pub?"

"Really?"

I nodded. "Least I can do for everything you've done for me, and for allowing me to snoop a bit."

"It's my job to look after you, Professor."

I smiled. "And you're great at it. Come on, the weather is only going to get worse. Let's gets some warm grub, and then you can tell me about your angle for the story."

"I'm in," he said. "I'm always up for a free meal."

I laughed. "I was the same way when I was your age."

I felt bad. This was also my way of picking the kid's brain about what he'd found out about Alice's past.

But he didn't need to know that.

Chapter Ten

After lunch, Ellis and I ran across the street to the apartment building. He wanted to show me some of the stories he'd found about our victim. But Paul met us at the bottom step with an umbrella. Had he discovered I'd borrowed Alice's key?

No. There was no way.

"Hello, Professor," he said in his usual jovial manner.

"Hi, Paul. Thank you for the umbrella. I don't mind getting a bit wet."

"Well, I thought, if it is okay, you might want to ask Ellis to come in to help?"

My mind whirled with possibilities. "I don't understand," I said.

"You've received several boxes from the States. I could use the help getting them upstairs."

"Already? That was fast. And I'm happy to help," I said. "You don't need to be going up and down the stairs." I turned to Ellis. "You've done enough. I can do this."

He shrugged. "I don't mind at all."

He followed us inside. Ten medium-sized boxes were stacked in the space near the desk. That was half of what I'd shipped over, but I had been told, because of customs, it could take as long as two months. I was surprised and happy. I loved having my books and a few of my things around me. And the rest of my winter wardrobe, which I desperately needed here. And by wardrobe, I meant dark jeans, boots, and the coats I'd seldom worn in Texas. At least I hoped that was what would be in the boxes. I had no way of knowing until I'd opened them.

The only other things I'd sent over were some of my favorite artwork and a couple of sculptures that a friend had made me.

I'd stored what I hadn't sold, just in case things didn't work out and I had to go back to the States and find another job.

With the three of us, it only took a few minutes to get the boxes upstairs.

"Do you want help unpacking?" Ellis asked. "And before you say anything, household errands and office services are in my contract."

I laughed. And then I handed Paul a forty-dollar tip.

"You don't have to do that," he said.

"I know. I'm just grateful to you for everything." Okay, and maybe it helped assuage my guilt in a small way to give him a bit of cash. "And I'm sorry it's American money; I still haven't been to the bank or an ATM to do an exchange."

"No worries," he said. "It's money and will spend as well as any." After thanking me again, he left.

I tried to give Ellis some money as well, but he shook his head. "That I can't do," he said. "It's in my contract. Meals are okay, and we were discussing university business. But the administration draws the line at tips and such."

"That hardly seems fair, especially for struggling college students. Well, I'll keep you well fed. I don't mind eating alone, but I prefer company."

"I never mind a warm meal. Is there anything else I can do for you?"

I started to say no, but then I held up a hand. "Just one more thing. I don't want to keep you, but could you email me links to the articles you've found on Dr. Rice when you get home?"

"No problem. You're doing your own investigation, aren't you?"

"It's more because she died on my doorstep," I said. "I feel this strange sense of responsibility to find out what happened to her."

"I would be the same way," he said. "I actually look at her a different way after finding out about her childhood. Can you imagine being in an asylum at such a young age?"

"No. It explains a lot, doesn't it?"

"About her behavior and the fact that she didn't seem to trust anyone," he said. "She was always hounding Gladys about different things."

"Didn't she have a TA?"

He shook his head. "She said she didn't trust anyone to help with grading and such. She did it all herself. And she treated poor Gladys as her personal assistant—though Gladys is extremely kind and never seemed to mind. She loves taking care of people. She's like a second gran to me."

I smiled. "I just found out she's married to Paul. I had no idea."

He nodded. "It's admirable that they both live a life of service. Not all of us are made that way."

"So true. Although you've done a wonderful job of taking care of me so far."

He blushed. "It's my job, and I'm excited to learn from you. Though what you did today . . ."

"Right. So, I'm someone who requires the absolute truth in a situation. Sometimes I go a step too far, and today was one of those days. The detective couldn't tell us everything, as it is his job to keep things close to the vest.

"But as a reporter, sometimes to get the truth, you have to be willing to take that extra step. Is it ethically wrong? Possibly. But if the detective told us the truth, then no harm done. If he didn't, well, we'll have proof of that. As a reporter, you can't trust anyone. Least of all your sources. You need information to back up every lead."

"That makes sense. But I would have never been brave enough to go through his files right there on his desk. What if he has a camera set up in his office?"

"Highly unlikely," I said. "I understand your point. I'm not saying you should ever do what I did. But sometimes we have to do scary things to get at the truth."

He nodded. Then he pointed to my laptop, which was on the table. "Were you able to get into the university server?"

"I was, and then I got locked out," I said. "I'm not sure what I did."

He smiled. "You probably just timed out. And the password for your laptop needs to be different than the desktop in your office. It's in—"

"The packet you gave me."

We grinned.

"Yes," he said. "But I'm happy to help."

I sat down at my laptop. "Give me just a second." I cleared my search history. I didn't want him to see anything about Dr. Rice.

I motioned for him to sit down across from me and then pushed the computer toward him.

"Give me just a second, and I'll get you in," he said. He typed quickly. "I don't know if you read your packet about the school files, but you have access to all student and personnel files on here." He glanced up over the screen at me and smiled.

"You mean, if I want to do a bit of snooping?"

We laughed.

Then he held his hands up in surrender. "I know I will be doing a bit of a search when I get to the university," he said. "But I don't have access to faculty information like you do. Well, I have some, but you have security for more of the files."

I didn't know why I hadn't asked earlier. For some reason, even though we lived in a digitalized world, I had assumed everything would be in file cabinets.

"I've bookmarked the server page for you," he said, pushing the computer back at me. "You need to put in your user name and a new password, and you'll be good to go."

"I'm sorry you had to show me again."

"It's okay. I understand that everything is new to you."

I found the info on the paper he'd given me earlier and typed it into the page. The welcome screen popped up. "Wow, that was quick. Thank you. I'm usually a bit more tech savvy." Our paper in Dallas had been fully digitalized and I'd had to learn all sorts of software, but this was different.

"No problem. Are you sure I can't help you unpack?"

"I'm good. Besides, I've taken up enough of your time today. Don't you want to get to work on your article?"

He nodded. "Most of the student staff who aren't back from holiday will be working from home. We're putting out a *welcome back* paper for next Friday. As we find out information about Dr. Rice, I'll update it, so we have the latest news going out."

"That sounds like a great plan. You know what you're doing, but if you need any help, let me know. I'm here for you."

"Thanks, Professor. We usually sent the mock-up to Dr. Rice once we had everything positioned. Will it be okay if we send it to you?"

"Whatever works for your team."

He laughed.

"What is it?"

"Nothing against Dr. Rice, but your approach is nice. She was into micromanaging every aspect."

"Yeah, well, I don't have time for that. I'm learning a new job and everything that goes with that."

And trying to solve a possible murder.

After he left, I forced myself to unpack and break down the boxes. If I didn't do it right away, I'd let the boxes sit there for weeks, possibly months, only digging out what I needed.

I didn't want to be judged by the housemaster, or anyone who might be coming in, like Rhys. I put the books on the shelves haphazardly and promised myself I'd organize them better when I had more time.

Then I remembered the book I'd taken from Alice's flat, the one about Welsh witches. I'd stuck it behind the couch cushion before the detective stopped at my door the night before.

In my defense, I felt so very guilty for taking something from a crime scene. I knew better. I'd just been so curious about Alice being involved or interested in the occult. She didn't seem the type.

As much as I wanted to thumb through the book, I stuffed it on the shelf with some of my other books. Once I had my place cleaned up, I'd sit down and do some real research.

After breaking down the boxes, I picked some of them up and headed downstairs. My thighs and calves were already feeling overused after hauling and unpacking the boxes earlier, but I needed the exercise.

"Oh, I can get those for you," Paul said when he saw me coming around.

"I can take them where they need to go," I said. "Besides, I probably need to know where to take my trash, right?"

"No, it is one of the services. It should be in your welcome packet from the university. We pick up daily; you just put your bag or bin outside your door in the evening, and our cleaner picks it up on her rounds."

"Oh. I should probably read the packets I was given for this place and the university. But it's been an eventful few days since I arrived."

"It has. I can promise our town is normally a sleepy little place. You know that from when you were here at university before."

I laughed. "I do remember. To me, those days were like a fairy tale, and I was lucky to live in it. Now it feels as though the real world has trod on those memories."

"Ah, I don't like to hear that. Dr. Rice is a bad business, but it's nothing to do with you. I don't care what others say." He smiled.

It took everything in me not to ask what he meant.

"Just put those against the wall. I'll take them out in a bit."

"Okay, thank you." I was used to being self-sufficient, but my home and work came with some great perks so far.

"My pleasure," he said.

"Paul, how did Dr. Rice treat you?"

He shrugged. "She was no-nonsense," he said. "Professors come in all types, as you will learn."

I sat down on the third step. He would know more about her than anyone, since he'd seen her every day.

"It's just that everyone I've talked to says she was unkind and took advantage of people. I wondered if she was like that with you. I'm sorry for that if she was."

He laughed. "It's not on you. You barely knew the woman. Besides, I have tough skin, as does my Gladys. She always saw Alice as a problem to be solved. For some reason, Gladys thought if she was kind to her, then the professor might learn to be a gentler person, but it never worked. My wife, though, always tries to believe there is good in people."

"That's admirable," I said. "I wish I was more like Gladys. I'm on the other end of that spectrum. It's tough for me to trust anyone. That comes from years of being a crime reporter and seeing the worst of the world."

"Well, that is understandable. It's like the soldiers who come back from war. They've seen the worst."

I nodded. "I would never compare myself to anyone fighting in a war, but I covered a few of them when I was younger. I don't know how they survive mentally."

"They are brave."

"Agreed. I think I asked before, but did Alice have any significant others? Anyone she might have dated or brought home? I understand it sounds nosy, but I keep wondering if there is someone out there who might be missing her and wondering what happened."

"There was a fellow who visited several years ago, but then one day he was gone and never returned. If she dated, she never brought them home."

As if realizing what he said, he grimaced. "Not that it would matter. To each their own." He smiled. "It's not my place to judge. But out of everyone living here, she was the one who was most alone. The others would have parties or the occasional guests, but not her. She was a lonely soul."

He frowned. "Her story is as sad as they come. If something happened to me, at least my Gladys would mourn me, but no one seems to care about poor Alice. I wonder if the university will even hold a service for her like they usually do when someone dies."

"I'm sure that's in the works," I said. "I think I remember the dean mentioning that they would do something when everyone was back from the holidays." What I wondered was if anyone who wasn't forced there because of propriety would actually show up.

"I'll take care of these boxes," Paul said.

"Thank you again. I'll bring down the rest."

After delivering the last set of broken-down boxes, I headed back upstairs for the fifth time that day, and my legs ached. I decided to try out my tub. I turned on some Kacey Musgraves, whose voice and storytelling songs I loved, on my phone and hooked it to the small speaker I'd brought from home.

It took a fair minute for the water to run warm, but I was soon ensconced in the heated bath with a few of my favorite salts thrown in. They were eucalyptus scented and great for soaking tired muscles and bones.

No matter how hard I tried to relax, my brain was a revolving door of those last minutes with Alice Rice. The surprise on her face as she fell forward.

She hadn't really sounded angry. Or maybe that was just time messing with my memory.

At some point, I must have dozed off.

I woke to a noise. The water was cool, and someone was banging on my apartment door.

After getting out of the tub, I grabbed my robe. "Just a minute," I said, exiting the bathroom and heading toward the door as they banged again.

I opened the door a crack. The detective was on the other side. "What now?" I asked, exasperated. "There are these things called phones where you can call and ask if it's a good time to come over," I said.

He frowned.

"Or even buttons on the phones to send these things called texts."

"Yes, I know how to use a phone."

"Do you?"

"If you check your phone, you'll see that I did text."

"I was in the bath."

He sniffed the air, then glanced down at my bare feet. "This time I believe you." As if he hadn't believed me the night before. I had to remind myself that except for that book on my shelf, there was no way he could know I'd been in Alice's room.

"What is it you needed?"

"Can I come in?"

"Uh, sure." I walked down the hall. "Let me get changed. Feel free to make yourself a cup of tea or coffee. I'll be back in a minute."

I threw on my old Columbia sweatshirt and a pair of sweats with some cozy socks. I grabbed my phone and saw that he had texted me.

When I came out, he was heating water for tea.

"What is so urgent that it couldn't wait until tomorrow?"

"We followed up on that lead you and Ellis gave us."

"What lead?"

"The CCTV outside the pub."

"Oh. And why are you telling me? From what I've learned about you so far, you aren't one to willingly share information."

He opened a file folder, then he shoved a picture across the kitchen bar. I sat down on the stool while he retrieved a couple of teacups from my cabinet. "Do you recognize him?" he asked.

The man in the photo had dark hair and was quite slim, but he was what some would call average. Nothing about him really stood out. "No. Why should I?"

"He was the man with Alice at the pub."

I was surprised he wanted to share that information.

"Okay, but is there a reason you would expect me to know him?"

He put the cups on the counter, then he handed me another photo. Same guy, standing outside the bookstore.

"I still don't recognize him. Why are you asking me?"

"Because the CCTV shows him following you around town," he said seriously. "And if you don't know who he is, well, that might be a problem, don't you think?"

I shivered. Who was this guy?

Chapter Eleven

I picked up the photo and stared at it again. I prided myself on my situational awareness. I'd lived all over the world and that talent had served me well, but I didn't recognize this guy. Had he been following me? Or was it a coincidence?

"Did he follow me back to my apartment?"

He shook his head. "After you exited the bookstore, he went the opposite way. He turned the corner at the end of the block, and that's where we lost him."

"How would he even know who I am?"

"Some predators have a type," he said.

I'm sure my eyes went wide. "Predator?"

"Well, he was with Alice at the pub, and now he's following you."

"Is he? And I don't look anything like Alice."

"You are beautiful, and some would say Alice was the same."

"You think I'm beautiful?"

"Are you fishing for compliments? I'm trying to make a point that your life may be in danger."

I bit my lip to keep from smiling. "Okay. Maybe she asked him to follow me. She wasn't happy about my appointment by the dean. What if he's some sort of private investigator and he was looking for dirt on me?"

"Now who is reaching?"

I shrugged. "I'm new to town. And you don't recognize him, which means he probably isn't a resident. When the students aren't in town, you have maybe ten thousand people who live here. My guess is you know the majority of them by sight."

"Again, you haven't been around long enough to make that kind of assumption."

I laughed. "I know good cops and bad ones. You're thorough and know how to do the job. My guess is you never go into a room without scoping out everyone who's in there, and you'd be great with faces. It's part of what makes a good detective."

"I think I'm flattered," he grunted. "But you're right, we have no idea who he is. My team is asking at the pub. Could be he signed a receipt, and we'll have a name."

"I don't know why he would be following me. I can't help you there."

"Did you have any unfinished business in the States?" He flipped open his notebook.

"You asked me that the night Alice died."

"Like you said, I'm thorough."

"No. I saw the writing on the wall two years ago when we had to slash a third of our staff. Back then, I told Carolyn what was going on. At the time, she told me that I'd make a great professor. I'd never thought of teaching, and I thought she was just being my friend." I sipped the tea he'd made. "Timing is everything, right?"

"What do you mean?" he asked.

"Her chairman was retiring. And then when I called her about my layoff—retirement—she said it was a sign and that she wanted to make me chairman of the department. She told me what she wanted to do, which was separate journalism from the literature department and create a go-to school here in Wales. I'm pretty sure I told you all this."

"Tell me again," he said.

"I explained, as I did with you, that I was certain she could find someone much more qualified. But she wanted someone who had been in the trenches and wasn't just an academic. I have no idea how she made it past the university board, but she offered me the job a week later."

"Right," he said. "And then a few months later you arrived, and now some guy is following you."

"You said he went the opposite way. So how do you know? Maybe he was just watching the bookstore or the new owner. Well, new to me. Rhian is quite beautiful. Do you think she might be in danger?"

"No. We're fairly certain he watched you."

I shrugged. "How could you know?"

"Because he followed you out of the pub and down the street."

I scrunched up my face.

"You're sure you don't know him? Maybe he's someone you met when you were a student here?"

"While I remember a few people who live here from decades ago, I don't recall them all. So even if I'd seen the guy, I wouldn't have known if he lived here or not. That's my point. I have no idea why he would be following me. I didn't leave any unfinished business, as you keep saying, back in Texas."

He glanced around the apartment and then frowned.

"Your things have arrived."

"Yes. Today, half of my boxes. Mainly books and clothes. That is pretty much the only thing I shipped over. I sold all of my furniture and put a few of my family's things that have been passed down into storage. That is, until I'm sure I'll be staying past this year."

"Why do you think Alice might have you investigated?"

I laughed. "You know the answer as well as I do. I took the job she thought should have been hers," I said. "Maybe she was looking for some sort of dirt on me."

"By following you into a bookstore?"

"He didn't actually go in—at least according to you. I'm a fairly boring person," I said. "I can't have been a very interesting subject to follow." Except that one time when I broke into the victim's apartment.

Why had I done that? The guilt was strong.

"What's wrong?"

"What do you mean?"

"You made a funny face. Did you think of something?"

"Oh. Well, if he was following me, that's one thing. But my days are running together."

"What do you mean?"

"Wasn't that the day after she died? If he killed her, why would he be following me? Unless . . ."

"What?" His eyebrows went up.

"Maybe he didn't know she was dead. If he doesn't live here, he may not have heard the gossip yet. And if he is a PI, you should be able to suss that out fairly quickly, right? He'd need a license. At least he would if he was in the US. I don't know the laws for that sort of thing here."

"You're right, I'll look into it. But do me a favor," he said.

"What's that?"

"Be more aware of your surroundings. And maybe make certain you're with a friend while walking around town or going to the university."

I laughed.

"What?"

"I'm quite independent, and I don't need a chaperone."

"You don't have to listen to my advice, but I do wish you would."

"Does this mean I'm off the suspect list?"

This time he smirked. "I never said you were on it."

"Ha." I covered my mouth.

"Have you had a chance to go through the files you took to your office? Was there anything in there that might be of interest to us?"

I shook my head. "I spent most of today unpacking boxes, and I left the papers in my office. I told you the only things I took were dissertations and some sort of list of accounts. I'm just making sure we have those grad students covered. And I'll have to ask someone else about the accounts."

He flipped the page in his notebook. "Do you know your neighbor very well?"

"Who do you mean?"

"Dr. Rhys Davies, who lives down the hall from you. He's the one who called the police the night Dr. Rice died."

"Because I asked him to. He asked what he could do, and I told him to call the police. Then he was helping me try to administer CPR."

"Did you know the victim was interested in him?"

"Not really."

"That's a nonanswer."

"What do you want me to say? He's a handsome guy; I'm sure he has lots of people who are interested in him. From the little bit that I've spoken to him, he's well read, kind, and helpful. Just because she was interested doesn't mean he was. I'm sure he would have mentioned it to you if they had a relationship that was more than professional. Did he?"

The detective raised his eyebrows.

I sighed. "No comment on your part, but I have a feeling I'm right. Besides, he explained to me the other day that he doesn't date his coworkers or anyone in town. He finds it easier to keep nosy people out of his business."

"And what about last night?"

I stared down at the photo and sipped my tea. "Uh, last night?"

"Did you hear him go past your apartment or any disturbance?"

"I was resting," I said. Hiding under the bed of the victim, but I couldn't tell him that bit.

"Riiight. You fell asleep on the couch."

"Yep. It's becoming a habit—you waking me up. Though tonight you may have saved me from drowning. I fell asleep in the tub. I don't think my body has adjusted to the time difference yet."

"Lots of water. That's what my nan used say. While she's a fan of tea and whiskey, she swears water can cure most anything."

"Did she travel a lot?"

He nodded. "Still does. She's on an Egyptian cruise with her friends at the moment. When my grandfather was alive, he was an anthropologist, and they traveled studying different types of civilizations. She was his assistant before they were married. She was quite the wild woman, from what I hear, though she's my nan, so I don't always listen to her stories."

I smiled.

"What?" he asked.

"I like her already. She sounds adventurous."

"That she is. To a fault sometimes. My mum and da keep hoping she'll settle down like a regular nan someday. But I don't think that will ever happen."

"Regular?"

He shrugged. "Their words, not mine. I've always thought she was amazing. And she has taken me on the best vacations of my life. Thanks to her, I've been all over the world. And she was the only one in the family who appreciated my calling to be a police officer.

"My mum and da think my job is too dangerous. Maybe it was when I was in Cardiff for several years, but not here. Except for the professor's death, the worst we usually deal with is drunk and disorderly."

It had been small-minded of me to think he was a man who'd lived here all his life and probably wasn't worldly. I was wrong.

"You mentioned your grandfather died. I thought I met him in the pub?"

He shook his head. "That's Granddad on my da's side."

"Oh."

"Listen to me prattling on. I'm the one who should be asking you questions. You didn't answer if there is anyone back home who might want to cause you harm. Maybe a coworker or employee?"

"I did answer you. I said no. I was careful when curating my reporting teams and columnists. They are all bright and wonderful journalists. And they all understood that losing their jobs had nothing to do with their abilities. They were professionals, and I wrote them all glowing recommendations."

"Anyone you might have written a story about and helped put away?"

I shrugged. "It's been a decade since I've done any real reporting. And yes, before you ask, I was on the crime beat for years. I did help the police put away a few criminals, but most of them were the white-collar variety. They would have served very little time. And why wait to catch up with me until I'm in a small town in Wales?

"Besides, no one back home really knew where I was going next. I didn't say because I wasn't sure it would work out. I told you that I've never been a professor before. As far as my friends know, I'm off traveling. I didn't lie. I just didn't give specifics of how long I would be away."

He frowned. "So the only people who knew you were here were at that party the night Dr. Rice died."

"Uh. I guess. Wait. No. The newspaper here ran an article about me. So anyone who might have read that would know."

He blew out a breath. "Something has been bothering me about the suddenness of her death."

"Detective, I believe that has been bothering all of us."

"Right. But she was poisoned."

"You heard from the ME?"

There was a long pause, and then he nodded.

Well, that's a surprise. He'd been honest for once.

"Yes. The timing is suspicious."

"Okay. What is it you're trying to tell me?"

"What if she wasn't the intended victim for the poison?"

I frowned. "You think it was meant for someone else? But we know she wasn't very well liked. I hate to say it, but she seems a likely candidate."

"Except no one had ever tried anything, at least as far as we know. We haven't found any threats. Well, there were more than a few student surveys that were unkind but most likely truthful. And there were a few emails from students saying what an awful instructor she was. And there were other emails not associated with the university. My team is still following up on those leads."

"I read through many of those surveys, and she was not liked as a professor. But it's a reach to go from a difficult instructor to wanting to murder them."

"True. But we may be concentrating on the wrong things," he said.

"I feel like you're trying to say something but I'm not following. Have I mentioned I'm exhausted?" I was being truthful. "I need you to spell it out for me."

"What if what happened to Dr. Rice was meant for you?"

Oh. My.

Chapter Twelve

The next morning, I glanced out the window to find the quaint town was covered in a foot of snow. I glanced down at my phone. I had an hour until Ellis came to pick me up. I'd tried to tell him that I'd walk; I didn't want him to drive on dangerous roads.

His answer was that the plows had already cleared the main roads. I pulled the box of pastries out of the fridge that I'd bought with Rhys at the bakery. While there was no microwave in the apartment, there was a small toaster oven. I popped in one of the Welsh cakes and then went to turn on the coffee maker. I was grateful to whoever had stocked the pantry and fridge, but I'd need to go buy some provisions soon.

For the first time since I'd arrived, my brain wasn't foggy. Even though the detective had made me wonder if I had been the intended target of whatever had happened to Alice, I'd slept hard after talking with him. Though who would want to do me in? No one, with the exception of Carolyn and her husband, had known me long enough to hate me.

The only person who had seemed to be troubled by my existence was the victim. Had she tried to poison me and accidentally killed herself?

It was a possibility, but I doubted it. At least that's what my gut said.

The detective had been smart to be suspicious that someone had poisoned her. But was he right about that poison being meant for me? And had that dark-haired fellow really been following me?

I shivered, and it had nothing to do with the cold.

While the coffee percolated, I went and pulled Alice's book from my shelf. I still felt bad about taking it and would find a way to put it back in her belongings. But I found it strange that an English professor, a fussy one, had so many books on the occult.

The book was interesting, with several chapters covering everything from myths and spirits to magic spells. While I'd thought most of the pagan rituals would have been from Celtic legends, I was wrong. Pre-Celtic, prehistoric landmarks were all over Wales. Then the druids came along.

As I read, I understood Alice's interest in the history of the country. There was a long-standing tradition of stories that were passed down orally, long before the written word. Any literature professor worth their salt would be interested in this kind of oral history.

The toaster oven buzzed, and I realized I didn't have a hot pad to take the tray out. I found a fork and rolled the pastry onto the plate.

Then I poured myself a cup of coffee.

There were sections on various goddesses from Celtic mythology listed later in the book. Many of the stories were about strong women who fought to protect their land and people.

By the time the alarm went off on my phone to remind me that Ellis would be here soon, I was well into the book. I put it back on the shelves among my own and promised myself I'd finish it later.

I washed the cup and saucer I'd used and put them on the drainboard. I couldn't remember what day the cleaners came in, but I didn't want to leave a mess for them. Then I thought about the book. What if one of them had cleaned Alice's apartment and noticed the book in my place?

It was highly unlikely, but I didn't want to take a chance.

I put the book in my backpack along with my laptop. I didn't need the computer at the university, as I had a desktop, but I didn't want anyone to peek at my research on Alice. If someone was following me—though I didn't think that was the case—I wasn't going to make it easy for them.

I had no reason not to trust the cleaners, but as a journalist, I was paranoid about keeping information safe. It was strange to think of so many people taking care of my needs, as I'd always been self-sufficient. Carolyn had explained that the university wanted their professors to focus on teaching and research, so day-to-day tasks were taken care of for them. It was something I'd have to get used to.

By the time I made it downstairs, the snow had started up again. I was glad I'd put on my fuzzy boots I'd bought at the last minute online. I also wore my puffer coat and a furry hat with flaps over the ears.

"Morning, Paul," I said as I passed the desk.

"Morning, Professor. Is everything okay?"

"Yes," I said hesitantly. Then I stopped. "Why shouldn't it be?"

He waved a hand. "No reason. I just noticed the detective stayed quite a while in your place last night."

I smiled. This man didn't miss anything. "We were just talking. He told me stories about his grandmother and how much she loves to travel."

He grinned. "That she does. Always has the best stories when she visits the pub."

"I can imagine. I'll see you later."

"Stay warm, Professor, and mind your step."

"Thanks," I said.

While I felt safer having a doorman, it had never occurred to me that he would be in the know about all of the tenants. I wasn't used to people being involved in my business.

When I opened the door, the wind nearly blew it out of my hands.

"Let me help," he said.

I passed through, and he shut it after me.

When Ellis saw me, he hopped out of his car and opened the door.

"You don't have to do that," I said. "I don't expect you to wait on me."

"My gran would be upset if she knew I wasn't being a gentleman," he said.

"Well, I won't tell."

He sighed when he sat down in the driver's seat. "It wouldn't matter; she always seems to know."

We laughed.

"How is the story going about Dr. Rice?"

"Tragic," he said.

I turned to face him. "Oh? What did you find out?"

"Nothing that I think we should print," he said. "Her early years with her family were quite traumatic."

"That is sad. Traumatic how?" Ellis had told me a few things, but I wondered what he'd found.

He turned the windshield wipers up, as the snow was coming down hard again.

"Her dad was some sort of financial bigwig, and there was a misappropriation of funds. It's confusing, though, if he was the one who was responsible. It never came out in the press. It's like they died and the story disappeared. He and his wife, her mother, were killed in a traffic accident. I think she was about nine when it happened. The story about the legal side of things seemed to die after that. There was some investigation into the accident."

"Oh?"

"In the end, the police said they didn't see signs of foul play. But why were they investigating if there weren't signs of foul play?"

"Good point, and you're right," I said.

"About?"

"Her early years being tragic," I said. "What if it is someone from the past who did her in?"

"You sound like someone from Cockney, England, with the *did her in*."

We laughed again.

"I do like *My Fair Lady* and *Pygmalion*. Did it say what asylum she went to?"

He shook his head. "Medical records, especially of children, are sealed."

"Right. But I wonder if this is something we should mention to the detective."

"Why is that?" he asked. "I thought our job was to keep our sources protected."

I nodded. "Yes, but there is also quid pro quo. If we share some information with the detective, he might be able to get into those records now that the professor is dead. Right? If it leads to something that had to do with her death."

"Ah. I hadn't thought of it that way. Do you think he'd actually share what he finds out?"

I coughed. *Absolutely not.* "It's worth a try. Do you have any idea where she went to live after the asylum?"

"No. The only thing I found was an old census report that had her listed as part of her aunt's family."

"What about more recent events?"

"I've been speaking with other faculty members. No one seems to have known her that well, even though she'd taught here for more than a decade. There were a lot of platitudes, but no one seemed to like her much. But we knew that."

"Did you find anything about her ex?"

His eyes widened, even though he stared at the icy road. "She was married?"

"Possibly. At least that's what I've heard. I haven't seen any records of a marriage license." Though I'd tried to look. "I found more information about her ex. He also had some sort of financial dealings that didn't go so well, and he ended up in jail."

"Interesting," Ellis said.

I bit my lip. Alice had been unpleasant to me, but I felt sorry for her. I tended to be a loner as well, but I'd made friends along the way. Most of whom I'd had all my life.

"Maybe we should look more into her ex," Ellis said. "I never remember seeing her with anyone, but my guess is the relationships may not have ended well. Given the way she acted."

"Ellis. What's our number-one rule?"

"Always seek the truth?"

I laughed. "Okay, number-two rule: Never assume anything. I've been doing a lot of that, and I know better. I've just never had to solve a murder before. White-collar crimes, sure, but I'm no detective. She may have had a perfectly normal life outside of the university."

I doubted it, but we couldn't know for sure. "We only go by the facts. It's okay to wonder and theorize, but when writing a story, you have to rely on facts only."

"You're right," he said.

I thought about the detective showing me the picture of the man he thought was following me. Was he? And why?

"But as you're doing your investigation, I want you to be extra careful."

"I'm always professional," he said.

I smiled. "I'm sure you are. But if someone used poison to kill her, they're going to want to keep that secret. Digging around in her past might put you in danger. Please don't investigate her exes alone. If you find anyone, you tell me first. Got it? That is something we will do together. I won't have you putting your life in danger for a story."

"Yes, Professor." He frowned. "But isn't that something that comes with the job?"

"Not while you're a student under my care. I mean it, Ellis. I want you to make me a promise. It will be your byline on the story, but we may be dealing with someone extremely dangerous. We do this together or not at all."

He nodded. "Do you have a gut feeling about who might have wanted her dead? I read your article about instincts and gut reactions."

I laughed. "I wrote that ten years ago. You really have been researching me, haven't you?"

"Yes," he said unapologetically. "Before I applied for the job. I have to admit that is why I wanted to be your assistant. I told you before, I feel like I can learn more from you than I can the rest of the faculty combined."

"Oh, that's not true," I said. "But thank you."

He shrugged again. "We'll have to agree to disagree. I can't wait for your classes, and I'm not the only one. The dean was right about bringing you onto the staff. We'll be the most prestigious journalism school in no time."

"So much flattery. My head will be too big to get through the door of my apartment."

We laughed.

"But do promise me you'll be careful. You still haven't said the words."

"I promise," he said. "And I'm a man of my word."

"I've only known you a short time, but I absolutely believe that."

"Oh, I forgot to tell you about your schedule tomorrow," he said.

"What about it?"

"All of the staff who just came back from holiday have set meetings with you. I can cancel if you like. But I booked them from about nine in the morning to noon. Is that okay?"

"Yes. I forgot about how to get into the schedule."

"Once you're on our server and signed in, it's one of the tabs at the top left. You can go in and change things or mark off time you need. That way I don't have to constantly bug you about things. Or if there are specific faculty members you need buffers with, I'm happy to oblige."

"Did Dr. Davies do that? Make you be a buffer?"

"Uh . . . maybe with a few of his students who might have had amorous intentions."

"Oh?"

Ellis laughed. "I'm a man, and I'm straight. But from what I understand, he's quite handsome. Some of his students may have tried to abuse his open-door policy—and it wasn't always just the females. So we made a new rule that all appointments had to go through me. It saved him a lot of bother, and I could keep track of those who only wanted to sit and talk to him and then those who wanted to flirt. Some of them were shameless."

Rhys was quite handsome. I could see how the student population might think so as well.

"Here we are," Ellis said as he pulled up to the door of our building.

I frowned. "I can walk from the parking lot."

He shook his head. "The dean would have my head if I made you walk in this weather."

I laughed. "Okay. But in the future, we don't have to tell her."

"Well, your first meeting today is with her, so I sort of do. If you go in all wet with snow, she'll know."

"Thinking ahead," I said. "I like that." I grabbed my bag from the floorboard, and he started to jump out of the car.

"Stay. I can get my own door." And then I was out before he could move.

Once again, the wind caught the heavy university door when I opened it, and it was all I could do to pull it closed.

In the office, Gladys was already at her desk. Today she was dressed all in blue. Her 1980s pantsuit was the perfect color for her complexion.

"You look gorgeous," I said.

She blushed. "You don't have to compliment me to get what you want," she said. "I'm here to help."

I laughed. "No, I mean it. Royal blue is one of my favorite colors."

"Mine too."

"That reminds me, and forgive me because I haven't read the packet, but is there a dress code for professors?"

She cocked her head. "I believe it says professional attire, but that does include jeans and jumpers. It's quite cold in our fair town, so nothing is too strict. People need to stay warm."

"Good to know. Um . . ."

"What?" she asked.

"Did the detective say anything more to you since the other day when they were here? I was just curious."

She shook her head. "Tight-lipped, that one. Though I tried to ask. You probably know more than I do."

I was confused. "Why is that?"

Her eyebrows went up, and there was a blush on her cheeks. "Sorry, it's none of my business," she said.

"Please, explain," I said.

"My husband, Paul, mentioned it at breakfast this morning. Only because he was worried about you. He doesn't want the detective pressuring you in any way."

I smiled. "I keep forgetting you and Paul are married. And everything is fine," I said. "We were talking about his grandmother last night. She sounds like an interesting woman."

She laughed. "She is. My mum was in school with her years ago. Said she was a wild one and had a bit of the witch in her."

"Oh?"

"That's not a bad thing around here. We like our witches," she said seriously.

"Uh. Oh. I had no idea there were witches in Wales. That's something I'd like to research."

"You should. Fascinating stories," she said. "I can make a list of books for you if you like."

"I'd appreciate that."

Her phone buzzed and she held up a finger. "Yes, Dean, she's here. I'll send her up."

She hung up the phone and pointed at me.

"The dean is waiting for you," she said. "She says it is an emergency."

I wonder what that's about. "Thanks. Remind me how to get to her office."

"I'll grab a map."

Chapter Thirteen

Luckily, Carolyn's office was in the same building, though on the third floor. There was an elevator somewhere, but I decided I should take the stairs to get some exercise—a decision I regretted by the time I reached the second floor. When I hit the landing of the third floor, I was out of breath, and I hoped the walk wasn't much longer.

I dabbed the sweat on my forehead with a tissue I pulled from my backpack, which I'd brought with me for two reasons: One, it contained a stolen item from Alice's apartment, and two, I wasn't sure who I could trust. Well, I trusted Ellis, but I didn't want him to know what I'd done. And Gladys was sweet but nosy. So the bag came with me.

At the end of the long hall, a sign above a door read DEAN'S OFFICE. This floor was dedicated to the admin of the university. The door was open, so I went inside. There were three desks but only one person inside the room. His head was down as he typed on a computer, but when I came in, he glanced up and smiled.

"You must be Dr. Griffith," he said. He stood and held out his hand. I shook it. "I'm Samuel, the dean's admin. It's nice to meet you. She was so excited when you accepted her offer."

I smiled. It was nice to be wanted, even if it was by my best friend. "It's nice to meet you, Samuel. Please call me Gwen. And I know everyone is proper around here, but I'm not."

He nodded. "She's waiting for you." He pointed to a set of double doors not unlike the ones for my office.

"Thanks."

I knocked.

"Come in," Carolyn said.

Her office was twice the size of mine, which was already huge. There was a large conference table and floor-to-ceiling windows, some of which were made of stained glass. Her desk sat in the middle of the room and was massive as well. She looked so tiny behind it.

Like me, she was dressed in dark jeans and a fuzzy sweater. She waved for me to sit down in one of the plush leather chairs across from her.

"How are you?" she said seriously. Her tone was weird.

"Fine," I said. "Why? Did something happen that I don't know about?"

"I talked to Detective Jones this morning."

I frowned. "And?"

"He's alerted campus security that you may have a stalker. I want to know why you didn't tell me. If you don't say anything, how can I keep you safe?"

I sighed. "Except for some film of a guy watching the bookstore I was in, he has no reason to think the stranger was after me. He shouldn't have worried you." I didn't share that I sometimes felt like someone was watching me. There was no reason for us both to be paranoid. Besides, I was new in town, and people were probably curious.

"Of course he should have told me. We can absolutely up our security on campus. I feel awful that you're dealing with so much turmoil. I thought we'd be making your life easier and safer when you moved here. We usually have no crime here, except for the occasional drunken brawl or disorderly conduct."

I smiled. "The detective said the same thing. I'm trying not to take it personally," I joked.

"I gathered this morning that the detective believes Dr. Rice's case is suspicious. He had many more questions about the people around her at the university and if there was anyone I thought might want to harm her."

"What makes you think I would know anything about that?"

She smirked. "I heard he was at your place last night."

"Did he say that?"

"No. But I have my sources."

Gladys and Paul. I might have a few words to say to the headmaster. I didn't like the rest of the world knowing my business.

"Well, we did talk about Alice a bit, but I don't know much more than you do. He does think she was poisoned. I'm sure he asked about what you served the night she died."

"He did, and I was shocked. We all ate the same things, unless someone there put something in her drink. By the time everything happened, the dishes had all been washed, so we weren't much use to the police in that way. I know she wasn't well liked, but to kill her? That's unbelievable to me."

"Did you know much about her past? Like that she spent some time in an institution when she was a kid? Her parents died in a terrible car accident, and I guess she had some problems. I mean, what child wouldn't? She was only nine or ten at the time. And they were involved in some sort of big financial scheme. Or at least they'd been accused of a crime. They died before the case went to court."

She shook her head. "I didn't know anything about that. We don't ask for any sort of medical history. It makes me feel sorry for her, though. She was a thorn in my side and was never happy here, but I wouldn't have wished any of this on her."

"I know. Did you by chance know her husband? Or ex-husband?"

"She was married?" That seemed to surprise her. "How do you even know that?"

"Ellis and I have been doing some digging into her past. He's working on a story for the paper."

She pursed her lips.

"What is it?"

"I'd rather we didn't bring out her worst moments in life. That hardly seems fair, since she isn't here to defend herself. It should run more like an obit."

I nodded. "While we're doing extensive research, Ellis doesn't plan to bring all her skeletons out of the closet. But we both wanted context. So, you never met the husband?"

She shook her head. "I don't remember if I did. Just a minute."

After she clicked a few buttons on her computer, her brows drew together.

"What is it?"

"On her initial paperwork, she was divorced, but the former spouse isn't named. She doesn't even have an emergency contact. How sad is that?"

"Well, I put you as mine."

"Yes, but we're friends. That makes sense. It breaks my heart that she wasn't close enough to a single person to be able to fill in that space."

"It is. By chance, is there a former address, before she moved into the faculty housing?"

Carolyn nodded.

"Can you write it down for me? Maybe Ellis and I can find some neighbors who knew her. He's having trouble finding quotes from anyone who liked her."

"I can give him a few. Send him up to me."

"I will, and that is kind of you. But I'd really like that address."

"I don't know if you should be poking around. You already have a stalker."

I sighed. "I don't have a stalker. I mean, I've only been here a few days. I'm telling you, the detective is jumping to conclusions." Though I would be more vigilant about my surroundings. But there was no reason for anyone to be following me.

Then an idea hit me. Maybe the mystery man had mistaken me for someone else. But I was keeping that to myself.

She wrote down the address and shoved the paper across her desk.

"Can I ask you something?" she asked.

"Anything."

"Why do you feel the need to investigate? I mean, between you and me. Tell me the truth."

I shrugged. "She fell on my doorstep and spoke her last words. And then she just died. I'm a reporter at heart, and I need to know the truth. You understand that better than most."

"I do," she said. "But I'm worried that there may be more to all of this than any of us might know. Maybe it was someone from her past—you said money was involved. People never forget that sort of thing if it was embezzling or a Ponzi scheme."

"I don't actually know what the situation was. Ellis found most of that out and I haven't read his research, but I plan to."

"I'm just saying, you've involved one of our best students in this, and I want to make sure you're both protected. Promise me you'll be careful."

"Promise. Can I change the subject."

She sighed. "If you must."

"I'd like to have another get-together for faculty," I said. "And I'd like to throw it. I thought maybe at my place, but maybe, given what has happened, it would be better to just meet up at the pub. I'd like to keep it low-key, just a chance for me to get to know the faculty and staff a bit better in a casual environment. I noticed they had a back room at the pub."

She smiled.

"What?"

"I knew you would be perfect as the chairman," she said.

I rolled my eyes. "I have no idea what I'm doing, and I will have a lot of questions for you. But I thought maybe if we meet in a more relaxed setting, not the dean's mansion, people will loosen up and I can really get to know them. I used to go out with my staff all the time. Friday nights at the bar became a ritual with many of them."

She nodded. "Am I invited?"

"Always. But you have to be one of us."

"I can do that. Are you saying I threw a stuffy welcome party for you?"

Yes. "Of course not. I just want people to be relaxed. I was thinking maybe on Friday night. I'm meeting with everyone tomorrow for one-on-ones, so then we could have a social gathering that helps them understand that while I may be their boss, I don't have a stick up my butt."

She giggled like she used to when we lived in the dorms here. "No one would ever accuse you of that. You're one of the kindest humans I've ever met."

I smiled. "You are prejudiced. And while I want them to like me, this is more about making them feel comfortable enough to come to me if they need some problem-solving or need to brainstorm on things."

"I think it's a great idea. And I really would like to come, as I'm hoping they feel the same way about me."

I laughed. "I already told you that you're invited." I said my goodbyes and headed back downstairs.

When I made it back to my office, Ellis was at his desk.

"Hey, can you get me an email list of faculty and staff? I want to throw a little get-together at the pub Friday night."

"On it," he said. "I'll email it to you."

"Thanks."

"Did you get in trouble?" he whispered.

"What do you mean?"

"I saw the detective when I was parking the car."

I laughed. "Thank goodness I missed him. No. Everything is fine. Where's Gladys?"

"She's in the break room putting tea together."

"Ah. Did you send over your info about Dr. Rice?"

He grinned. "I emailed you some of the articles I found last night about the court case that never went to trial. It sounds like her father was embezzling, but he blamed his partner at the firm."

"So the partner never went to court either?"

"No. Once the Rice family died, the case just disappeared into the ether."

"How much money was involved?"

"That's the thing. Several millions. If it had been stolen or embezzled, wouldn't the firm want to find out what happened? Or the courts? And if I was one of the clients, I would have had a fit."

"I agree." I pulled out the paper that Carolyn had given me with Alice's former address. "I'm busy the rest of today and tomorrow, but how about we go check this town out? This was her residence before she moved here. Maybe we can find something out about her ex-husband and that relationship. And we can check the newspaper morgue there. They have more than what we found online."

"Good idea." It was easy to see he was excited.

"There is one thing, and I know we've discussed this, but the dean is worried about us doing some sort of exposé. She doesn't want us dredging up the past. She wants something that respects Dr. Rice's privacy."

He frowned. "But what if someone from her past is the one who killed her?"

"Well, that's a different story for another day, and would be more about the killer. Also, I told the dean we would be careful."

He nodded. "I'll do some research on the town to see if I can find us any leads."

"Okay. But don't go there until I'm free to travel with you."

He opened his mouth, but I held up a hand. "I know. But we should both look out for one another. And if anything happened to you, I would never forgive myself. That and the dean would murder me where I stood."

I thought of something and pulled my phone out of my other pocket. "I'm curious if while you were searching, you saw a picture of this guy." I'd taken a picture of the photos the detective had shown me, telling him it was so I would recognize the guy if I saw him again.

He squinted and then took the phone from me. He shook his head. "No. Is this from CCTV?"

"Yep. The detective thinks this guy might be following me. I disagree."

He glanced up. "You have a stalker? But you've been here less than a week."

I laughed. "I honestly think it's a coincidence, but the detective swears he was following me when I went to the bookstore the other day. I think it's a bunch of nonsense. But I was curious if you'd seen him, and if the detective is right, maybe we keep a lookout."

"I don't like this," he said. "If the detective is taking it seriously, maybe you should as well. And please stop arguing about me picking you up and taking you home. From now on, I'm glued to your side."

I adored this young man. "Fine. It's not my intention to make anyone worry."

Gladys came in with a huge tray. There were small cakes, biscuits, and some sandwiches. My mouth watered. "Oh, good, you're here," she said as she put the tray on the big table in front of the window.

"Is this all for us?"

She nodded. "Part of my job is making sure we have a good tea throughout the day. We never know when a student, faculty, or staff may have missed a meal. Well, that was the former chairman's directive. Unless you want to change it." She sounded like she wouldn't be very happy about that.

"I . . . uh. It seems like a lot of work for you."

"I enjoy putting it together. Today I have a rose hip tea that is delicious."

"That sounds lovely. And I'm fine with the tea being served, as long as it isn't too much of an inconvenience for you."

She smiled. “Not at all, Dr. Griffith.”

I sighed. “I’d really be okay if you both call me Gwen,” I said.

She and Ellis glanced at each other and laughed.

“Decorum and professionalism are hallmarks of our department,” she said.

“That’s Gladys’ way of saying it’s never going to happen.”

I grinned. “Fine. But Professor is okay too.”

“Well, Professor, your tea is ready,” Gladys said.

While outside the walls, the world might be a little crazy, it was nice to be made to feel at home—even if it was a formal home with a great deal of politeness. I was used to the raw energy of the newsroom and reporters seldom watched their language, even in these days of everyone being canceled.

After grabbing some tea and sandwiches, I headed into my office. Today I’d planned to go over my class lists to make sure I had everything ready for them. Ellis had already uploaded my syllabi and notes to the website that covered my curriculum. I just wanted to double-check that everything was up and could be easily downloaded.

But my mind kept drifting to my phone and the book in my backpack. I’d stolen something from a dead woman’s apartment. What had I been thinking? After locking my doors, I sat down, then I pulled the book out of my backpack. I’d read quite a bit of it. When I went to put it on my desk, I dropped it on the floor. A piece of paper floated out.

It was another list of accounts. Some had been marked with a yellow highlighter.

Unlike the other logs, this one indicated several hundred thousand in various accounts.

What were you doing, Dr. Rice?

Chapter Fourteen

After Ellis dropped me off at home that afternoon, I waited in the lobby for him to leave. Then I headed down the block to the bookstore. I'd left my email with the owner, Rhian Morgan, and she had reminded me that the book club for singles was meeting on Saturday afternoon.

I refused to live the life of a shut-in like I had in Dallas, where I was so exhausted by work that I seldom went anywhere. I mean, I met up occasionally with friends, but I was far from social. I wanted a different life here in Dillynaidd. Also, the more integrated I became into the culture of the town, the less time I'd be an outsider.

But I needed to pick up the book the club would talk about on Saturday. The snow had stopped, and it was a balmy forty degrees. The sun was even out, though not for long. Days were very short this time of year.

Like before, the brass bell rang over the doorway. Rhian was at the desk. "Gwen, it's good to see you. Can I help you with anything?"

I told her about wanting to join the book club.

"Oh, that's wonderful. It's a fairly small group, but we have a lot of fun."

"You didn't mention the book you would be talking about."

She pointed behind her to the shelf of Agatha Christie books. "We read thrillers and mysteries. It's the only genre the members all agree on, and we like to mix it up with classics and newer authors. This month it is a Hercule Poirot mystery, *Death on the Nile*."

"I haven't read that one, though I saw a couple of the movies. But I love Agatha Christie."

"Don't we all. Do you need a copy?"

"I do."

"I have it in the single volume, but we also have a beautiful boxed set." She wasn't lying; the leather-bound set was gorgeous. Then she pointed to the price, which seemed like a mistake. There was no way it was that cheap.

"How can I resist? Also, you should know this about me: I'm easy when it comes to books."

She laughed. "If I didn't own a bookstore, I would go broke buying them," she said.

"Do I need to bring anything, like food, to the chat?"

"No. Tea, coffee, and biscuits are provided. Just bring yourself. You don't have much time to read the book, though."

I laughed. "I'm a fast reader." As a former journalist and editor, I'd honed those skills long ago.

"I'm excited that you've decided to join us. We are a close group, and I have a feeling you'll fit right in. There are even a few professors from your university, so you'll have a chance to get to know them as well."

"Wonderful. Thanks."

She put the boxed set in a canvas bag and sent me on my way. It was heavy, but I decided to stop by the bakery. I'd avoided the cookies during Gladys's tea service, but I wanted something sweet.

I crossed the street but glanced back halfway across. I had an odd feeling that someone was watching me. Tires squealed to a stop. When I turned, the hood of a car was about an inch from my hip.

A man with a gray beard jumped out of the driver's side and ran toward me. "Are you all right?" he asked.

My nerves had taken a sudden turn toward breakdown, but I was fine. "I'm sorry," I said. "I didn't see you."

"When you stopped, I thought you meant for me to pass," he said. "Thankfully, I wasn't going too fast. Are you sure you're, okay?" He looked from his car to me. He had a right to be angry with me. I should have been paying attention, but he appeared more worried than mad.

I nodded. "It was my fault. I shouldn't have stopped in the middle of the street like that." I glanced behind me, but no one was there. I was definitely losing my mind.

"Let me help you," he said as he guided me the rest of the way to the sidewalk in front of the bakery.

"Thank you," I said.

He nodded. "We aren't a very busy village, but there is some traffic on Main Street, so mind your way."

"I will. And thank you for not running me over."

He laughed and waved.

I shook my head and then put a hand on my chest. My heartbeat had sped up considerably. I took a deep breath and let it out. Then I glanced up and down the street. There were a few people on the sidewalks, but none of them looked like the man in the picture, and they certainly weren't worried about me.

After grabbing some more Welsh cakes and croissants from the bakery, I headed down to the pub. Before I sent out the invites, I wanted to make sure the room was available for the faculty party I wanted to throw.

Catrin waved me up to the bar and motioned for me to take a seat. Then she set a pint on the bar in front of me. "Are you okay?" she asked.

"What do you mean?"

"This one"—she pointed to one of the regulars I'd been sitting by the last time I was there, the one called the Captain—"says you were nearly mowed down by a car. You should have called the police."

Nothing in this town happened without everyone knowing. "If we'd called the police, I would have been the one in trouble. I was distracted, and I stopped in the middle of the road. But I'm fine. He didn't hit me."

"Well, that's a blessing," she said.

I sipped the beer. I'd planned to make a sandwich at home for dinner, but the scents from the kitchen were too enticing. "What's the special tonight?"

"She's made her famous cawl," the Captain said. "Best you've ever had."

"Go on, you. You don't have to flatter me for a second bowl."

I didn't mention that I'd had it a few days ago and that he'd recommended it. He was older and might not remember. "Sounds good to me."

"Another storm is coming," the Captain said when Catrin walked away.

"That's good to know. I've been so busy I keep forgetting to check the weather."

"Are you sure you're okay? You wouldn't be the first pedestrian old Harvey has hit. They should have taken his license years ago."

I grinned. "I'm fine, thanks. He didn't hit me, so all is well." Then I thought of something. "You didn't by chance see someone following me?"

His bushy gray eyebrows rose. "Do you mean the fellow with the dark hair who ducked into the alley when you turned around?"

I shivered, and it had nothing to do with the temperature of the pub. "You saw him?"

"I did. Tall bloke in a navy coat."

I pulled out my phone. "Was it this guy?"

He squinted at the picture. "My eyesight isn't the best, but could have been. He had his head down, so I couldn't see his face. Is he causing you trouble? We have laws against that sort of thing. Maybe you should go to the police."

"They are aware. Thank you, though. I thought maybe I was going crazy, but I sensed someone behind me."

"You're sane as the rest of us, which isn't saying much." He laughed at his joke, and I couldn't help but smile.

Catrin brought out a steaming bowl of the aromatic stew. I closed my eyes as I breathed in the scent of it. "Yum. I could eat the air."

"Less calories, but won't fill you up," she said. "Are you certain you're okay?"

"She's not," the fellow beside me said. "She has a stalker."

"Oh dear."

I shook my head. "Not a stalker," I said. "But I did feel like someone was following me. And my new friend here confirmed it."

"Everyone calls me Captain," he said.

I had remembered, but he seemed to want to be friends. And I needed all of those I could get.

"Well, thank you, Captain. I really was beginning to wonder if I might be paranoid. And I don't think the guy is out to hurt me." Though I had no way of knowing that. "He may be trying to get information about a story one of my students and I are working on."

"Ah, that's right. You're the new journalism professor," he said.

"I'm Gwen," I said. We shook hands.

"She's the chairman of the department," Catrin added. "Just came over from America."

"Which reminds me," I said. "I actually came in to see if I could rent out your back room for Friday night. I'd like to invite the faculty for a casual get-together."

Catrin pulled out a book from under the bar. "Let me look." She flipped a few pages. "It's free. And it doesn't cost anything to have the room; we seat larger parties in there all the time. Just let me know ahead of time so we can get the tables ready for you."

"That's great, thank you."

"We're happy to have the business," she said.

After that, I ate my stew. I paid my tab and the Captain's.

"You didn't have to do that," he said.

"I did. You helped to settle my mind. You have no idea how valuable that information was."

"Well, then, at least let me walk you home." He was off his stool and heading to the coatrack before I could respond.

"Thanks," I told Catrin, and followed him. "I just live across the street."

"Then we won't have far to walk." There was no changing his mind.

True to his word, he walked me to the steps in front of the building and glanced both ways down the street. "I don't see anyone, but you stay safe," he said. Then he patted my shoulder as he left.

Paul was still at the front desk when I came in with my baked goods and books.

"Can I help you take those up?" he offered. "I heard you had a run-in with a car this afternoon. We've been worried about you."

I shook my head. "I'm fine. It was my fault." I was about to head up and then paused.

"Paul, there's something I need to speak to you about."

"Of course, Dr. Griffith."

"I'm a very private person," I said, "and I'm used to that. Do you understand what I'm trying to say?"

"I can't say that I do." He seemed genuinely confused.

I sighed. I didn't want to offend him. He truly was the kindest man. "I feel like things that happen in our building shouldn't be for the public interest. I think you can understand how that might make me feel uncomfortable."

He shook his head again. "I'm not following," he said.

I blew out a breath. "I adore your wife, Gladys, but she seems to share information a bit more freely than I'm comfortable with, and I wondered if perhaps you could maybe not mention what goes on in the building."

His eyebrows drew together.

"And now I've offended you and made you angry."

He shook his head. "Not at all. But it will help me if you give me specifics. I forget sometimes that my wife likes to share a story."

"Right. Like if I have visitors—not that I will have many—I'd like those situations to stay private. More for their sake than my own."

He nodded. "I apologize," he said. "I promise she means no harm. We just talk about our day."

"Totally understandable. And please know that I'm not upset. Nor do I want to upset you, but I value my privacy. As a single woman in a new town, I would feel safer if everyone didn't know my personal business."

He grabbed his chest as if he might be having a heart attack. "That wounds me," he said. "I've never thought about it like that. We absolutely want you to feel safe. And I will not share the goings-on with Gladys. Again, though, she means well."

I smiled. "I know you both do. I'm a cards-on-the-table kind of person. I hope you understand that. And there is another reason why I need to keep things private."

"What's that?" he asked, and appeared genuinely curious. I set my bags down on the step and then pulled out my phone. I showed him this picture. "Detective Jones caught this man on CCTV and thinks he was following me. Today when I stopped in the middle of the road, I had it confirmed that he might have been doing it again. I'd rather he not be able to get information about my private life."

"You need to tell the detective about it today."

"Since everyone in the pub already knew, I have a feeling he does as well. Just keep an eye out for me?"

"Of course. And sorry about the bother."

I smiled. "It's really okay. But I have to look after my safety, right?"

"You do. And you are perfectly safe here at Afon House."

"Thanks, see you later." I headed upstairs with my bags.

But I couldn't stop thinking about Alice. She'd probably thought she was safe in Afon House as well.

Chapter Fifteen

I was nervous the next morning as Ellis drove me to the university. I was about to meet with the rest of the faculty. I'd heard they were all quite wonderful, but after Dr. Rice, I had to see for myself.

The Captain had been right about the weather, but so far it was only a wind so strong it was difficult to stay upright.

"Your schedule is busy until one," Ellis said. "Then I thought we could go to Crumby to do our research on Dr. Rice."

"That sounds like a good plan, but what about the weather?"

He laughed. "You used to live here, so you'll understand that if we wait for decent weather, we'll never get there."

I smiled. "True. As long as you don't mind driving in it."

"Not a problem."

Once we were inside the building, we headed for the office. "You didn't have to wait for me, Professor."

I feared facing Gladys, but I didn't want to tell him that. I had a feeling I'd be on her bad side this morning. When I entered the office, she glanced up and gave me a tight nod.

Best to face this head-on.

"Gladys, can you please come in my office?" I said, keeping my tone friendly.

She gave me another tight nod. Ellis was at his desk with his head down. He was a smart kid.

She followed me inside, and then I shut the door.

"Look, I know that Paul probably spoke to you. And I hope he explained why I need my privacy."

"He didn't explain," she said. "He only yelled at me for sharing information about you."

I chewed on my lip. Great, I was the reason they'd argued. "Right. That is not how I hoped things would go down. Let me show you something." I pulled my phone out of my backpack. I showed her the picture.

"While I can't know for certain, the police believe this man is following me. And I have no idea why. He was seen again yesterday. It makes me beyond uncomfortable to think a stranger might know my comings and goings and personal information. While I know you would never do anything to cause harm to another person, privacy is important."

Her mouth was a thin line, but she nodded.

"Please know how much I appreciate you and everything that you do. I'm not Dr. Rice. I don't hold grudges. And I realize in small towns, bits of information do get circulated. But I don't feel safe right now, at least until we figure out what's going on. I'll be honest, I didn't take the police seriously. After yesterday—well, I've changed my mind."

Her shoulders dropped, and her face turned from anger to worry. "Dear me," she said. "I would be worried too. Do you have any idea who he is?"

I shook my head. "I wish I had some clue. I emailed the detective again and sent him the name of a witness who saw him following me yesterday."

"But I feel like that is something we should circulate," she said. "At least to our university police. If he is on campus, we should know. I could take care of that for you, it you would like. You just need to email me the picture."

"Uh, I believe the police are already on it. And again, that's a personal problem. It's a small thing, the privacy, but it is important to me."

"You can count on me," she said. She made like she was zipping her lips, but then she smiled, though it didn't reach her eyes.

"Thank you, Gladys, and know that I'm sorry for any grief Paul may have given you."

She shrugged. "I stopped listening to him as soon as he raised his voice."

Then she turned and headed back out to reception.

That could have gone better. I hoped she understood.

* * *

I left my door open as I visited with the rest of the staff. They were a great group of people. While the personalities varied from shy to outgoing, they were intelligent. I looked forward to working with them. And they'd all answered yes to my RSVP for the drinks party.

I was particularly fond of Laura and Becca, who were also fairly new to the department. They couldn't have been more different, but they were funny and kind.

At lunch, Ellis came to my door. "You ready to head out?"

"I am." I shut down my computer and grabbed my purse and backpack. "We'll be out the rest of the day doing some research," I said to Gladys.

"Oh?" She fully expected us to tell her why.

"Yes, something Ellis is working on and I'm supervising. See you tomorrow."

Her smile dissipated, but she waved.

Ellis pulled the car around, for which I was grateful. The wind was still blowing like crazy.

"I'm trying not to be nosy, but I'm curious about what happened with Gladys," he said as he pulled out onto the main drive away from the university. "She hasn't been her cheerful self since your chat."

I sighed. "Since I should probably have the same conversation with you, it's like this: I like my privacy. You both are privy to more than most, but I'd appreciate keeping my life close to the vest. I don't like people knowing my business."

I went on to explain why.

"Until we find him, I meant what I said about sticking to you like glue." For someone so young, Ellis was protective. He was a great kid.

I smiled. "Thanks."

"As for Gladys, please don't think too badly of her. Gossip in this town is currency. She grew up in a different age where that was their main form of communication."

I nodded. "I get it. And I hope I didn't upset her too much."

He shrugged. "She'll get over it. Did your faculty meetings go okay? I had my headphones on so I couldn't hear."

I laughed, and so did he.

"I am curious about you, though, Ellis."

He frowned. "What do you mean?"

"It's a personal question, and given what I just said, you have every right to tell me to stuff it."

He laughed. "I'm an open book, Professor. What do you want to know?"

"Why do you want to be an investigative journalist?"

"Puzzles? When you begin an investigation, it's like there are a thousand pieces, and you have to put them together in the right way to find the truth."

"That's a good analogy."

"I'm also extremely nosy," he said. "I have to know things. It's innate."

I laughed.

"What?" he asked.

"I say the same about myself. I have to know the truth. There are those gut instincts that come into play. But there are times in my life when I haven't understood why I've felt so strongly about finding the truth when everyone else was saying it didn't matter."

"Well, we have that in common," he said. "I wasn't Dr. Rice's biggest fan, but the idea that someone might have killed her—I have to know what happened. And it makes me feel slightly weird because that need is so strong."

I smiled. "You're right. We are on the same page."

"And about your private life. You should know I had to sign an NDA. Even if I wanted to share, and I don't, I'd get in a lot of trouble."

"An NDA?"

"A few years ago, an administrator shared information about a student with the local paper. Since then, most of us who have access to personnel files have to sign a nondisclosure agreement. You probably signed one."

"I really should read things before I sign them."

We laughed.

"Now, where are we going to begin today?"

"At the local newspaper archives, or as we like to call them, the morgue. They're a bit old-school and don't have any files online from their old print editions. It's sad that can be said for a lot of small-town newspapers. And with the economy, as they are shut down, all that information is lost, unless they donate it to a local library."

"Hmmm. That is sad. I'd never thought about that. Back home, the libraries also keep old microfiche files."

"I don't know what that is," he said.

"Now I feel really old. But we might look into acquiring old papers' morgue files at the university if one of them closes. Our university could be a hub for that sort of thing. Lots of American universities keep files on all newspapers in Ireland and Wales. That could be a great resource. Students can transfer files as part of coursework and internships. I'll talk to Carolyn about it."

"See, that's why she brought you here. That's something we should have done years ago."

As we were driving, I glanced behind us. There was a navy sedan following, but it was a two-lane highway. Well, more like one-lane in some spots. Most back roads in Wales were like that, so I didn't think anything about it.

Ten minutes later we pulled on to the main drag of Crumby, which was quaint and even smaller than Dillynaidd. I noticed the navy sedan parked a few spots down from where we pulled in. I tried to see who was driving, but the windows were tinted, and I felt like I was being paranoid.

Several signs in the front windows of the newspaper office announced that the paper was celebrating its 150th year. Inside, an elderly gentleman sat behind a desk. He was the only one in the office, and he typed quite slowly on a computer keyboard.

He held up a hand as if to wave but kept typing. We waited patiently.

A few minutes later, he stood and made his way slowly to the front desk. "How can I help you?"

"I'm Ellis. I called yesterday about needing to look at the archives. I'm working on a story for the university paper." He showed his press ID.

The man nodded.

"And you would be?"

"His professor and fellow researcher," I said. I still wore my lanyard with my university ID. I showed it to him.

"Chairman? Well, we have honored guests today. There's just one problem."

"What's that?" I asked.

"I'm the only one here today. Two of my staff, including the one in charge of the archives, are out with the flu. And I'm working on putting out our weekend edition by myself."

Ellis's face dropped. He was so disappointed.

"Right, that's too bad about your employees," I said. "I've been there myself through the years. But I'm fairly good with finding things in morgues. It's why I came to help Ellis today. I promise we will put everything back where we found it."

The man cocked his head and stared at us for what felt like a full minute. I kept eye contact. "Fine," he said. Then he turned and headed to the back of the office.

Ellis and I looked at each other, not certain if we were meant to follow or not.

"Well, come on," the man said.

We were about to follow him when I noticed something out of the corner of my eye. I turned, but no one was there. I could have sworn I'd seen a figure out the window.

I blew out a breath. I really was paranoid. Stalker or not, no one would know we were here today. Ellis and I were the only ones who knew.

The morgue had the scent of musty paper and ink. I would never grow tired of that smell.

"Boxes are mostly sorted by year and then month. Gloves are in a box at the corner. Make sure the lids are put on tight to protect the paper."

At least the old issues had been put in special boxes to protect them.

"Thank you," we said at the same time.

"I'm leaving at three today and will have to lock up."

"Is anything on microfiche?" I asked.

The man shook his head. "Never saw the sense in spending the money. These boxes do well enough."

"Right. Thank you."

I glanced at my watch. We only had two hours. Hopefully, that would be enough time.

The gentleman left, and Ellis and I started perusing the boxes.

"What year do we need to begin?"

"Late 1999," he said. "That is when the first article about her parents came out. Then a few months after that, they died."

"Right. Let's get to it."

When we found a box labeled with the right year and month, we put on some gloves. These would keep the oil from our hands from destroying the paper.

"Remember, it's old and brittle. Be gentle," I said.

"I will be, Professor."

We divided the stack in half and started going through them.

"I found something." Ellis turned to put the paper on the table behind us. We'd been searching for about half an hour.

I stood there as he gently unfolded the front page. There was a photo of a car smashed to bits and a headline that read

"Rice Family Tragedy." We read the story on the front page. Then Ellis looked up at me.

I nodded. "I'm done. Go to page twelve."

After scanning the article with an app on his phone, he gently turned the yellowed pages. The story was much more in-depth than anything Ellis had sent me.

Alice's father had been indicted for embezzlement at a banking firm. Several hundred thousand had gone missing from client accounts. The defense for her father stated that he was completely in the clear and that someone had framed him. They would be proving that in court.

The family, including the father, said, 'No comment,' according to the reporter who wrote the story.

While the reporter made it sound like there was something fishy about the car crash, the police said it was an accident. The car skidded off the road during rainy weather and went off a cliff.

"Wow," Ellis said.

"It's sad. And I wonder if the reporter was right. The timing seems strange," I said. The paper also stated that the father and mother had been headed to the piano recital of their young daughter.

"All the bad thoughts about Dr. Rice just left my brain," Ellis whispered. "Can you imagine being nine, and then your parents don't show up for your recital and you find out they are dead."

"It's beyond sad," I said. "And I know that is a terrible saying, but it seems to fit here."

"Agreed."

"You mentioned there was an article that said she'd gone to an asylum."

"Right. A short article. But there wasn't much in it that we don't already know."

"Let's see if we can find anything else, and maybe if she has any living relatives."

He nodded.

It took a bit more searching, but we found another follow-up article.

The reporter had relied completely on hearsay, which annoyed the heck out of me. Facts when reporting news were the only thing that mattered.

The article was about Alice being released from the asylum and going to live with her aunt, the father's sister. The hearsay came in regarding the money her father had embezzled, which had not been recovered. The reporter conjectured that Alice might know where the money was hiding—as if a nine-year-old would know anything about that. The reporter said he had a source who confirmed that the girl knew about the accounts.

It was idiotic.

But the reporter's name was familiar. I'd seen it on the desk plate in this very office as we passed by. Gerald Lewis.

"Take a picture of that for Dr. Davies," I told Ellis. "It will make great fodder for his ethics class. You keep searching. I want to have a chat with Mr. Lewis."

I took a deep breath and headed into the office. The older gentleman was still pecking the computer keyboard.

"May I ask you a question?"

"You can ask," he said grumpily.

"You wrote one of the articles we're using in our research. I'm curious if you could share any other information."

"Nope. I don't share my sources."

"I'm not asking you to share your source. I want to know why you thought a nine-year-old girl would know where her father had hidden embezzled funds."

"Sounds like you want to know my source to me."

"So you remember writing it?"

He shrugged. "I've been doing this for fifty years. I don't remember every story I wrote. Do you?"

Yes. I did. But that was beside the point.

"You said that Alice Rice knew where her father's embezzled money might be. I want to know why you wrote that."

He shrugged. "I remember the name and the girl, but not the story," he said. "And I'm not sharing my source."

"Fine. Do you know if Alice still has any relatives in town? I'd really like to speak to someone who knew her back then. I mean, Ellis would."

He snorted. "Why should I help you?"

I sighed. "Because it's the decent thing to do."

Ellis came out of the back room. "It's okay, Professor. I know where we need to go next."

I glanced back at him. He smiled.

"Okay. Let's go." We left the grumpy old man behind.

When we were in the car, I let out the breath I'd been holding. "I can usually keep my temper in check, but I wanted to punch him. Problem is, I'm not sure if it's over the old article or because he's a jerk."

"Probably both." Ellis laughed.

"So, where are we headed next? Did you want to check out the ex?" I asked. That was the main reason we'd come here.

"A care home," he said. "I may have snooped in the employee files and found a former address for Dr. Rice. Though I would not have used the information in a story."

"At least you understand there should be boundaries. Now spill the rest."

"That house was owned by her aunt and was sold. There was a real estate listing in the paper for it. There were no records after that, so I called around to some of the local care homes. And I found the aunt."

"Brilliant."

He smiled. "Thanks. I was worried you'd be angry I was into the employee files in the newspaper office."

I smirked. "Don't make a habit of it. And don't share the info with anyone else. As with any other story, you protect your source."

"I will."

I glanced around to see if the navy car was still there. It was gone. My paranoia was getting the best of me.

Still, I kept checking the mirror just in case.

Chapter Sixteen

The care home was in a one-story stone building a few miles outside of Crumby. It seemed to ramble as if it had been built onto over the years, but it was surrounded by a beautiful garden, even though it was the dead of winter.

A nurse stood behind the front desk when we went in. I'd never been a fan of places like this. Absolutely necessary, but they reminded me of hospitals, which I disliked. That antiseptic smell never seemed to go away, even hours after leaving.

"Hi," Ellis said. "We're here to visit Winona Rice." He was polite and charming.

The woman appeared shocked. "Are you family?"

"Friends of the family," I spoke up. "Her niece."

"Oh, that was a terrible business. She was devastated. Alice came to see her once a week like clockwork every Sunday. They played games and did puzzles. Winona cherished those times."

It seemed odd to imagine anyone enjoying time with Dr. Rice, but we were all different with our family. Or at least I had been, when my mom was alive. Even though work had taken over my life, I'd tried to visit her a few times a year, and we had a call every Sunday.

"We just wanted to check on her," Ellis said, "and let her know we were thinking of her."

"What a kind soul you are, young man. I wish all the youth had your manners. And it's good for her to have new visitors. So many of our patients don't." She handed us a marker and two peel-and-stick name badges. "You'll need to wear these while you're in the building."

She glanced up at the clock and then down at a clipboard. "She'll be in the community teaching a class. But if you don't mind waiting, I'm sure she'd love to see you."

"Thank you," I said.

She pointed us through some wooden doors. "Go through there and head straight past the cafeteria. There is a sign above the door."

We headed in that direction. "That was smooth," I whispered to Ellis.

"And mostly the truth," he said. "I do feel sorry for her. Now that Alice is gone, she may not have any visitors."

"True." The nurse was right; Ellis was a good soul. He cared about people, which might become a problem in his chosen career. Sometimes we had to write unpleasant things during our search for the truth. It was best not to get involved with the subjects of one's story.

When we neared the community room, we glanced at one another with surprise. The class was low-impact aerobics.

"Is that her?" I whispered.

He nodded.

The woman teaching the class wore athletic wear and was extremely fit. She didn't appear like she needed to live in a care home. The others in the room were a variety of folks. Some had walkers but were still doing the movements; others sat in chairs.

"Lean to the right," Ms. Rice said as her arm went over her head. "And then to the left. And then shake those hips. Just not too hard, Naomi, with that hip replacement."

Everyone in the room laughed.

They went on for five more minutes as Ellis and I leaned against a far wall. When it was over, they all clapped.

Several people went up to Ms. Rice and thanked her. She toweled off her face, and Ellis waved at her.

We headed over.

"That was amazing," he said.

She laughed. "What, old people can't move?"

"No. Uh . . ."

"I'm only joking, son. Who did you come to visit today?"

"Actually, you, Ms. Rice."

Her head jerked back in surprise. "Me?"

"Yes, ma'am. I worked with your niece, Dr. Rice. She was one of my instructors at school. I'm working on her obituary, and . . . I don't mean to be insensitive, but I was hoping to get some quotes from you about her. I couldn't find any other family."

Her eyes narrowed at me.

"I'm the new chairman of the department," I explained. "I didn't know Alice long, but I wanted to come with Ellis to add my condolences. We are so very sorry for your loss."

She frowned but stuck out her hand to meet mine. "That is kind of you both." She motioned toward the seating area. "Why don't we take a seat? These old legs of mine need a rest."

"Of course," I said.

We sat down at a table near a window.

"Do you by chance know what happened with my niece? That handsome detective from Dillynaidd came by to ask a few questions, but he wouldn't tell me anything—other than she collapsed suddenly and they were unable to resuscitate her. She was always so healthy. I can't remember her ever staying home from school sick. I just can't believe she's gone."

I didn't feel like sharing that it had happened at my place. "That's what we heard as well," I said. "What Ellis was hoping to get was a bit about her history here in Crumby. What was she like as a child and that sort of thing."

"The professor is right," Ellis said. "As you probably know, Dr. Rice was quite private and not terribly social with her peers. I hate to say, but it's been difficult finding anyone who knew her well."

"I'm not certain what I can tell you," Ms. Rice said. "Though she did come by once a week and bring me some cheese. It's the one thing I can't live without. It's why I still exercise. We'd play cards or do a puzzle. My memory isn't what it used to be; that's why I'm here. Can't remember to take my meds or what happened yesterday. Alice had read that games and puzzles help the memory." She pointed to her head.

"It's okay if you can't remember," Ellis said. "I was just hoping to get something kind from one of her relatives."

"I'm the last of us, I'm afraid. I'll do my best to help you. Alice was like a daughter to me."

Ms. Rice seemed to have loved her niece deeply.

"She came to live with you when she was quite young, is that correct?" Ellis said.

She nodded. "My brother and his family died tragically. Well, except for Alice. The police called me that night. I'd been teaching a ballroom dancing class." She stared off into space and didn't speak for a full minute.

"Um. Ma'am?" Ellis touched her arm lightly, and she seemed to jerk back to the present.

"Did I mention my memory is going?"

"Yes, ma'am," he said politely.

"Where was I?"

"The night your brother died."

"Right. I went to pick up Alice at the music school, but she was catatonic. One of the officers had told her what happened. By the time I arrived, she was unresponsive. I rode in an ambulance with her to the hospital. There was nothing to be done. The doctors said it was shock.

"They made me admit her to the psychiatric hospital, but I visited her every day. I spoke with her, even though she didn't talk back. I wanted her to know she was loved and cared for." Ms. Rice sniffed and then shook herself. "About six months later, I went to visit, and she hopped out of the chair she'd been in and hugged me. And that was that. I brought her home and did my best to raise her."

"We all thought she was quite brilliant as a professor. Was she always into her studies?"

I glanced at Ellis in surprise. He might have stretched the truth there a bit, but I understood what he was doing.

Alice's aunt smiled. "You don't have to say nice things about her," she said. "I know how my niece was with most people. Not me, mind you. But to her peers, she was always standoffish. A child who went through what she did doesn't come out of it without scars.

"I was called to her school more than once because she was unkind with other children. But I loved her, and she adored me. You are right about her being quite bright. She always had her nose in a book."

She stared off into space again.

"Do you think there is any chance someone might have wanted to harm her?" Ellis asked. "I mean, someone who may have held a grudge?"

She stared at him blankly.

"Ms. Rice?"

"Oh. Sorry. Lost in thought. What did you ask?"

He repeated the question.

Her brows drew together. "You think someone hurt my niece?"

"We're just covering all the bases until the police reports are complete," I said. "Did she have anyone special in her life we could maybe speak to?"

"My Alice was private about such things. I worried about her, though. It's not good to be so lonely."

"Did you ever meet her husband?"

She seemed shocked. "You know about him?"

We nodded in unison.

"Piece of work. I hope he's still in jail. They were only married a few months. The divorce took longer. He took all her savings. Found out about her father, and when they split, he said he'd only been after the money her father stole. He was in for a big surprise."

"What do you mean?" Ellis asked.

"Swear you won't print a word I'm about to say. I don't want to dredge up the past and tarnish my niece's name. She spent her life trying to ignore that craziness."

"It will be off the record," Ellis promised. "But perhaps it will give us context into why she didn't trust people. I think that's fair to say."

"You'd be right about that. My brother was accused of stealing. It was complete nonsense. I don't say that because he was my sibling. He was always one to do everything the proper way. Never cheated on taxes or failed to put money into savings. Tithed to the church. He'd been that way since he was old enough to earn a wage. Someone was trying to set him up. What's the word?"

"Frame him?" I suggested.

"That's it. But he was onto them. Whoever it was, he had an idea. He wouldn't tell the family in order to protect us, but I know that's what got him killed. And whoever it was got away with it. I told that detective if there was anything strange about my niece's death, he should look into it. His former partner Russell Winthrop. There's a name burned in my brain."

"You think he might have been the one to set your brother up?" I asked.

"Yes. Nasty piece of work. Headed to Spain or somewhere as soon as there was trouble. Said he had to distance himself for the sake of their clients. I've always thought he left to hide the money."

"We'll look into that," Ellis said.

I gave him a look, but he shrugged. It was one thing to look into Alice's death, quite another to investigate a forty-five-year-old financial fraud case.

"And that ex of hers was certain she had the money hidden away somewhere. But there was no money. No hidden accounts. There was a bit of life insurance that we used for her university, but she was raised on my salary as a dance teacher, which wasn't much."

Secret accounts?

Ellis and I glanced at each other. And I wondered about the pages from the logbook I'd found. I hadn't shown them to anyone because of the way I'd found them. Had those been from her father? The numbers meant nothing to me.

"That's terrible," Ellis said. "It must have been difficult for everyone for them to die so tragically."

"Except for Alice dying, it was the worst day of my life. Promise me you'll let me know if someone hurt my Alice. Promise me."

"I . . . uh . . ." Ellis stammered.

"We will," I said. "I promise."

A bell rang in the hallway. "Oh, that's first bell. I need to get ready for tea. Please excuse me." Then Ms. Rice walked away.

"I wasn't finished," Ellis said. He stood, but I grabbed his wrist gently.

"Let her go. That was a lot for her."

We made our way out to the car, but I decided there and then I would come visit with Winona Rice again. I hated the idea that she had no one else. I might not have liked Alice, but her aunt was a charmer.

Snow fell again and it was dark outside, even though it was only four in the afternoon.

"Are you going to be okay to drive home?" I asked worriedly.

"I'm fine," Ellis said. "I'm used to it, truly, Professor."

As soon as we were in the car, he turned to me.

"Do you really think Dr. Rice was murdered?"

"I do."

"Me too. What I don't know is if it was something that was going on currently or if someone from her past found out something."

"Or thinks there are still hidden accounts?"

He nodded. "It's weird learning about her like that."

"That's why it's always a good idea to talk to everyone involved in a story. It helps you gain perspective about your subject."

"Her aunt made me feel even more sorry for Dr. Rice. I didn't think that was possible." His eyes went wide. "That was a terrible thing to say. Sorry."

"You can speak freely with me, Ellis. But only me. Okay? I don't want to spread any rumors. If anything, it will only make it more difficult to get to the truth. But she was seeing someone at the pub. We need to find out who that was."

"I might know a way," Ellis said as he turned on the car, then put the heat on full blast.

"What do you have in mind?"

"Did the police take her computer from her office?"

"I don't think so. I think they just copied the hard drive. Why?"

"I was thinking most people meet online these days. Maybe she was logged in to some sort of dating site. If I can get access to her computer, I could take a look."

"I believe her office is still a crime scene," I said.

"They took the tape down this afternoon."

"Okay, then. I know what we're doing tomorrow morning." I laughed.

This idea of solving Alice's death because I felt guilty she died on my doorstep had morphed into something else. The more I learned about her, the more I needed to know the truth. And I had a feeling Ellis felt the same way.

Chapter Seventeen

The next morning, Ellis and I acted like we did every day, but as soon as Gladys went to make the tea, Ellis snuck into Alice's office. I had a master key and I'd given it to him. This was all his idea. Still, I felt guilty. If anyone found him in there, it would be difficult to explain. But I would take the blame.

"Ten minutes max, okay?"

Ellis nodded. "Like the police, I'm just going to transfer everything onto this." He held up a thumb drive. "I'll be out in a few minutes. That said, you're the lookout. If she comes back early, speak loudly."

"Got it. And you don't have to do this. If I understood exactly what it was we needed, I'd be happy to take over."

I felt like I should be the one giving the orders.

"No. I've got this. A real reporter would risk anything for his story, but it isn't just about that. We need to know what happened." He quickly went inside. I stood in the doorway staring down at my phone. If someone came by, I hoped they would think I was reading a text.

But less than five minutes later, Gladys came back with the tea tray.

Crud.

"What are you doing out here?" she asked, obviously confused.

"Trying to get a better signal," I said loudly. I held up my phone.

"Just ask Ellis to check the modem. Could be the internet is down again. Unless you're trying to make a call—then it's sometimes easier to just go outside. The walls and windows of the university are thick, and service is uneven on the best of days. I usually use the landlines when I'm here."

"Ah, that makes sense." I said it so loud that she jerked a bit. The items on the tea tray rattled. "Oh, that tea looks wonderful. Do you have those little orange and chocolate biscuits you had the other day? I love those."

She went to set the tray down. "I do not, but I can get some from the kitchen." She seemed pleased that I'd complimented her food choices.

"I don't want you to go to any trouble. It had been years since I had them, and I think I might be addicted."

She laughed. "Well, let's feed that addiction. There are some left; I'll run and get them."

"Are you sure?"

"Be right back," she said in the hallway.

As soon as she turned the corner, I knocked on the door of Alice's office.

"Get out of there," I said loudly.

When the door opened quickly, I might have jumped a bit.

"Good call on the biscuits," he said as he followed me to my office.

"Did you get what we need?"

"I believe so. Luckily, she used her computer here for personal emails and texts. It's against university policy. I'm kind of surprised. She always seemed to be such a rule follower."

"Well, as we've been learning, there are many sides to people."

"There you are, Ellis," Gladys said from the doorway. "The professor is having trouble with her internet."

"Oh? Uh, let me look into that," he said as he slipped the thumb drive in his pocket. "But you said you wanted to go over the invite list for tonight. The pub called earlier, and I confirmed. She wanted to know if you wanted to do a tapas sort of thing."

"Oh, that's a great idea. It's always a good idea to serve liquor with food. I'll call her back."

"I've got it. But first, let's fix your internet."

"Don't forget your tea," Gladys said. "I've put your favorite biscuits on there."

"You are wonderful, thank you."

She blushed. "It's nice to be appreciated."

"Well, I'm not used to people feeding me throughout the day. It's absolutely charming and a huge bonus in my eyes."

"It's my pleasure," she said. "Now I need to run upstairs. The dean wants the finalized list of classes. I emailed, but her assistant wants a printout as well. I'll be back soon."

"Take your time," I said as she left.

Ellis and I grabbed some items off the tea tray. I made sure to grab most of the cookies I'd asked for so Gladys wouldn't be suspicious—though I hadn't lied about the addiction.

"Okay, show me what you found," I said.

"Your desk or mine?"

"Let's use my computer. If anything happens, I want the blame to fall on me." He followed me into my office.

"Okay, you sit down and show me what you found."

He booted everything up and clicked on the dating website.

"How do you know her password?"

He showed me a piece of paper he pulled from his pocket. "Like most people, she kept them under her keyboard. I hope you do not do that, Professor."

I usually kept everything on my phone. "I don't." It probably wasn't much safer, but at least they couldn't be found as easily.

He clicked on her profile. She was smiling.

"Okay, so I'm in," he whispered.

"It feels wrong to read her private conversations, but are there any?"

He clicked on a tab that said "Chat."

We both sighed when he pulled it up. "It's a number and username," I said. "That is disappointing."

"I think that is to protect the people on the site," he said. "That way they can talk anonymously and get to know one another."

"You seem to know a lot about it," I said.

He shrugged. "Like I said, most of us meet online in some way, though I can't afford dating sites like this. I meet most of my friends while gaming online."

I smiled. He was so wise I sometimes forgot he was a young man.

"Go ahead and click on the profiles where they had chats."

There were a few different conversations. Most of the chats were about likes and dislikes. Thankfully—since Ellis was reading with me—there wasn't anything sexy or inappropriate.

He clicked on the first one. The gentleman had gray hair and appeared at least twenty years older than Alice. "It doesn't look like they went out," he said.

"How can you tell?"

"There are emojis to say how the date was. And there are none."

I couldn't imagine being on a site like this where it appeared you were graded by those you dated.

"Can anyone see those? If she gave someone low marks, they might have taken offense."

He shook his head. "I think it is only for the individual user, so they can remember how things went."

"Okay. Let's check another one."

He went down the line. Every time he brought up one of the photos, I took a picture of the face and their username with my phone.

"Are you going to show those to the detective?" He asked as he brought up the last one.

"Not unless absolutely necessary," I said. "I'd have to admit to what we did."

He brought up the last username. I sucked in a breath when I saw the photo.

"What is it?" Ellis asked.

I took a quick picture. "The detective said this guy was following me. I didn't believe him at the time. But look."

I showed him the photos side by side.

"That's the same fellow."

"It is."

"Do you think he might have killed her?" he asked.

"Let's not jump to conclusions. I want to check at the pub and see if Arnell and Catrin have seen him. Do me a favor and copy and paste their chat so I can read through it later."

He nodded.

"Thank you for this," I said.

"It's weird to think of her dating these men," he said.

"Well, she didn't date them all. She was quite particular. Oh, look at the occupation for the last guy."

"Self-employed security," Ellis said.

"I wonder what that means."

"Maybe he's a security guard trying to make himself sound better."

"Could be. I've never used one of these sites, but I could see people doing whatever they must to make themselves look better."

"Like I said, I've met through gaming and social media," he said, "but never on one of these sites. They cost money, and I don't have any."

"Said most every student in the world."

"True. It's easier on social media to find people who share your interests."

"I can see that. I'm not on sites because I'm a very private person."

"That explains a lot," he said, and then he shut everything down.

"What do you mean?"

"While I found articles about you, and the ones you wrote, oh, and research papers, I didn't find any sort of online footprint on social media sites."

"It was a conscious choice. A lot of reporters have them now, and they have huge followings. But I always felt like if you wanted everyone to like you—and that seems to be what social media is about—then how can you do what's necessary to get to the heart of a story?"

"I never thought of it that way," he said. "Should I delete all my socials?"

I shrugged. "That's your choice. As you said, it also makes it easier for people to find you. When you're working on crime stories, as I was at your age, I didn't want people to be able to find me."

"Also a good learning experience. There is something I wanted to talk to you about."

"What's that?"

"You sent me an invite for tonight."

"Are you busy? That's okay," I said.

He smiled. "No. It's just that I thought you might want to keep it a faculty evening."

"You are a member of the faculty, and you're teaching an undergrad class. It's part of your coursework."

"Okay. The former chairman was a bit more formal and only invited his friends to this sort of thing."

I laughed again. "Well, as we've established, I have no idea what I'm doing. I need all the friends I can get. I don't want people to think of each other as competition. I want us to all work together to create something special for the students. And as I say that, I know it's sounds Pollyanna-ish."

"I don't know what that means. But I like the idea of inclusivity. It's something we've been missing here."

"So I've been told. But you and I are going to change that, Ellis. I'm glad I have you on my side."

He lifted his fist, and we fist bumped. "Just so you know, I'm not much of a fist bumper."

He laughed. "Noted. I'll call the pub and finish making the arrangements."

"Thanks."

Gladys knocked on the doorframe. "Were you able to get everything settled? I can call IT, or Ellis can. I should have offered that before."

I wondered how long she'd been standing there listening. We should have shut the door.

"All done," Ellis said as he walked out.

"Good. Let me know if you need anything else."

"You're a blessing, Gladys. Thank you." It seemed our little disagreement from the conversation with Paul was over. At least I hoped so.

But I did have one more thing to ask her. I followed her to her desk and then handed over my phone.

"The other day when I was going through Dr. Rice's files, I found copies of a logbook. I wondered if you might know if it has to do with the university or if it's something else."

Her eyes opened wide. "Oh? What did the police think?"

"They have the same files, but I didn't ask the detective. I wasn't sure if they were important. Can you take a look?"

I pulled up the photos on my phone.

She pulled her glasses off the top of her head and still squinted. "They are a bit blurry," she said.

"Yes, I was trying to take pictures quickly."

She smiled up at me. "Look at you playing investigative reporter, but I can't help you."

"Are you sure?"

She glanced again and then shook her head. "No, sorry. They don't look familiar. Maybe they were her private accounts."

"Okay, thanks. It was worth a try."

* * *

Later that night, Ellis dropped me off in front of my apartment. I wanted to freshen up before heading over to the pub.

I was nervous, even though I'd already met all of the faculty. This was my first time to throw a party in years. And I was glad it was meant to be casual.

I waved at Paul as I headed upstairs. He gave me a short nod. Gladys might be over our little argument, but it appeared Paul held a grudge.

I'd have to figure out a way to charm him back to my side.

I freshened up and changed into my newest pair of jeans and a caramel-colored sweater that was incredibly soft. Then I pulled on a pair of boots. The snow outside had stopped, but the sidewalks were still covered.

I glanced at my watch and realized I only had a few minutes. I didn't want to be late to my own party.

When I headed for my front door, there was an envelope on the floor. Either it had just been delivered or I'd missed it when I came in.

I started to toss it on the breakfast bar, but I was curious. It was just a white envelope with no writing. I couldn't resist.

Using a knife from the kitchen drawer, I slit the top of the envelope open.

There was a single piece of paper inside.

I opened it up. In typed block letters, it read STOP INVESTIGATING OR DIE.

Chapter Eighteen

I didn't have time to freak out over the note. Okay, I freaked out a little. Throughout my career, I'd been threatened more than once. It came with the job. Especially if one was a decent reporter.

I didn't have any plastic bags to put the letter in, so I put it back in the envelope and folded a tissue over the whole thing. Then I stuffed it in my bag.

I took a deep breath and opened my door.

"Oh." I jumped.

Rhys was there with his hand raised again. "Sorry," he said. "I didn't mean to scare you. I wondered if you might want an escort across the street."

"Right. Uh. Sure. Thanks."

What I really wanted to do was call the detective, and I would. But I didn't want to show up late to my first big faculty party.

"Are you okay?" He frowned.

"What do you mean?" I glanced down to make sure I'd remembered to dress properly.

"You seem a bit pale," he said.

"Oh, I'm fine. Do you have any advice?" I asked as I locked my front door.

"About the faculty?"

"Yes." I buttoned my coat.

"You'll find there is an array of personalities, but they are a good lot. And they all love teaching."

"Well, that is promising."

Downstairs, he waved at Paul. "Night, Paul. Don't wait up," Rhys joked.

Paul frowned and just nodded at him.

Rhys opened the door for me. When we were outside, he glanced back at the building. "I wonder if something happened. Paul seems upset."

"That's probably due to me. I mentioned that I didn't appreciate him gossiping with Gladys about my private business."

He chuckled loudly. "Oh. I bet that went over well."

"I feel it's important to set boundaries early on, and they were making me uncomfortable."

He held up his hands as we crossed the street. "Absolutely respect what you've done. That situation has been a problem for all of us who live there. I, for one, am grateful."

"Well, hopefully, he'll forgive me soon. All it took with Gladys was asking for more of the chocolate and orange biscuits she makes."

He laughed again. "She does like to feed us. Tomorrow, maybe think about bringing him some Welsh cakes from the bakery. They are his favorite."

"Thank you for that information."

"You've done us all a grand favor. It's the least I can do." He put a hand on the pub door. "Are you ready?"

I took a deep breath. "Let's do this."

"Hi, Docs," Catrin said as we entered the warmth of the pub. "Some of your guests have arrived. Can I get you a pint?"

"I'll take one," Rhys said.

"Me too."

"Head on back. We put up a buffet with the tapas you requested."

"Thank you," I said. "That's perfect."

"We try," she laughed.

When we entered the back room, the professors turned toward me.

"Hey," I said. "Thank you for coming." I shook their hands.

"We're grateful for the invite," Dr. Becca Kelly said.

"I can't say your predecessor ever met us at the pub," Dr. Laura Thompson said. She had a heavy Welsh accent, long, curly hair, and a widow's peak. I imagined she and Becca had more than one student who crushed on them.

"Oh?"

"He was a bit more formal, but I love this. We're all so busy during term, I think it is important to get together," Laura said.

"I agree," I said. "I'm not one for formality. Maybe we should do this once a month."

"I'm in," a man said from behind us. I turned to see Dr. Nathan Glynn walking into the room. He was very tall and had a full head of curly hair. He was in his early thirties, and from our chat the day before, I'd learned he was a big nature buff. He spent his holidays in Patagonia, which sounded fascinating.

I wasn't so into the great outdoors. Walking down the block to the bakery was pretty much my idea of an excursion.

The gathering was relaxed and filled with laughter, which made me happy. We ended up around the table Catrin and Arnall had set up.

The conversation eventually came around to Alice.

"It's weird that she's gone," Becca said.

"Were you friends?"

They all glanced at one another and then at Rhys.

He sighed. "As I've mentioned, she was a loner."

"We shouldn't speak ill of the dead," Laura said. "But she went out of her way to cause trouble, and she was unkind. We all know it."

"It's true," Becca added. "We all get along, but she refused to make any effort. Do you know about the rumor that someone murdered her? I could see that. She had a habit of making people angry." She made a face. "Sorry. I was just so surprised to learn she was gone. She was always complaining to our former chairman that I allowed my students too much freedom."

"In what way?"

"Questioning authority," she said. "Whether it was a professor or the dean of the university. The job of a reporter is to ask those hard questions."

"I couldn't agree more."

"It didn't help that her students constantly complained about her to us, and to the dean," Laura added. "It was like she wanted people to hate her. I never understood it."

After learning more about Alice, I could see why she would be standoffish and distrustful. She'd also probably been afraid people might learn about her past.

"I heard you were involved in the investigation," Nathan said. Then he sipped his beer.

They all stared at me.

"In what way?"

"We heard she died on your doorstep," he said. It wasn't accusatory, more curious.

I sighed. "She did."

"The chairman did her best to save Alice. I was there," Rhys said. "She kept on until the emergency team showed up. It was quite heroic."

"Did she say anything?" Laura asked.

"She didn't have a chance," I said.

I explained what happened.

People gasped around the table.

"That's terrible," Becca chimed in. "I'm so sorry you had that happen to you so soon after arriving."

"Thanks."

"Your assistant, Ellis, seems to be thorough," Nathan said. "He came by the office yesterday and questioned me. He's already a great reporter."

I smiled. "He is. I've been overseeing his research for his article. He's impressive."

"Can you tell us what you've learned so far?" Laura asked. "None of us knew much about her."

"Ellis has sworn me to secrecy. But after delving into her past, I will say it is easier to understand why she didn't socialize much. She had her reasons."

"You sound like you feel sorry for her," Rhys said. He'd been unusually quiet the last half hour.

I shrugged. "I don't know that *sorry* is the right word. Understanding of her is better. She had a difficult life, and it quite obviously affected her."

"Now I feel bad," Becca said.

I shook my head. "Well, as you all know, she went out of her way to be difficult. Lots of people have hard beginnings and they're still able to be civil human beings.

"I do wonder if you all saw her with anyone, as in dating. Did she ever bring a plus-one to events?"

Once again, they all glanced at one another.

"No," Nathan said. "She was always alone."

"This room is in the cone of silence, let me assure you," I said, bringing up the *Get Smart* sitcom from the sixties. Some of them stared at me, but others laughed. I continued, "Do you know of anyone who might have wanted to hurt her?"

"I don't know what 'cone of silence' means," Laura said.

"It's a joke from an old TV show," I added. "It means none of the information will be shared."

"We all knew that her students were not her biggest fans," Laura said. "But I can't imagine anyone being angry enough to hurt her."

"Maybe the former chairman," Nathan said.

Silence blanketed the room as everyone stared at him.

He seemed to realize what he'd said. "Oh. Sorry. He constantly complained about her. More than once he mentioned he just wanted her to go away. I did see her here with a man a few times, though."

"Oh?" I grabbed my phone out of my bag. I pulled up the picture of the man who had supposedly been following me, which then reminded me about the letter in my bag. I needed to take that to the police station when we were done here. I shivered but then pushed the thoughts away.

"Did he by chance look like this guy?" I passed my phone across the table. "There are two photos." One was from the CCTV. The other was his dating profile.

Nathan glanced at the picture. He frowned.

"Could have been," he said. "Other than being surprised she seemed to be on a date, I didn't pay much attention. I was here with my mates for a stag party." He passed my phone around.

"Did any of the rest of you ever see her with him?"

As they looked, they shook their heads.

"Do you think he's the killer?" Becca asked. She shivered.

"I honestly have no idea. But thank you all for looking. The detective inspector found some photos of him and was curious. He may speak to you all individually now that everyone is back from holiday."

Becca shook her head.

"What is it?"

"Things like this just don't happen here. This is a small university town, and it's always been so safe. It's hard to think that someone killed one of us."

"We still don't know that for certain," I said, though I was indeed certain. The news from the ME hadn't come out yet.

"But you think so," Rhys said. He knew better, and I'd been grateful he kept my secrets.

"You are all journalists; you know we never assume. I'm waiting for all the facts, just like the detective."

"That's why you're the boss." Becca raised her glass. "To the boss."

"The boss," they all cheered.

"Thanks. And please don't think of me that way. I'm your friend as well. I'm here to support you and help with whatever you need. As some of you already heard at the previous party, I'm here to create the best journalism school in Wales, if not the UK."

"Let's do it," Laura said.

"I'm lucky to have such a strong team."

We cheered again.

Everyone seemed reluctant to leave, but I needed to go to the police department. Eventually, they left.

"I'll walk you home," Rhys said. It was a joke, since he lived there as well.

"Actually, I need to go to the police station."

His eyes flashed with alarm. "What happened, and why didn't you tell me?"

I told him about the envelope I'd received.

He helped me into my coat. "I'll come with you."

"It's late and that isn't necessary. It's only a block up the street."

"You received a death threat. I will be coming with you. From now on, you need to make sure you don't go places alone. It's dangerous. Her killer might be after you." He appeared genuinely concerned.

The wind whipped around us as we made our way up the street, and the cold stole my breath.

Inside the station, it was bright and warm. I was surprised to see the detective speaking with the sergeant at the front desk.

He glanced up and frowned.

"What happened?" he asked.

"I could just be here to visit," I said. Then I smirked.

He glanced up at the clock. "It's after nine, I doubt you are here for social reasons." He nodded toward Rhys. "And you have an escort, which is a good thing. So, what happened?"

I pulled the tissue-wrapped envelope from my purse. "When I was leaving for the party I was throwing at the pub, I found this under my door."

He frowned and pulled a pair of gloves from his pocket—it appeared he always kept them in there—and carefully unwrapped the tissue. He stared at the blank envelope with surprise.

"It's what it says inside," I said.

"Get me an evidence bag," Gareth said to the sergeant. Then he opened the letter and read the contents. He sighed. "This is what happens when you snoop."

"We were researching, not snooping," I said.

"Same thing," he and Rhys said at the same time.

"Hey, I expect you to be on my side," I said to Rhys.

"I am, but now your life has been threatened," he said. "And what about Ellis? His life might be in danger as well."

I hadn't thought about that.

"I need you to make a list of everyone you've spoken with, and I want copies of everything you've found."

Now it was my turn to sigh. I couldn't show him everything, because then he would know I'd broken the law by snooping in Alice's apartment.

"Okay. But tomorrow. I'm exhausted tonight."

He shook his head. "First thing," he said.

"Okay."

"And you don't leave your flat without an escort." He glanced at Rhys.

"I'm happy to take you wherever you need to go," Rhys said.

"I'm not a child, and I can defend myself." But what they said made sense. I was feeling uneasy. He was right. Ellis and I had obviously hit a nerve with someone we'd spoken with, but that was a good thing.

It meant we were getting closer to finding the killer.

Chapter Nineteen

The next day, I made the list for the police detective. I felt like I could steer him in a certain way by what I did share without harming Ellis's story. Thankfully, Gareth was out of the office when I arrived, so I left the list with the desk sergeant.

"Where to next?" Rhys asked. He'd insisted on walking with me.

"The bakery. Paul is still giving me the eye. Then, later this afternoon, I'm going to the bookstore for the singles book club."

"Oh, that's on my plan for today as well. And I never mind going to the bakery."

"You're in the book club?" I pretended not to know.

He nodded. "I've been friends with Rhian for years," he said. "She makes me go, but I enjoy it. Some of the other professors are in it."

"Oh, I didn't know. Do you think they'll mind me crashing?"

"Crashing?"

"Well, it's personal time for them. I'm the boss, even though I don't really think of myself that way."

"They won't care. We love talking about books; that's the only requirement."

I laughed. "Books happen to be one of my favorite subjects."

After the bakery, we went back to the apartment building. I had a box for myself, and then I handed Paul the other box.

"Paul, I truly didn't mean to offend you the other night," I said. "I've had a rough start and, as a single woman, I was feeling vulnerable. I hope you and Gladys understand. And I hope you'll accept my peace offering."

His brows drew together, and then he opened the box. A smile spread across his face. "Never meant to make you feel uncomfortable, Professor. You were in the right."

"Let's don't worry about right or wrong. What happened was extraordinary circumstances, and I understand we are all shocked."

"That we are," he said.

"Okay. Just know I'm grateful for all you do."

"Understood," he said. "And thank you for these."

Well, that was one problem solved.

A few hours later, there was a knock on my door. I was expecting Rhys, but it was the detective.

"Oh. Uh . . . what's wrong?" I asked.

I had my coat on and was holding my backpack, where I'd put the book I'd read for the club.

"Were you heading out?"

"Book club," I said.

"Are you going alone?" He frowned.

"No. Rhys and I were walking over together. Did you find out who put that letter under my door?"

"It's being processed for fingerprints and type of paper. Hopefully, we'll have answers soon."

"Is that what you were coming to tell me?"

He shook his head. "I read through your list, and I know you left some people off, like the victim's aunt. I was at the nursing home this morning speaking with her. She said she'd spoken to some young people, but she couldn't remember their names.

"So I asked to see the security tapes for the lobby, and imagine my surprise to see you and Ellis."

I blew out a breath. "I'm trying to protect Ellis' sources. And I was trying to protect her as well. You met her, so you know her memory is going. I didn't want anyone to bother her."

"You didn't think the information about the victim's past might be valuable for our investigation?"

"Are you more upset that we were there or that you're a step behind? Besides, she said you'd already spoken to her. I think she remembered you as the handsome detective from Dillynaidd." I grinned.

He stared at me, and then his eyebrows went up.

"What I want is for us to work together. Your life has been threatened."

"And it isn't the first time I've been through something like that," I said. "Though it's been a few years. I'm more worried about Ellis. He's young and has his whole life in front of him."

"Right, but I checked, and he didn't receive a threatening letter."

I'd have to talk to Ellis about that. He shouldn't have felt intimidated by the police detective. He had a right to protect all of his sources.

"Okay, in the interest of sharing, I have something for you. Maybe check the CCTV in Crumby Thursday. While I didn't see who was driving, I could have sworn we were being followed."

He pulled out his pen and notebook from his pocket.

"Why didn't you tell me last night?"

"I was tired. And I thought it might be nothing. But it was a navy sedan. Two-door, I think. I didn't get the make. And we visited the newspaper office." I gave him the time. "Maybe, if they got out of the car, you can see who it was. I did feel like someone watched us through the window there."

He shook his head.

"What?"

"This is the sort of thing you should be sharing right away," he said. "Next time you think someone might be following you, call me." He wrote a number on the paper from his notebook and handed me one of his cards. "That is my personal cell. I'd appreciate if you'd take this matter more seriously."

"Do you know what kind of poison?"

"Will you keep it to yourself?"

"As you've seen, I can keep a secret. If you want me to share, I need to know you'll do the same."

"Fine. It was thorn apple. Unusual around here but found in different kinds of birdseed."

"Birdseed? How would that even work?"

"The report said it was in her food, and possibly tea. Her entire kitchen is being tested. It appears she was dosed over time."

I shivered. "That's terrible. So somebody was poisoning her. That means it has to be someone who was close to her."

"It also means there is no way you could be a suspect." He cocked his head.

"I thought I was already off your list."

He shrugged. "Like you, I wait for facts to be confirmed."

"Is there anyone around you know who is into birds? I mean, I'm a late-in-life birder, but I don't have anywhere to put a house up for them." I'd grown fond of birds because my mom had been a birder. Her feeders in her backyard were always filled, and she would sit out there for hours. Whenever we traveled to a new place, she would look out for various species and check them off a list she kept.

"We are looking into things."

"So you still don't have a main suspect."

"Other than the person who is following you?"

There was a knock at the door, and the detective answered it.

Rhys looked from me to him. "Am I interrupting?"

I shook my head. "Nope. The detective was just leaving."

"That I was. Though I want to reiterate, do not travel alone. While I understand you are perfectly capable of protecting yourself, it never hurts to have a friend with you."

I sighed.

"I'm taking her to book club," Rhys said. He smiled.

"Tell Rhian I said hello," the detective said. Then he turned and left.

"Was he harassing you again?"

I shook my head. "No, not this time. He just came to tell me they were processing the letter."

"That's good to hear. Are you ready?"

"Let's go."

* * *

I was surprised to see the small group included about ten people and that two of them were Becca and Laura.

They were funny and kind, and they had brilliant insights into the book. I found myself drawn to them, but I worried they would just see me as their boss. That is, until they invited me to a dinner at an Italian restaurant down the street.

"What about me?" Rhys asked.

"Hens' night," Laura said.

"What she said." Becca laughed.

"Fine." Rhys smiled. "I had plans out of town with Henry and the dean, but you need to make sure the chairman isn't on her own. The police want her to have an escort every time she steps out of her flat. Call me when you are leaving, and I'll be there."

They frowned.

"What happened?" Becca asked.

"The detective inspector is being overly protective," I said.

"Tell them the truth," Rhys said. "We all want the best for you. And you can trust these two."

"You can," Becca said.

"I received a threatening letter, and the police think I'm being followed." Okay, I thought that as well, but I understood how paranoid I would sound if I said it out loud.

"That sounds serious," Laura said.

"It is," Rhys said at the same time I said, "It's not."

We laughed.

"No worries. It's freezing outside," Becca said. "I live on the second floor—well, actually, we both do. And I have a car that I keep in the garage behind our building."

"There's a garage? I had no idea."

"There is. It's free if you live in the building," Rhys said.

"Good to know." Not that I planned on getting a car. While I hadn't had a chance to use it, there was a good bus service as well as the train that stopped at most of the small towns all the way to Cardiff. I'd used both a great deal when I'd been an undergrad.

I was about to leave with Rhys when Rhian waved me down.

I went over to her. "Thank you for inviting me," I said. "It was great fun." And that was the truth. The time had flown by.

"I'm so glad you made it. I heard you're going to dinner with us tonight."

"Oh, you'll be there as well, yeah?"

She smiled. "We try to get together once a month for Italian. It's good to have women friends, right?"

"I couldn't agree more." I'd been slightly worried they'd invited me to make the boss feel welcome, but maybe they just wanted to get to know me. I would give them the benefit of the doubt. Besides, it was better than sitting home alone with my thoughts.

* * *

As we walked home with Rhys before dinner, I had that weird sense that someone was watching me. It was the four of us who lived in the building. I didn't want to appear paranoid, but as we passed the bakery, I stopped and turned around.

I saw someone duck around the corner about a half a block down. I took off running—a big mistake, since I'm not big on exercise. By the time I made it to the corner, I was out of breath. But when I peeked around, there was no one there.

The others came running behind me.

"Is everything okay?" Rhys asked. He stared around the corner.

I bent over to catch my breath. "Someone—" I took in a deep breath, which actually hurt. "Watching."

Becca held her handbag like a weapon. "Where are they?"

I smiled. She was fierce. "Gone. Maybe it's just me being paranoid, but I know I saw someone."

"No. You aren't being paranoid," Laura said. "As women, we have to be on guard, even in our sweet little town. Jerk. I wish we could have caught him. I would like to practice what I learned in self-defense."

I smiled. These were my people.

"Are you okay? You are pale," Rhys said.

I laughed. "I'm not used to running like that."

"Well, you're faster than me," Becca said. "I still wish we had caught the person. I'm mad they are trying to scare you. That letter would have been enough to keep me in my flat for the rest of my days."

I sighed.

"I know," Rhys said. "Don't be mad at me for sharing. But after that letter last night, I'm genuinely worried. I feel like the more of us who know, the better we can look out for you, and each other. I'm just trying to be a good friend. I know you value your privacy. I told them that."

"And yet . . ." It was difficult to be angry. He was only doing what he thought best.

"The other women in our building needed to know someone is leaving threatening letters," he said. "We should be looking out for you and each other. I'm worried about everyone's safety."

He made a good point. "Come on," I said. "After all that running, I need a nap before going out tonight."

They laughed nervously, but I could tell they were uncomfortable. At least I wasn't alone.

"Did you tell anyone else?" I asked as we headed home.

"I didn't tell the dean, but she knows," he said. "She texted me early this morning and ordered me to stay by your side. I have a feeling the detective called her."

I rolled my eyes. I was surprised Carolyn hadn't shown up today.

"Let me guess, she and Henry are out of town again?"

"Yes. They've gone to Cardiff for the weekend for some conference Henry is speaking at. She almost came back, but I promised we had you covered—though I'll be heading that way in a few hours to help with Henry's speech. He can be a bit all over the place, and as his friend, he usually asks me to help."

I was so used to being alone. But in a weird way, it made me feel even more sorry for Alice. If she had been a kind person, all of these people might have cared about her as well.

It was sad.

I wished I could tell them about her, but it didn't feel right. Not that I saw any of them as suspects. Becca and Laura had been out of town, and Rhys just wasn't the murdering type. Charming. Handsome. Kind. But not a murderer.

A strange thought floated through my brain. We all thought, because of the man who had been following me, that she'd been killed by a man.

In the past, poison was usually used by women, though that train of thought had become outdated. Most poisons were easily accessible. I wanted to do some research about the type and how easy it would have been to buy the birdseed needed.

Alice had so many enemies, but which one wanted her dead?

Chapter Twenty

Later that night, there was a knock on my door. I opened it to find Becca and Laura there. They smiled, and I couldn't help but grin. They were both dressed up in colorful, frilly blouses.

"Should I change?" I glanced down at my uniform of sweater, jeans, and boots. The rest of my clothes were in the second shipment, which hadn't arrived, and I didn't think my boring black suit was appropriate for a dinner with friends.

"You're perfect," Becca said. "We're wearing jeans as well. And I'm going back upstairs to grab my boots."

"Yes, we have a good-news/bad-news situation," Laura added.

"Oh?"

"My car won't start," Becca said. "And it wasn't the battery this time. It had to be towed. So we need to walk."

"That's no big deal," I said. "It's just three blocks down. What's the good news?"

"Well, since I don't have to be the designated driver, I can drink all the wine I want," Becca joked. We laughed.

"That is good news. Besides, after eating pasta, it's probably not a bad idea to walk."

"Agreed," Laura said.

"I'll meet you two downstairs," Becca said. "Give me three minutes to change my shoes."

We headed downstairs, and I was surprised to see a different man behind the desk. He waved at us but was busy sorting some papers on the massive desk.

"Who's that?" I asked.

"Davy," Becca said. "He only works weekends and the odd night when the desk guys are off on vacation. He's nice enough, but kind of shy." He also appeared young—well, compared to Paul.

She introduced us.

He nodded and then went back to his paper sorting.

It only took us ten minutes to walk to the restaurant, and we entered with pink cheeks and a bit out of breath.

This place hadn't been here when I lived in Dillynaidd, and I was interested to try it out. I loved pasta. The lights were dim, and white tablecloths covered the candlelit tables, which had wineglasses at each place setting. Maybe it was good we were walking.

Rhian waved to us from a table set for four. We headed over. The other girls hugged her, and I followed suit. Well, she reached her arms out to me, and it would have been weird if I didn't reciprocate.

The hostess handed us menus, which had a long list of dishes.

"What's good here?"

"Everything," they said together. Then they laughed.

"Well, that's always a good thing," I said.

"Chef Antony is from Naples, but his dishes are from all over Italy," Becca said.

"He's also the hottest single man in Dillynaidd," Rhian said.

"She's not wrong," Laura added. "He is very easy on the eyes."

Becca cleared her throat as she glared at her friends. "Not that we objectify men," she said.

"We do a little," Laura whispered. "There are so few that are actually datable in town."

"There is that," Becca concurred. "But none of us is brave enough to ask him out."

"Mainly because we can't live without his food," Rhian said. "If things went wrong, it would be weird to come back. So we just come and gaze lovingly at him and eat whatever he puts in front of us. You'll see."

I laughed hard. I couldn't remember the last time I'd done that. After months of stress, it felt so good. "I can't wait."

A sommelier stopped by the table, and since she knew the other women, I let them choose for us. I preferred a good glass of whiskey to wine, but I liked the latter just fine.

A waiter came by with a giant plate of different kinds of bread and poured some olive oil in small bowls for each of us. Then he returned with fresh buffalo mozzarella and a bowl of olives.

"I don't need to order anything else. I'm okay with just these," I said.

"We always end up with extra to take home, so eat as much as you want," Becca said. "We also usually order the chef's special. It's a surprise but is always delicious."

"She says that because if you order the surprise, the chef comes out with the dishes."

"Now I'm really curious about this guy."

"Just wait," Rhian said. "I promise we aren't talking him up too much. He's been in magazines. We have no idea why he settled here in our small town."

"I heard it's because his mom was from here. And his dad was Italian, and he was a mama's boy," Becca said. "They make all the pasta fresh daily."

The last thing I expected in Dillynaidd was to find a restaurant like this.

When the waiter came, we all asked for the chef's special.

"Becca, I meant to ask earlier, but what part of Ireland are you from?"

She grinned. "I grew up around Dublin. I came here for undergrad, and I loved the town. After working for papers all over Ireland, and also grad school, I ended up applying for a position about four years ago. I really love it here. It is my size of town."

"Agreed," Laura said, and held up her glass. We all did the same. "To the charm of Dillynaidd."

We clinked glasses.

"And how did you end up here?" I asked Laura.

She blew out a breath. "I was working for a paper in London and hated my job. I lived in a one-room flat where the heat never worked. One day I saw a job posting for an adjunct professor. I took it as a side income because it was online. After the first semester, the dean met with me and asked if I'd be interested in a full-time position. It was a no-brainer, as you Yanks like to say."

"And you know how I ended up here," Rhian said. "Granddad left me the bookstore. I can't imagine doing anything else. And while the dating pool is small, I wouldn't want to live anywhere else."

We laughed. "So what I'm hearing is, if I want to date someone, I probably need to visit some of the other towns around here."

They nodded.

"I think Rhys said the same sort of thing."

They giggled.

"What?"

"He is quite popular among the faculty and the students, but he does make it a rule to never date anyone in town," Laura said. "He never brings a plus-one, and we've always wondered about his type. Oh, listen to me. He's a charmer and so kind. I don't want to gossip about him. But some men are too handsome."

"I don't think I've ever heard that before," I said. "But I do see what you mean."

I had no desire to date anyone. My plate was full learning a different job and adapting to a new home.

"Here he comes," Rhian whispered.

Chef Antony came out from the kitchen holding two plates on each arm. The women around me hadn't lied; he was handsome. Tall, black hair, a charming smile and beautiful, thick eyelashes over chocolate-colored irises.

"The bellas have a new friend," he said as he put the plates in front of us. His accent was heavy and his voice deep. I understood the attraction.

They all blushed.

"Hi," I said. "I've heard wonderful things about your food."

He put his hand over his heart. "Ah, thank you. I am grateful." He bowed his head. "Now, mangiate. And order dessert. Our pastry chef has outdone herself tonight."

The women around me watched him leave. And then we all laughed.

"He has the charisma of a movie star," I said, and I meant it.

Rhian pointed at me. "That's it. Whenever he's around, I forget to speak. All I can do is stare at him."

I grinned. "Some people have that power over others. It's a shame he has to hide in a kitchen all day."

"Well, maybe not for long," Rhian said.

The other women turned toward her. "What do you mean?" Becca asked.

"When he was in the bookstore the other day, I overheard him talking to his pastry chef, who came in with him. Chef Antony mentioned working on a cookbook. He already has a publisher. They were in there looking at different formats of cookbooks and bought several."

Laura frowned. "I hope he isn't lured away from our sweet town."

"Me too," Becca said.

"It didn't sound like it. The pastry chef asked him if he'd be opening up more restaurants. He said no. He likes the idea of making one place excellent, and they are going for their first Michelin star."

After a few bites of the creamy pasta dish, I could understand the fuss. It was honestly one of the best meals of my life, and I'd been to Italy more than once. That said, I could only eat half my dinner, as I'd already had too many olives and too much fresh mozzarella.

"I see why you all come here, and it isn't just for the views," I said.

They smiled.

"As a town, it feels lucky to have a place like this and the bakery. I've already eaten my weight in Welsh cakes," I said. "And the pub has great food."

"There's also Conway's, which is just outside of town," Laura said.

"Oh? What kind of food is that?"

"A lot of seafood and more traditional Welsh dishes," Rhian added. "It's very good and not too expensive."

"I'm so used to being surrounded by hundreds of different restaurants," I said. "That's not bragging, just something I will have to get used to. I don't really cook, so if I couldn't order it, I didn't eat. I may have to learn how to cook if I want to shake things up around here."

"Laura and Becca are both great cooks," Rhian said.

"We only learned out of desperation," Laura said. "The community center has cooking classes all the time. That's where I learned how to make pizza and homemade pasta from Chef Antony."

"And Catrin, who owns the pub, taught a class on soups and stews," Becca said. "My favorite recipes are where you dump a bunch of ingredients in a pot and cook it for a bit."

I smiled. "That sounds up my alley. I'll have to check it out. Where is the community center? Is that new?"

"It's in the old church behind the bakery. It's still a church, but they turned the reception hall into a community center, where they teach everything from cooking to crafts. It's also a great way to meet people," Rhian said.

I'd promised myself I'd get out and about more than I had when I lived in Dallas.

I couldn't eat another bite, but I ordered tiramisu to take home with the rest of my food. By the time we left, I was bloated and grateful for the walk home.

"That was a lot of calories," I said.

I walked on the street side.

"Well, this is my stop," Rhian said in front of the bookstore.

"You live here?"

She shook her head. "Behind the store there is a row of houses. I have my granddad's old place."

"She makes it sound old, but it's a beautiful town house," Becca said.

"Awww, thanks," Rhian said. "It's easier to go through the building and out the back than to walk down the block. And I'm sleepy. I'll see you all soon."

We waved goodbye.

"Carolyn was right," Laura said.

"About?"

"You," Becca answered.

"What do you mean?" I asked.

"She said you'd fit right into our little group. If she isn't out of town with Henry, she usually joins us for our get-togethers."

"Well, I'm glad you all asked. Did Alice ever join you?" I knew the answer before I asked.

They shook their heads. "We only ever saw her at the university or faculty parties. She always thought she was better than us," Laura said.

"Laura," Becca chastised.

"You know it's true. She was going for your position, Gwen, and we are so grateful that Carolyn made the right choice."

"How do you know I'm the correct person for the job? I've just started."

"Because you already know how to get along with people, which is a big part of the chairman's job," Laura said. "We have a lot of different personalities, but she rubbed everyone the wrong way."

"It makes me uncomfortable to talk about the dead," Becca said. "She was an unhappy person. Her life was sad, as far as I'm concerned."

"No one's life is perfect," Laura added. "That doesn't mean you have to be a jerk. You asked us if we might know of anyone who would want to hurt her. She offended everyone she met. Students, faculty, staff, take your pick."

The roar of an engine caught my attention. As I turned to look, I was yanked away from the curb. I landed on my bum along with Becca, who had pulled me to safety as the navy car sped by.

My heart raced, and a sweat broke out.

"Are you okay?" Laura asked as she reached a hand down to help me up. "I bet it was a drunk driver. It was like he was trying to run you over."

Becca was still on the sidewalk, but she pulled her phone out and dialed a number.

"Who are you calling?" I asked.

"The police. Laura is right. They were coming straight for you."

My stomach churned, and I felt quite sick. "You didn't by chance get the license plate numbers, did you?" I asked, but my voice cracked.

"It was too dark, and it happened so fast," Becca said. "I'm sorry if I hurt you."

"Don't be. You saved my life."

I must be close to the truth where Alice was concerned. Now, if I could only stay alive long enough to find out who killed her.

Chapter Twenty-One

By the time we made it to our apartment building, Gareth was waiting for us in the lobby. Davy appeared overly interested in our conversations, so I invited the detective and my new friends up to my place.

After lighting a fire and turning on the kettle, I settled in and waited while he interviewed the other two women. They were pale and frightened, and I could relate. It took a good fifteen minutes for me to catch my breath.

"They didn't even try to slow down," Becca said. "I turned and saw the tire hit the curb and then nearly yanked poor Gwen's arm out of the socket getting her out of the way. They took off."

"You keep saying *they*," Gareth commented. "Did you see the driver?"

She shook her head. "The glass was tinted, and it was dark right there. It was as if they waited until we were between the lampposts. I couldn't make out anything."

"And the license?"

"I don't think there was one," Becca said. "The car was either navy or black, hard to tell."

I knew it was navy. I'd been falling down, but I'd caught a glimpse. It was the same car that followed Ellis and me to Crumby.

The detective talked to my new friends for a bit longer and then excused them. "I need to speak to Dr. Griffith alone," he said.

"Will you be okay?" Laura asked worriedly. "I feel like we should stay with you tonight. That was absolutely frightening."

"I'm fine. You two go ahead. And thank you for saving my life and the wonderful dinner." My hands still shook as I opened the door and ushered them out.

When I closed it, Gareth was shaking his head.

"You need to stop investigating on your own. Whoever is doing this means you harm. Do you understand?"

He made me a cup of tea like he owned the place and put a liberal amount of sugar in it. Then he handed me the cup as I sat down on the barstool.

"I . . . uh . . ." I didn't know what to say. He was right. Between the note and the car, it was obvious someone meant to do me harm.

I shivered.

"Drink the tea," he ordered.

"You're so bossy."

"I'm trying to keep our newest resident alive. I need you to tell me everything. And I do mean everything. Like why you were in Alice's apartment that night the housemaster heard a noise."

I stared at him. Was he guessing?

"Please, don't bother lying. You'd been in there. I smelled your perfume. It's vanilla and quite distinctive."

I sighed. "I guess my career as a cat burglar is over." Though I refused to actually say I was in there. "Are you going to arrest me? Perfume doesn't seem like something that will stand up in court."

"I'm not going to arrest you, though I should. More for lying to me. What did you find?"

It was more a relief to be able to tell him. "If I'd been there, ya know, hypothetically . . ."

He sighed.

"I might have found a box of personal items under her headboard. A box full of memorabilia. Some were letters, there were photos, and then a bunch of numbers that don't make any sense to me."

"What do you mean?"

I pulled my phone out of my purse and showed him the photos I'd taken.

"There were copies of some kind of logbook. I thought it might have something to do with her dad's trouble when she was younger. Maybe she found something to prove his innocence and someone killed her for it."

"That's a reach," he said.

I shrugged. "Well, he was under investigation for financial fraud when he died. His sister and his daughter never believed that he had done anything wrong. The sister blames his former partner."

He smirked.

"Oh, that's right. You spoke to her as well."

"And she wouldn't be the most credible of witnesses with her memory problems," he said.

"Right. I understand that, but she knew her brother better than most people. And I feel like she would be truthful if she'd known he'd done something wrong."

I remained silent for a moment, thinking, then continued.

"What I don't understand is why someone wants to kill me. I've shared very little, as you know. And no one knows all of the information. Ellis knows some, as do you. But I haven't shared the entirety of it with anyone."

"I believe now is the time," he said. "I'm going upstairs to get the box. You wait here."

He was gone about five minutes, and then there was a knock.

"Take this," he said when I opened the door, handing me the box from Alice's room. "I need to take the key downstairs. But don't open it until I get back. I need to log it for evidence."

I nodded. I was so tired, but it felt good that someone besides me would finally know the truth about what I'd found.

I'm lucky he didn't arrest me.

I'd been kind of dumb exploring like that on my own.

He returned quickly. "Okay, let's open the box. Then I want you to make a list of everyone you've spoken with, and don't pull the 'protecting sources' act on me. Someone tried to kill you tonight. You need to let me help."

"Except for the visit to the Crumby newspaper, you're aware of the rest," I said. "And I'm not trying to protect sources. I'm telling you the truth. That reporter at the newspaper wasn't happy with me calling him out on his writing about Alice when she was a child. I found that appalling. But I can't see him trying to kill me over it."

"Still worth checking out."

I shrugged.

After putting on a pair of gloves and handing me a pair, he opened the box.

There were a few photos. I pointed to one. "That guy looks familiar to me," I said. "I'm wondering if that is her ex-husband."

He turned the photo over. There was only the name *Alan*.

"Darn."

"What?" he asked.

"I forgot to do a search at the county clerk's office to see if they had a marriage record for her. It was closed when I went by. And the letter has a prison stamp."

"They do have a marriage certificate. We have it on file. But his name wasn't Alan. This man does look like the one in the photos from the CCTV. The man who was following you."

I shrugged. "But why? How would he even know who I was, then? I'd been in the country for maybe twenty-four hours at that point."

"Could he have been driving the car tonight?"

"Like my friends, I didn't see anything. Mainly because Becca pulled me so hard and fast, I was trying to keep my face off the pavement. By the time I looked up, the car was past. And it was dark, but I swear it was the same make as the one that I thought followed us to Crumby. Don't you have some sort of database where you can input a photo and it tells you who it is?"

He laughed.

"What?"

"This isn't one of your American television shows," he said. "Though I'm partial to a few of them."

"Oh?"

"But we do have a criminal database; it will just take a while for a result. Nothing happens quickly here."

"Okay."

"Do you remember seeing him anywhere else?"

"No. I keep feeling like someone's watching me, but when I turn around, no one's there. I'm probably being paranoid."

"No, you aren't. Someone tried to run you over tonight. Which reminds me. No going out alone." He held up a hand. "You have to be smart about this until we find out who tried to kill you tonight. And who wrote that letter."

"I wasn't going to argue," I said.

"Well, that's a first."

We laughed.

"Let's get back to it," I said. So, the accounts are the only thing in here I couldn't figure out. Maybe one of your officers will be luckier; I've never been great with math. But I think it's weird she had pictures of different accounts, especially if they aren't hers. The amounts also seem high for a university professor.

"Her aunt said the only money they had was from her dad's life insurance, and that was used for Alice's studies."

"And you believe the aunt?"

"Don't you? With the way her memory is, I don't think she's capable of lying."

"You make a good point."

As we went through the box, he put things in plastic baggies and logged them. He had a system, and I didn't interrupt.

Well, until I yawned.

He glanced up with a worried look in his eyes.

"You've had a tough night. I should go."

"Thanks for not arresting me."

His eyebrows rose. "There's still time. Try not to get killed. And do not go anywhere alone. Understood?"

As he left, I fake saluted him.

My shoulder already ached, and I had a feeling it would be worse the next day. But I still wanted to go with Ellis to check out the man we thought might be Alice's husband.

I should have told the detective.

But he could have looked the information up. Besides, we hadn't spoken to the husband yet, so why would he have a reason to run me over?

I leaned against the door.

Someone had tried to kill me. I'd been scared, but that had morphed into anger. I was determined to find the person who'd tried to hurt me—and who had probably killed Alice.

I was too close for comfort. I just had to put the puzzle pieces together.

Chapter Twenty-Two

The next morning was gloomy and overcast. The wind continued to blow, but at least it wasn't snowing. I'd made Ellis stop at the bakery to get us some coffee and pastries.

Then I told him what happened the night before. He skidded to a stop on the side of the road. "What?" He turned to me. "They really tried to kill you? Are we safe? Did you tell the detective what we were doing today?"

I blew out a breath. "That's a lot of questions. Yes, they really did, and I don't think it was random. And I told him almost everything, except that we were going out today. Including something I haven't mentioned to you." I told him about the accounts.

"You should have shared them with me. I'm not that bad at math. My da made me take accounting classes. He doesn't see journalism as a real job. Though when he read my first story, he changed his mind."

"I'll share everything with you when we're done today. No more secrets. Now tell me what you know about her ex."

"I can't believe they tried to run you over. That's scary."

"It was. But I'm okay. I've honestly been through worse when I was your age and reporting on various conflicts around the world. My life was always in danger. I just didn't expect that living here.

"But you have to promise me you'll be careful as well," I continued. "Since we've been working together, whoever did it might go after you next. I can't have that. Be extra careful and don't go anywhere alone. Understood?"

He nodded and then pulled back out on the road. "As you suggested, I went to the county clerk's office and found the marriage certificate for the professor and a James Malcolm Baughan. She kept her name. They married and then were divorced two years later when he went to prison for financial fraud."

"Oh, that is unfortunate. Especially after everything that happened with her father."

"Hard to know because it was a decade ago, but she seemed to put distance between them quickly."

"Wait. Alan. That was the name on the letters in the box."

"The box?"

Crud. I hadn't told him that bit. "Right. So the detective found a box in her apartment. It was filled with all sorts of things. We found letters, which were written from prison. He signed the letters *Alan*. But her husband's name was James. That doesn't make sense."

"Unless it's one of those weird nicknames," Ellis said.

He made a good point. People often had strange nicknames. I worried about dragging Ellis into this. Maybe we should have told the detective where we were going today.

"This might be a bad idea," I said.

"What do you mean?" he asked. "We're following a lead. A good one, I think."

"Right. But if he's a felon, he might be dangerous. He's certainly not going to want to answer questions about his ex."

Ellis shrugged. "He might if she divorced him when he went to prison. She didn't stand beside him."

"Right. We know why, though."

"True. Let's just go and we'll see," he said. "Worst case, we can ask around town about him. Or maybe one of his neighbors. We're already halfway there. Besides, look at this."

He handed me a file folder from the back seat.

I opened it and gasped. "It's him."

"Right," he said. "The man who was following you."

"That changes everything. I have to know why. But you are staying in the car. I refuse to put your life in danger."

"I can decide that for myself, Professor. I won't let you speak to him alone."

"Ellis, you are a student at the university; you will not put your life in danger."

"If you were me, would you let anyone get in the way of your story?"

I opened my mouth and shut it. "You have me there."

"I'll find a way to come back alone," he said. "I, too, need to know what this is about. If he's the one who tried to kill you, not that he'll admit it."

"You have a hard head and are way too smart," I said.

He laughed. "It's the truth. There is a reason I want to learn from the best."

"Yes, but not if it gets you killed. Young men your age think they're invincible. There are some very bad people out there. I have a feeling this James Alan, or whatever his name is, might be one of them."

"Then it's best if we talk to him together. That is, if he even opens the door."

"There is that. I say we lead with that we're doing a story on the ex-wife, which is the truth. Then we slide into the question about why he was following me."

But when we arrived at the top of the street where James lived, it had been closed off by police. Gareth was there talking with some of the other officers.

I pointed to a parking space at the corner. "Park there, and let's go see what's going on. Do you have your camera?"

"Yes." Ellis held it up.

"Right. Let's see what the detective has to say. This is way too much of a coincidence." As we walked down, an ambulance arrived.

"Someone's been hurt," he said. "Well, that was a bit obvious."

I smiled. "You're just commenting out loud. I wonder what happened."

When Gareth saw us, he frowned and shook his head. He said something to the other officers and then walked toward us.

"I feel like we're about to get into some trouble," Ellis said nervously.

"You may be right. I'll take the blame. I dragged you here if he asks."

"But . . ."

"Just do what I say."

"What are you two doing here?" Gareth asked sharply. "I distinctly remember telling you to stay home and out of trouble."

"No. What you said was if I left my apartment, I should have an escort. That's why Ellis is here."

Gareth gave Ellis the evil eye, and the poor kid stared pointedly at his high-top sneakers.

"So you found out the gentleman in 1202 was the victim's ex, and you came to interview him."

"Yes," I said. "He's also the man in the picture. The one from the CCTV. And he was also on her dating profile but under a username. I didn't put two and two together until this morning."

He cocked his head. "And how do you know that? About the dating site."

"I was perusing the site myself and found her. It lets you see emojis about dates from all sexes. It's odd, though, that she would have linked interests with the man she divorced, right?"

I couldn't tell him we'd signed in under her account. I prayed he didn't know anything about dating apps. Or at least the one Alice had been using.

"You were already on dating sites? You haven't been here a week," Gareth said.

Ellis made a sound that turned into a cough.

I patted him on the back.

"Uh. I wasn't *looking* looking. Just curious. Every woman I've met says the dating pool in town is quite shallow. I was bored last night, so I looked around."

"You were exhausted last night when I left."

Ellis coughed again.

I sighed. "Why are you giving me the third degree? What does it matter?"

"Well, I ran him through the database and was surprised by how quickly a response came back. When I arrived to question him this morning, I found him unconscious in his snug. Looks like blunt-force trauma to the head. He's breathing, but there is a lot of blood."

Ellis's head snapped up. "Do you think someone tried to kill him?"

"They may succeed yet. It doesn't look good. Now, why exactly did you think it was a good idea to question a known criminal?"

"I wanted to ask why he was following me. I feel like the answer to that question would solve our problems. I also wanted to ask him why he left that threatening note and how he did it."

"Well, he won't be answering any of our questions today, if ever."

"Does he have a navy car?" I pointed to the garage behind the house, which was closed.

Gareth pointed his pen at me. "We'll check."

He walked over to the other officers and said something. They followed him to the garage.

"Do you think it will be in there?" Ellis whispered.

"I kind of hope so. Even if I don't know the why, at least I'll know the who."

"True."

The officers used a pair of bolt cutters to cut the chain holding the door closed. But when it rolled up, I sighed. Inside was a small, very dirty, white pickup.

"Well, that's disappointing," Ellis said.

"Agreed. None of this makes sense. If I could figure out why I'm a target, maybe the answers would fall into place."

"Like you said, you haven't been here long. Who would want you dead?"

"It has to be that we've come too close to the truth, but we haven't realized it yet."

The detective strolled over to us. He'd overheard my last remark. "I keep saying that you've talked with someone and asked them something that hit a nerve," Gareth said.

The EMTs rolled out a gurney with the victim. At least I thought it was him. The dark hair matched, but his face was bloated and covered in blood. What we could see, that is, as they'd put an oxygen mask on him.

Gareth moved over to help.

"Do you think whoever is after you did that?" Ellis asked.

I glanced up at his pale face. "Hey, you okay?"

He nodded. "It all just feels very real."

"I couldn't agree more. And I'm so sorry I dragged you into this."

"I think it was the other way around. I'm the one who wanted to do the story on Dr. Rice. The detective is right. We need to sit down and go through everything we've done step by step. Who we told what and that sort of thing. Someone we talked to knows we are close to the answer and wants you dead."

I shivered. He wasn't wrong. "We're all thinking the same thing."

We waited for Gareth to come back to us.

"I'd hoped the car you've been seeing would have been in there," he said.

"We felt the same way."

"You both understand that you need to stop with your investigation. Ellis, I'd be grateful if you'd turn over any files you might have regarding my case."

The young man stared at me.

"I can't, in good conscious, allow him to do that. We protect our sources at all costs. And he already shared his notes."

Gareth shook his head. "When it involves your safety, I think you'd both be more willing to share. You saw what happened here. Someone dangerous is involved in this. He or she has killed once, and they are doubtful Mr. Baughan will pull through. He may not have long to live. You might be able to help us pinpoint his attempted murderer."

I blew out a breath. "Right."

"I'm trying to find a killer here. You may have something that pulls this all together. At least I could look at what you have to see if it helps our case. Your lives are in danger."

"It's up to Ellis," I said. "I will back you no matter what."

"I really want to help," Ellis said. "If that makes me a bad reporter, so be it. Someone tried to kill you last night. Maybe, if we pool our resources, we can find the killer."

"Okay. We'll head back and pull our notes together."

"I need to finish up here," the detective said. "I'll call when I'm done."

"Two things," I said.

"Tell me," Gareth encouraged.

"Alice's aunt said her ex always thought there were secret accounts. Maybe look to see if he has any copies of the logbooks like I found."

"Right. What's the other thing?" he asked.

I thought for a moment. "The poison. Or books about it. He may have looked it up on the internet. But that's the thing that bothers me. He doesn't seem like the killer, because it would have to be someone who saw her more often, right? And if he was the murderer, then who was after him?"

"You have something there," he said. "Now, please leave us to investigate and be vigilant."

Ellis and I slugged back to the car.

He sat for a moment staring out the window. "I understand if you want to fire me. I'm certain I've disappointed you."

"Not at all. I'll be honest, if the roles were reversed, I'd want to help the investigation as well. If someone had tried to kill you last night, I'd do whatever it took to find the truth."

He let out a breath.

"And it isn't like we're just handing everything over," I said. "He's willing to bring what he has to the table as well. We'll be working together."

"It's scary to think someone was so vicious they tried to kill that man. What if we'd been there?" he asked.

I shivered.

He was right. This was all way too scary.

Chapter Twenty-Three

Ellis parked in front of my building, and then we walked across the street to the pub. We'd just missed the afternoon rush, so we had the place to ourselves. Catrin came out of the kitchen and waved.

"Sit wherever you like," she said. "I'll be back in a minute to take your orders. Do you want a couple of pints?"

"I'd actually like some coffee," I said.

"I'll take the same but cream and sugar," Ellis added.

She nodded.

We sat by the fireplace, which roared with flames. Even though we'd had the heater on in the car, the weather outside was wet and miserable. The fire warmed me quickly.

We'd made a bargain in the car. Over lunch, we would try to forget about the case and give our brains time to process.

"Are you nervous about teaching?" Ellis asked out of the blue.

I laughed. "How long did it take you to come up with a question not related to the case?"

He grinned. "Until just now."

"Of course I'm nervous. I've done public speaking throughout my career. And I've even been on television as parts of round table discussions. This is different. Every class needs to mean something, and I have to get information across that will make the students think. You've taught some undergrad classes; do you have any advice?"

He appeared shocked. "Me?"

I nodded. "Yes. I read through the feedback from the courses you taught, and it was quite positive. You engage well with the students, and they liked that you had a sense of humor."

"Even though I had access to my surveys, I never read them," he said. "The idea of it made me nervous. One of my favorite classes is Dr. Davies' ethics course. It could be a yawn, but he uses a lot of case studies to make it interesting. And he puts the students into situations where they have to find a clever way out and tell the story in an ethical fashion."

That was good to hear, but I wasn't surprised. "His scores were higher than all the other professors." I'd thought it had to be that he looked like he should be on the cover of a magazine, but it turned out he was a great professor as well.

The teaching part of this job really was the scariest for me. "I like the idea of involving the students more in the curriculum," I continued. "I know we said we wouldn't talk about the case, but I wondered if there were any students of Dr. Rice's that might have wanted to truly do her harm. Not just complain, but to commit this sort of crime."

"Once I became Dr. Davies' assistant, I steered clear of her," Ellis replied. "They didn't share an office. But you hear things."

"She didn't have an assistant, right?"

He shook his head. "When I first worked for Dr. Davies, there was a girl who lasted a couple of days. No one could stand to work with her. I think she eventually gave up and dumped most of her admin stuff on Gladys."

"Poor Gladys."

"Agreed. She has a hard time saying no, though I have encouraged her more than once. 'I'm here to help,' she always says. Dr. Rice took advantage of her."

"Do you think Gladys . . ." I couldn't even finish the sentence. We laughed.

"That would be a big no. She might kill someone with kindness or tea cakes."

"She makes a mean tea cake," I joked.

"True."

"Okay, enough about the case. What is your big plan once you have your PhD?"

He blushed. "I'd like to teach eventually, but first, real-world experience. I'd like to work for one of the online papers here in Wales or maybe even in another part of the world. I'm looking at Spain as well."

"Are you bilingual? I didn't know."

"I speak and write Spanish, French, and Welsh."

I laughed.

"What?"

"I know bits and pieces of the first two languages, but I tried to learn Welsh when I lived here before. It just doesn't stick in my brain."

"I always say it's harder than the other two combined. And it takes locals years, so don't give up."

When Catrin came to take our orders, I showed her the picture of Alice's ex-husband. "I know it was a while ago, but is this the man you saw with Alice Rice at the pub?"

She took my phone and stared at it a few seconds. "Could be. I know he's actually been around a few times, but not with her. Came in alone. He was here last week, I think, when you were here that first time."

So he had been following me? But why? It involved Alice in some way, but I might never find out if he didn't survive.

After our meal, Ellis and I headed over to my place.

"Afternoon, Professor, and Ellis," Paul said. It appeared the Welsh cakes had worked their magic. "Have you been off on adventures?"

"We were at the pub stuffing our gobs," Ellis said.

Paul laughed heartily.

We headed upstairs. Just as I unlocked the front door, my phone buzzed.

"It's a text from the detective. He'll be here in half an hour," I said. "Do you want some more coffee, or do you prefer tea? I have both."

"Coffee is good. I need my brain. What should we do?"

"Do you have your notebook?"

He pulled it out of his coat pocket.

"I think we start with a timeline for each of us, beginning from the time of Alice's death to today. Maybe if we come up with more than one coincidence, it will show us something."

"Because there is no such thing as a coincidence; I read that article you wrote: 'Occam's Razor in Journalistic Practices.'"

I laughed. "I'm going to admit it is strange to have someone who has read so many of my trade articles. Most of which I wrote more than a decade ago."

He shrugged. "I keep telling you I'm excited to learn from you firsthand."

"Right. But we wouldn't always share our sources. This is a special case."

"If it helps them or us find a killer, I don't see the harm," he said. "It isn't like the detective hasn't talked to most of the same people. He might share something that makes it click for us. I thought about it in the car. I'm calling it a meeting of the minds. Besides, the only off-the-record conversation I had, you were there."

"With the aunt?"

"Yes."

"Okay. Let's make our timeline before he gets here."

* * *

A half hour later, there was a knock on the door. I answered and found the detective on the other side. He held a paper bag and cup.

"I had to pick up lunch on the way. Sorry I didn't ask if you wanted anything."

"We already ate," I said. "We've been making separate timelines of people we've interviewed. The problem is, at least from my perspective, the only person I thought might actually be a killer was her ex. Now that doesn't seem to be the case."

We put our notebooks together and compared the list. Ellis had talked to twice as many people for his story. He'd even called a few students. I didn't know many of the names, but he had made notes beside them.

"There is one person you both have left off your list, and I know you've spoken to him."

I frowned. "Who?"

"Dr. Davies."

I choked and nearly spat out my coffee. The detective patted my back. "Are you okay?" he asked.

I nodded. "Why would you suspect him?"

"Opportunity," he said. "He lives just down the hall. He saw her daily. And he says they were friends. And yet no one I've talked to has ever seen them together. Well, except for university social functions."

"He tried to help me save her life," I said. "While I worked on her, I glanced up; he was pale and in shock."

"Even murderers sometimes have a conscience."

I rolled my eyes. "You don't have anyone else, so you're blaming him because he was here?"

"Like I said, opportunity. Also, he was her Secret Santa. The tea he gave her had some of the poison in it."

Ellis and I gasped. Then I held up a hand. "Wait."

"Like I said, opportunity."

"Maybe, but if it's loose tea, anyone could have added the poison after the gift exchange. You can say what you want about Dr. Davies, but he is an intelligent and thoughtful man. I can't see him using a weapon that could be traced back to him."

"Killers aren't always careful."

"Okay, but what was his motive? He's known her for years, and then all of the sudden poisons her?"

"I can never look at him the same way," Ellis said sadly.

"Don't listen to the detective, Ellis. He's just trying to close his case. If it was Rhys, how did he bludgeon Alan? Or even know about him? He's with Carolyn and Henry in Cardiff at some convention. He was helping Henry draft his speech."

Gareth's eyes opened wide.

"You didn't know that was where he was, did you? You assumed because he didn't answer his door that he had done some kind of runner. I'm telling you that he isn't your man. He seemed to be the only one who was genuinely sad about Alice.

He felt sorry for her. And he's not stupid enough to poison tea he gave her."

I drummed the table. "It has to be someone close enough to . . ."

Pieces of the puzzle came together in my brain, but everything wasn't quite set.

The detective seemed upset I'd shot down his theory about Rhys and shoved fried fish into his mouth.

"The wheels are turning," Ellis whispered, and then pointed at me.

"It's just right there. Something big is missing, but I feel like we've already seen it. Let's go through the evidence that we know about besides the poison."

The detective pulled out his phone and found the evidence list. Nothing rang a bell for me or Ellis. By that evening, we were all exhausted.

Ellis left, and Gareth moved toward the door.

"Do me a favor and don't arrest Rhys," I said. "I can promise you it wasn't him. He was truly upset that night. And he has no motive—other than she was annoying, which was something we all copped to and believed."

"Promise me you won't put your life in danger," he said. "Do not leave your flat without Ellis or one of your friends. Do you understand?"

"Promise." My head hurt, but it was too late to drink more coffee. I stood by my fire.

"And lock the door when I leave."

I nodded.

Whenever I was stuck on a problem, the best thing I could do was to walk away from it.

I remembered the witchy book in my backpack. When I picked it up, it slipped from my hands and landed on the floor.

Another piece of folded paper stuck out the back. This was the second one I'd found in this same book. It had to mean something.

I carefully opened it. It was a list of accounts that looked much like the ones I'd seen in Alice's private box of things. Accounts to where? And why did she keep them in hiding places?

These were the key to everything. I just didn't understand how.

Chapter Twenty-Four

The next morning, I woke up fully dressed on my bed and was surprised it was daylight. I'd had a terrible time going to sleep. I kept seeing Alan's bludgeoned face every time I closed my eyes. I hadn't allowed myself to synthesize what had happened, and my dreams had been fitful. Someone ran after me, but I could never see their face.

The subconscious was a wondrous thing; I only wished it had given me the answers I needed. I glanced at my sports watch. I had just enough time to shower before Ellis showed up. It was Monday, and classes started in a week. There was a lot to do before then, but my mind was plagued with killers chasing me from every corner.

Davy was at the front desk, and I stopped short. "Is everything okay? I thought you worked nights and weekends."

"Oh, hey, Professor. Our Paul had an appointment this morning. He'll be in soon. Do you need me to relay a message?"

I shook my head. "No. Have a great day."

He waved as I stepped out of the building.

It was a typically overcast day, but the clouds were dark.

"Looks like more snow," I said. And then I glanced at Ellis. His hair was disheveled, and I was fairly certain his sweater was on inside out and backward.

"Are you okay?"

He frowned. "What do you mean?"

I didn't want to call him on his appearance, but something was definitely wrong.

"It just appears you dressed in a hurry," I said.

He glanced at himself in the rearview. "Oh." He tried to smooth down his hair with his hands.

"Also, your sweater, or jumper, as you call them, is inside out." He pulled it out from his body and laughed. Then he took it off and turned it around. "I couldn't sleep last night, and I forgot to set my alarm. I'm sorry."

"Hey, don't worry about it. I had the same problem."

"You don't believe the detective, do you? I mean, Dr. Rhys, of all people. It just can't be him."

"I promise you it isn't. I haven't known him long, but he's no killer. Take him off your list."

"I just worry about the police ruining his life."

I nodded. "Which is why we have to look elsewhere and find the real killer. Maybe these will help." I showed him the piece of paper.

"More account numbers?"

"Yes, and the amounts next to them vary greatly. We've been thinking the numbers were tied to her past, but what if she was involved in some sort of scam with her ex? I mean, maybe that's why he was attacked. I wonder how he's doing."

"I called the hospital and said I was his nephew. He is still in a coma and had surgery this morning to relieve pressure on his brain." Ellis paused. "Did you send those accounts to Detective Jones?"

"Uh, I thought I'd wait until I can figure out what bank they go to."

"How do you plan to do that?"

"Stop being logical, Ellis. I haven't made it that far yet. I need some coffee and hopefully some of Gladys' cakes and pastries. I missed breakfast."

"Me too. Don't forget you have your department meeting with the dean tomorrow. She expects you to send an agenda."

"Ugh. She's always trying to make me do my job."

He laughed.

"Any chance you have an idea of what kind of agenda I should be setting?"

"I do."

"You're a godsend, Ellis. I don't know what I'd do without you."

He laughed. "Evidently, I need you around as well. Otherwise, I'd show up to school with my clothing on backward."

"And inside out."

We laughed again.

I truly was grateful for him. Then something hit me.

"Other than oversleeping, has there been anything wonky going on with you?"

"Wonky?"

"Strange. People trying to talk to you who normally wouldn't. Anything out of place in your car or at home. Weird notes left on your doorstep. That sort of thing. You've been just as involved. I worried you might be holding back or afraid to say something. You can tell me anything. I hope you know that. And I understand lots of people say that, but I will keep your confidence."

He stopped at the roundabout and waited for a car to pass. "Are you asking me if I killed the professor?"

I burst out laughing. "No. No. Though if you did, your secret would be safe with me. I might try to talk you into going to the police, but the decision would be yours. I protect my sources as well."

"For the record, I didn't. My brain doesn't work that way. I wonder sometimes if that is why I'm having so much trouble deducing who is behind her death. But too many people wanted her gone. It's impossible."

"And the other part of my question? Do you feel like anyone might be watching you? Have you seen the navy car I mentioned?"

He shook his head. "I've been keeping an eye out. And nothing has been dropped on my doorstep like you. Which is strange when you think about it."

"Why is that?"

"Well, I've been working the story hard and talking to people, and no one has come after me. But they did go after you. So what have you said that made someone think you were dangerous to them?"

I blinked. "I hadn't thought about it that way."

"If you text me a picture of those accounts, I can ask a friend of mine to help find out where they are."

"Really?"

He made a face.

"What?"

"Well, my friend might not exactly use legal means. She's a hacktivist who owes me more than one favor."

"Just don't tell me any more, okay? If I end up passing the accounts to the detective for him to check out, I want to be able to keep a straight face."

"We should give him everything. Then maybe someone will stop threatening you and killing people."

He made a good point.

At the university, Gladys was setting up a tea tray as we came inside. "There you are," she said. "I made some more of your favorites. I thought we'd try a new rose tea today, and I saw that you love coffee, so we have some of that as well."

"You're spoiling me," I said. "I've never worked in such a lovely environment, and certainly no one was feeding me."

She laughed. "It truly is my pleasure. I enjoy looking after others."

I dumped my bag on my desk and came back to grab some biscuits and coffee. I was starving and loaded my plate.

"The dean called earlier," Gladys said. "When you have some time, she'd like to chat."

"Is she back from Cardiff?"

"No. But she still wanted to talk to you. She heard you had some sort of accident and was worried."

"Accident? Oh." I'd forgotten all about Saturday night.

"Are you okay?"

"Yes. Probably someone texting while driving. They ran up on the curb. But I'm fine."

"Goodness, that must have been scary." Gladys frowned. "We can't lose you. It would break our hearts."

I smiled. "Thank you, Gladys. I'll give her a call so she doesn't worry."

Since my cell didn't work great inside the university, I used the landline. Carolyn picked up on the second ring.

"I just spoke with the detective inspector. Why didn't you tell me someone tried to run you over?" she asked.

"Hello to you too." I laughed.

"Don't joke. I'm worried sick. Henry is finishing up here, and then we are heading back. I think you should move in with us until they find the killer."

I smiled. "It's good to be loved, but I'm fine." I told her about helping Ellis with his story and some of what we'd found out.

"That is frightening. Leave it to you to land in the middle of major drama. Our town is so boring. How did that even happen?"

I laughed. "There is something I wanted to send you. It's probably nothing, but I keep finding account numbers. I'm handing them over to the police later today, but I'm wondering if they have anything to do with the university."

"Is there anything else I can help you with?" she asked.

"No. That's it. Ellis and I are handing everything over later today." I explained about how we'd tried to protect the sources.

"Well, I'm glad you've decided to cooperate. It saves the university getting into the legal side of things. Though I have contacted the legal department to make sure you and Ellis are covered in case anything comes up with the police."

I hadn't thought about the ramifications for the school. "Thank you."

"I need you to promise me something," she said.

"What's that?"

"Don't do anything that puts your life in danger. And please think about moving in with Henry and me. We would love to have you. Oh, there's Rhys and Henry. They've been working on his speech, and it's time for us to head down. Be safe."

"I will."

It had been a long time since anyone had cared about me and my safety. I didn't take her caring lightly. And she was right. Things had gone too far.

I glanced up to find Gladys at the door.

She waved. "I didn't want to disturb you," she said, "but Ellis had to leave to follow a lead. At least that's what he said. He asked if you could find a ride home this afternoon. I told him I'd be more than happy to take you."

"Oh?" I frowned. Ellis was supposed to be taking me on his interviews. "Did he say where he was going?"

"Courthouse archives," she said.

"Okay. Good to know. And I can walk this afternoon. It's really only a few blocks." Some very cold blocks.

"Oh, it's no bother. I'll be heading your way anyway. Don't forget you were meeting Dr. Kelly in her office at ten. She's on the second floor and to the right. Ellis asked that I remind you."

I'd completely forgotten. "Thank you."

I stuffed some of the biscuits in my mouth and chugged my cold coffee. Then I grabbed a notebook and pen and headed upstairs.

I found Becca's office and went inside. No one was in the room, but I peeked in around one of the other doors and found her with her head down. I knocked on the doorframe.

She jumped and stood up. "I would have come down to yours," she said.

"It's fine. I'm trying to refresh my memory so I can remember where everything is."

"Isn't it strange being back, but not as a student?"

"It's surreal for sure."

"How are you?" she asked. "I had so much fun on Saturday. Right up until someone tried to run us over."

"I'm good. I'm glad we all survived." I tried to play it off as no big deal. "Was there something specific you wanted to talk about today?"

"I do. It isn't for this term, but we don't have a media relations class here. I realize most people see it as more a public relations sort of thing, but I think it is important for journalism professionals to see that side of things. The more the students know on how to deal with other media professionals, the better."

"Absolutely. And you're right, that is one thing we aren't covering here."

"The idea came from you the other night. You were talking about some of the top journalism schools in the US, and I went through some of their courses. I'm teaching feature writing and editing courses this term, but I'd like to add the new one for next autumn."

I nodded. "I'll have to run it by the dean, but I love that idea. And good for you going beyond the norm. That's the kind of thinking I like."

She smiled brightly.

We chatted for a few more minutes before I headed back downstairs. I realized I'd forgotten to text Carolyn the picture of the accounts. When I made it down to the office, the desks were empty. I glanced at my watch. It was noon and Gladys was probably at lunch.

I headed into my office and searched through my backpack for the slip of paper I'd found. I needed to give it to the detective.

It wasn't in there.

Had I left it at home?

I dumped the contents of my backpack out on my desk and went through everything again.

Darn. I must have left it on the breakfast bar in the kitchen.

It would have to wait.

I made myself another cup of coffee and sat down to work.

It was around four when Gladys knocked on the door. "I'm finished for the day. I don't mind staying a bit longer if you need to finish what you're working on," she said.

I glanced up at the window and realized it was dark outside. "I didn't realize how late it was. I'm happy to head home. I'm sorry if I made you stay late."

She waved. "Dealing with scheduling the next few days, I could work for the next twenty-four hours straight. But my old bones need a rest."

I smiled. "I'm right there with you." I gathered everything and shut down my computer. "Okay. I think I'm set."

We headed outside. It was chilly, and the wind whipped around us. Glady's green coat flew up at the bottom. She laughed.

Inside the car, she quickly turned on the heat. "Thankfully, it isn't a long drive. I have something to ask you, though," she said as she pulled out of her parking spot.

"Anything," I said.

"Well, I wondered if you've had a home-cooked meal since you arrived. I've had a stew in the slow cooker all day, and I'm making soda bread. I'd love for you to come to ours for tea."

She was so sweet, and I didn't want to be rude.

"Unless you have other plans—a beautiful woman like you probably does. Or if it makes you uncomfortable eating with Paul and me."

After the awkwardness from last week when I'd tried to set boundaries, I felt guilty. "Not at all; it's very kind of you. I'd love to come to dinner."

"Lovely. We'll do tea at seven-ish. Paul will bring you around to ours." Welsh people called all meals tea.

I hoped I could make amends with them and keep those boundaries firmly in place.

But first, I needed to find that paper with the accounts.

Chapter Twenty-Five

After freshening up, I searched for the piece of paper with the account numbers. I couldn't find it anywhere. Had I lost an important piece of evidence? And then I remembered I'd taken a picture of it to send to Ellis's friend. I wondered if he'd had any luck with that.

I stuffed my phone in my pocket and then went downstairs. Rhys was coming down the hall with his overnight bag.

"Hello," he said. "How is everything?" He was quite dashing in his navy peacoat and matching beanie.

"Good. I'm heading over to dinner with Gladys and Paul."

"Ah. You're in for a treat. Gladys is a wonderful cook."

"I'm sure they wouldn't mind if you joined us," I said. "She said there was plenty."

"Maybe another time. I'm exhausted. Creating a speech for Henry that could keep him on topic wasn't easy."

I laughed. "I had no idea you were a speechwriter."

"Years ago, for politicians. Being a journalism professor is a much better job—though politics was my way into my new career as a journalist."

"You don't seem old enough to have done all that."

He laughed heartily. "Good genes, I think, from my mother. But thank you. I'm an old man. And I'm exhausted." He lifted his bags. "I should get unpacked. Enjoy your dinner."

"Thanks."

As he passed, his pine scent filled my nose. The freshness fit him and his personality.

The detective was nuts for thinking Rhys could harm someone.

Downstairs, Paul was speaking to Davy. "I'll only be gone an hour or so."

"Don't worry about it," Davy said. "Have a nice meal," he said to me.

"I hear I'm in for a treat."

"You are. My Gladys is quite the chef," Paul said proudly. I followed him down a long hallway. I hadn't been in this area. There seemed to be some storage and utility spaces. I thought we were going out the back door, but when we reached it, he turned to the right and headed up a steep stairway.

I couldn't imagine him and poor Gladys climbing these steps daily.

When we reached the third set of stairs, I was out of breath, but I still followed. At the landing, Paul pulled out his giant key fob from his belt. When he unlocked the door, we were assailed with the scents of stew and fresh bread.

"I could eat the air," I said.

Paul laughed. "Now, that won't fill you up."

"What's that, luv?" Gladys asked, appearing in the doorway.

Paul kissed her cheek. "The professor says she could eat the air, and I told her it wouldn't be very filling."

They laughed like that was the funniest joke ever.

"Don't forget your phones."

Paul turned to me and held out his hand. He sighed. "Sorry, Professor, rules are no phones during dinner. They'll be in the basket by the door. My wife likes dinner conversation uninterrupted."

I pulled my phone from my pocket and gave it to him. "No problem. My mom was the same way when I was young." But back then it had been handheld video games. I'd been fond of Mario and Animal Crossing.

"Go ahead and have a seat at the table," Gladys said. "I'm almost done. Get her a drink, luv."

The apartment was one big room with a small table and chairs in the corner of the kitchen. Paul and Gladys's home was maybe half the size of mine and not as well outfitted. I felt a bit guilty. I'd never use my fancy kitchen, and Gladys was using every inch of hers.

It was decorated as if a florist shop had exploded. The wallpaper, the furniture, and draperies were covered in bright flowers. It was very Gladys, and very sweet.

"Do you prefer wine or whiskey?" he asked. "We have both."

"I'm quite fond of whiskey," I said.

He smiled. "Good on you. Prefer the stuff myself. As does the missus."

He poured two fingers into a crystal glass and handed it to me. "Lechyd da," he said.

I repeated it as we clinked glasses. I remembered the phrase meant *good health* or something close to it. "I hope I didn't offend you too much with my Welsh. It's on my list of things to learn while I'm here."

"Not at all," he said.

The whiskey was strong but had an earthy taste. "That's excellent," I said.

"One of my favorites," he added.

Gladys set down a large bowl of stew and warm bread with butter in front of me. It was the first homemade meal I'd had in days. The occasional sandwich or bowl of cereal didn't count.

"This looks and smells amazing. Thank you for inviting me."

Gladys smiled. "It's a simple meal, and we are simple people."

I took a bite. "Well, it's simply delicious."

* * *

An hour later I was full and sleepy. I could barely keep my eyes open. We sat on the sofa and talked about rugby and soccer—or football, as they called it here. I'd become a big fan of Wrexham after watching the television show, not that I knew that much about the sport.

But having history in Wales had made me sentimental.

"Well, I should get back to work," Paul said. "Can I walk you back, Professor?"

"Um, sure," I said. "Thank you, Gladys." I couldn't help but yawn. My stomach was so full it hurt.

"It was nothing, Professor. Thank you for coming." She handed me my phone.

Going down the stairs was even more difficult. I felt a bit dizzy and woozy. "That whiskey really did me in," I said. I'd had three glasses, which was absolutely my fault.

"That combined with a belly of my wife's stew would have anyone sideways."

We laughed.

By the time we made it down to the lobby, my legs were jelly. I tripped over the rug and would have done a header if Paul hadn't caught me.

"You okay there?" Davy asked.

"I've learned that three glasses of Paul's whiskey is two too many."

We all laughed.

"I'll help her upstairs," Paul said. "Be back in a minute."

I waved him away. "I'm fine. It's only a few more steps."

"Are you sure?"

"Yes. I'll be fine. Next time, warn me." I laughed.

By the time I made it to my door, I was ready to pass out. My head hurt, as did my stomach. I'd barely made it inside before I ran for the bathroom. As my brain tried to dissolve in my head, my stomach retched over and over again.

Something was very wrong.

The last time this happened, it had been food poisoning.

But would it happen so fast? And why hadn't Paul and Gladys been sick?

Oh. Crud.

I fell from my knees to the floor, barely able to keep my eyes open.

I pulled my phone from my pocket and texted.

Poisoned.

And then I hit send. The problem was, I couldn't see who I'd sent it to. My eyes were blurry, and then everything went black.

Chapter Twenty-Six

I held my hand up against the bright light. I tried to speak, but my mouth wouldn't work. There was a tube down my throat. When I tried to open my eyes, it was impossible.

"She's coming around," a voice said. "Dr. Griffith, can you hear me? Blink your eyes."

I tried to force them open again. I managed a squint.

A pen light blinded me. "I'm Dr. Morgan," she said. "You've been brought into A&E. I need you to follow my penlight with your eyes."

I did my best to do as she asked.

"You're breathing on your own now, so we're going to pull the tube. I need you to take a deep breath and then cough as hard as you can."

Everything was happening so fast, and my brain was still fuzzy. Before I realized what was going on, it felt like the doctor had ripped a lung through my throat. I coughed hard.

"Good job," she said.

Another face leaned in. A woman dabbed spittle from my chin.

"Get her some water," the doctor said. "Sip it slowly. The police need to speak to you, but I can put them off until tomorrow."

"No," I squeaked out. My throat felt like gravel and glass. "Gareth."

She nodded. "I think he is one of the officers. You have quite the crowd in the waiting room. That's a good thing."

"Poison," I said.

She nodded. "We've done some tox screens. They haven't come back yet, but you stopped breathing on the way here. You gave us quite a scare. Your stomach has been emptied, and you may feel some pain over the next few days, but your heart rate is back to normal. All signs are good.

"If you hadn't thrown up, it might have been a different story. Did you take the poison on purpose?" She held up a hand. "I have to ask."

I shook my head. "No. I don't know who did it." Well, I had a good idea.

"Dr. Morgan, you're needed, code blue." An announcement and an alarm went off.

"I'll be back," she said.

"Morgan?"

She stopped and turned back.

"Bookstore?"

She smiled. "I'm Rhian's cousin. I promise you're in good hands. She, along with her friends, are in the waiting room. I have to go."

She left quickly.

Before the door shut, Gareth walked into the room. He frowned. "You look rough," he said. "But better than you did when I found you."

"I texted you?" I'd honestly had no idea whose name I pulled up.

He laughed. "You texted everyone on your phone. I was just first on the scene. Everyone you know in Wales is out in the waiting room. I need you to tell me what happened."

I sipped the water the nurse had given me. She was still checking my vitals.

"Can this wait?" she asked.

"No," he and I said at the same time.

"I had dinner with Paul and Gladys, and then I started feeling really ill. At first, I thought I had too much whiskey. But then . . . that's all I remember."

He spoke into his walkie-talkie on his shoulder. "Bring the Gunthers in," he said.

"Boss." A voice came over the box. "They're gone."

His eyes went wide. "What do you mean gone?"

"Looks like they cleaned up fast. Patrick had gone up to talk to them, and they're gone. They've done a runner."

"Everything is cut off," Gareth said. "They won't get far."

"What do you mean, cut off?" I asked.

"Snowstorm. Closed down the roads."

"Why would they try to kill me? I thought last night was to smooth over when I tried to set boundaries."

"Those are answers I don't have yet. We need to find them. Is there anything else you can tell me? What exactly did they say to you last night?"

I shrugged. "It's kind of a blur. I thought we were having a good time. We talked about football, and I ate everything she put in front of me. I thought I'd made amends. Do you think they tried to kill me because . . ."

"What?"

"The accounts. The missing paper. She was the only one who was in my office."

"Doc, you aren't making sense."

"I found a slip of paper in Alice's book." I realized what I'd said. "Which I was going to turn over to you as soon as possible."

He frowned. "And?"

"I left it in my bag at the university. But when I came back, it was gone. She took it. She knows about the accounts. How can she know? No. No. That isn't possible."

"You okay? You aren't making sense."

It was all a jumble in my brain. "When I showed her the first set, she denied knowing what they were, but what if she did? Maybe, like Alice, she's been poisoning me this whole time. Those darn orange and chocolate biscuits."

"Again, not following."

I drank more of the water. Then I blew out a big breath. "I need Ellis. I need you to bring me Ellis. And get me out of here. I don't like hospitals."

"We haven't been able to find him," he said. "Dr. Montgomery called several times, and I sent one of my men over. Do you know where he might be?"

"She told me he went to the courthouse to do some research." I closed my eyes. "I've been so stupid. Poor Ellis."

"Dr. Griffith, I need you to pause and take me from the beginning."

"We don't have time. What if they have Ellis? Dear me, if they've killed him, I'll never forgive myself."

"You think Gladys and Paul have killed your assistant over some accounts?"

"Yes. He wasn't going to the courthouse; he was headed to a hacker friend. She lied."

"Okay. Again, I need you to start at the beginning."

"I don't have proof. But I believe Alice caught Gladys stealing from the university. I don't know why she didn't take that information straight to you."

"Maybe she was greedy," he said. "If I'm following. She wanted them to cut her in. And like you, they poisoned her."

"Right. We need to find Ellis, now!"

"Give me some ideas where we can check."

"Get me out of here," I said. "I can help find him."

"You nearly died. That isn't happening," he said. "You scared us. You're staying here until they release you. Tell me where you think they might have hidden him."

Wait. He sounded like he cared. "Um, at the university. Gladys knows every room. She's constantly giving maps to people. Maybe she poisoned him and stuck him somewhere."

I prayed he was alive. I didn't think I could live with myself if he wasn't. "The garage behind the apartments. There is a row of them. Gladys had a car. She gave me a ride home, but she dropped me off in the front of the building. Why wouldn't she just park in the garage? That's where you should check first."

My stomach roiled, and the pain was excruciating. I moaned and crossed my arms.

"I'm getting the doctor."

"No. No. I'm fine. Look, you need to find Ellis. Start at the garage. Please. She was strange about that. Said she didn't want me to have to walk across the street. What if he's dead?"

"Marcus, check the garages, directly behind the flats. We're looking for Ellis Hughes. Six three, Black male. He may have been kidnapped."

"Sir. Heading that way."

"Get university security to check the journalism building. Every room. Got it?"

"Yes, boss."

"Go," I said. "Please. I can't do anything, but you might be able to find Ellis. Go." I made a shooing motion with my arms.

"Fine. But let them take care of you," he said.

I nodded.

He left, and Carolyn and Henry ran inside.

"What happened?" she asked. "I overheard one of the nurses say you almost died on the way over."

"I promise to tell you everything, but later. Right now, I need your help. The killers might have Ellis. You have to help find him. The police are checking our flats and the garages. But take everyone and go to the university."

Henry glanced at her.

"What?" I asked.

"Sweetie, there is a terrible storm. All the roads have been shut down. It isn't safe."

I sighed. "You don't understand. I think they kidnapped him."

She frowned. "Who?"

"Gladys and Paul. They poisoned me tonight. And I'm fairly certain they killed Alice."

"Gladys?" The question in their voices was clear.

"Trust me. I know how it sounds. We're three blocks from the university. Please. Please. Go check our building. Look in storage facilities or anywhere she might have hidden him."

They glanced at each other again.

"Take the others with you," I said. "Please. And stay together. I know it's hard to believe, but they are dangerous. Do not go alone. Pair up. Please. It's Ellis. If I could get out of here, I would go myself. We have to find him."

"It's a wee bit o' weather. We can do it," Henry said. "I'll tell the others."

My eyes were watering, but I didn't cry. "Thank you. The police are looking as well, but if the weather's bad and they took off . . . I'm just worried about him."

The nurse came back in and put something in my IV.

"What's that?"

"To help with the stomach cramps," she said. "Doctor ordered them when the detective said you were in severe pain."

"I . . ." Crud. It was making me feel drowsy.

* * *

The next thing I knew, I woke up and the room was dark. I hit the lights over my bed, then glanced up at the clock on the wall. I'd been asleep for a couple of hours. Had they found Ellis?

I fumbled around with the nightstand next to the bed. I had hoped to find my phone, but it wasn't there.

Darn.

"Well, you're looking fit," a voice said from the dark corner.

I swallowed hard.

"Hello, Gladys."

Chapter Twenty-Seven

The woman who'd tried to kill me stayed in the shadows.

"The police are looking for you and Paul," I said. "Where is Ellis? Is he even alive? How could you do that? He's just a sweet boy."

"Who was getting answers about business that was not his. It's your fault, you know. I told Paul you were bright. I could tell the first time I met you. And you're kind. Someone who has been through the things you have, most of the time they turn hard."

"Like Alice. Why did you kill her?"

I had to keep her talking. I thought I could take her if she attacked me, but I was weak. I could barely move my arms.

"She found my retirement fund. That's all it was. I make a pittance compared to the rest of you, and I work twice as hard. So does my Paul. Works himself to the bone. We both do." Her voice had changed, and she sounded so very mean.

"Most people would ask for a raise."

"I have. I wasn't appreciated. I took what I was owed. It's as simple as that. She was always so nosy. Left my book out one day, and she peeked."

"Why didn't she turn you in?"

She grunted. "Greed, Professor. She wanted me to give her half."

"So you killed her."

"Slowly but surely. Found out her favorite tea. Slipped in a bit of nasty. Technically, she poisoned herself."

"She came to my apartment that night. She wanted to tell me something."

"Wasn't about me," she said. "That would have ruined her fun. She liked torturing me, though. Paul heard her that night. He was halfway up the stairs. Heard what she said to you.

"But then it was God's divine timing. She was struck down, and I thought we were in the clear. She'd made copies of my books, and we couldn't find them. I was ready to quit. We'd already decided to move to Spain. We have a nice little bungalow waiting. But we couldn't leave any evidence behind."

I remembered Paul on the phone that next night saying he couldn't find them. He'd been in Alice's apartment searching it.

"Why are you here? I already told the police everything I know."

"Hearsay, though, if you're dead. And they won't find any proof; we've taken care of that. And Ellis . . ."

"You horrible woman. Where is he?"

"Still alive. Barely, though. He didn't puke up my concoction like you did."

She'd poisoned him.

"Okay. So, if you're going to kill me, tell me where he is." I grabbed the IV pole next to me. I might be weak, but I would go down fighting.

"Paul has him well in hand."

"The roads are shut down, and you can't get away."

"We're just poor old Gladys and Paul. We'll say you had too much whiskey at ours, but we have no idea where you got the poison. The police will believe us."

"You keep saying that, but I'm a journalist. And as I said, I told the detective inspector everything."

My stomach cramped, and I doubled over in pain. That's when she made her move. She came at me with a butcher knife.

"Ugh," I grunted. I knocked the IV pole toward her and struck her on her temple. She stumbled back just as a nurse came in and whacked her with the door.

"Oh!" the nurse said as the knife clattered to the floor.

Glady's had already been falling over. And the door took her down.

"Grab the knife," I groaned. "She's trying to kill me."

The nurse did one better; she kicked it away and hit the alarm on the wall. It blared down the corridor so loud it made my head hurt all over again. A stampede came running down the hall.

Gladys was on her knees as they rushed in, the detective leading the charge. He took one look at her, then one at me. She was in cuffs a few seconds later and being read her rights. And then he dragged her out.

She was mumbling, but none of it made sense.

"Run after him," I begged the nurse. "Tell him to find out where Ellis is."

"The young university student? He's in the room across the hall," she said.

"Go check on him. If she came to kill me, she might have gone after him first."

The stampede of doctors and nurses ran across the hall. I dragged my IV pole with me to the doorway.

"Vitals are good," someone said. One of the staff turned around to find me leaning on the doorway. Then she led me back to my bed.

The tears may have fallen a bit. "He's okay? You're certain?"

"He's severely dehydrated and covered in bruises from being stuffed in a car, but he's okay."

Oh. No. Had he been stuffed in her car? The one she'd driven me home in?

I needed answers. I was about to say so when the detective returned.

"Is she okay?" he asked the nurse.

"Shouldn't you be questioning Gladys and her husband at the station?" I asked. "What did they do to poor Ellis?"

He laughed and shook his head. "To answer your first question, they can sit for a bit. They aren't going anywhere."

"Where did you find Ellis?"

"In the trunk of the blue car that has been chasing you all over the place. It was in the garage behind your flat. It was a rental they planned to take to Spain. At least that was what Paul kept saying over and over."

"Is Ellis really okay?"

"The doctors say he will make a full recovery."

I leaned back on the bed. A tear slipped down my cheek, and I took a deep, shuddering breath.

He handed me a tissue.

I sniffed. "I'm not crying," I said.

"Of course you aren't. It's probably a side effect of the poison."

"Yes. Gladys told me why. Those were her illegal accounts. She stole from the university. And she killed Alice."

"I know. And they tried to kill her ex-husband, who Alice had told about the accounts. I found that out from Paul."

"How did you discover the rest?"

He pointed to the corner of the room and then to another. There were cameras. I hadn't noticed them.

"Emergency keeps a video recording of everything that happens. I was already running down here to keep her from stabbing you. We didn't catch the knife until she moved. You did a good job of getting her to talk. You would have been a good detective."

I shook my head. "It's the job of the journalist to look at a story from all angles. I needed the last point of view. Thank goodness Ellis is okay."

"The suspects are in custody, but I'm putting a guard outside your door."

"And Ellis's."

"Right. You know he's just across the hall."

"Can't be too careful. I really like working with him." I cleared my throat. "It's hard to find a great assistant."

"Right."

"Don't you have more questions for me?" I winced when the stomach cramps returned.

"Yes. But first you need to heal up. We've got time." He turned to leave.

"Gareth?"

He stopped at the door and glanced back at me.

"Thanks," I said. "For everything. Mostly for saving my life. And for finding me so fast."

"Thank you for actually catching the killer. You did, you know. That IV pole was brilliant."

I laughed and it hurt.

"I'll talk to you later." He waved and was out the door.

I settled back against the bed.

We'd caught a murdering duo, but they had nearly killed my assistant.

I wondered if I'd still have a job tomorrow.

Chapter Twenty-Eight

Two days later, Ellis and I were in Carolyn and Henry's kitchen. She'd insisted we both stay with them. We'd been fed and cared for, and Carolyn hovered like a mother hen.

We all sat around their breakfast bar, or what they called a bench. "I think it's too soon for you to go home," she said. "You both need time to heal."

I shook my head. "I'm fine," I said. "I have been. And I have to get back to work. Classes begin in a few days."

"We can find someone to cover the first few days."

"Carolyn, I love you. I'm grateful that you've taken care of me and Ellis. And that you didn't fire me."

"Fire you? Why would I do that?"

Ellis and I glanced at each other.

"Uh. No," she said. "You two uncovered a murderer working in our university. She killed Alice. Yes, you both could have died, but you're fine now. And Ellis's story has gone all over Wales."

"He's famous," Henry added.

Ellis snorted and ducked his head.

"It's time to let our little chicks fly from the nest," Henry said. Then he hugged his wife.

"I just . . . I asked you to take a job, and you nearly died." Carolyn sniffed. "I don't know if I'll ever be able to forgive myself."

I stood up and wrapped my arms around her. She put her head on my shoulder.

"I'm fine. I've been through worse. Remember Kandahar?"

"No, because you would never tell me what actually happened, and the state department wouldn't allow it."

I'd forgotten about that part.

"Well, I've been through worse. Now, Ellis . . ."

He waved a hand. "I'm going to miss the food, I have to admit. This is the best I've eaten in years."

"Oh, Ellis," Carolyn said. "Why didn't you tell me that your mother died last year? I had no idea you were all alone."

He shrugged. "I'm a professional," he said. "You don't bring your private life to work. It's one of Dr. Griffith's rules of journalism. Objectivity at all times. People look at you differently when they find out you're an orphan."

"He's not wrong," I said.

The doorbell rang.

"I wonder who that is?" Henry went off to answer the door.

When he returned, Gareth was with him. I'd spent a good deal of time the last few days with the detective inspector. We'd handed over all the evidence we had to help the police make their case. It helped that there was video of Gladys trying to kill me. And the poison she'd used on Alice and me had been found in her home.

But what helped the most was Paul. He hadn't been on board with his wife's plan for murder and told them everything for a lesser sentence. They were both going to prison for a long time.

"Hi," I said.

Gareth nodded. "I wanted to let you know that we found out it was Gladys driving the car that tried to kill you. She tried to blame Paul, but he was working that night. And the day you went to the newspaper, she followed you. I thought you'd both like to know that we have a solid case against them."

He could have texted, but I'd learned he was kind. More than once he'd stopped by just to see how I was doing.

"See," I said to Carolyn. "I can go home."

"I can't believe you want to live there," she said. "Someone tried to kill you. We need to find you a new place."

I sighed. "No. Basically, all I did was puke in my bathroom. I love my flat. It's beautiful and my stuff is there. Plus, you assured me we were getting a new doorman, or whatever you call them here. I'll be okay. I want to go home. And I'm ready to head back to work."

"Fine. But you have to text me every night before bed and tell me you're doing well."

Everyone laughed. "Deal," I said.

"I'll give you and Ellis a ride," Gareth said.

Ellis's eyes went wide. "I can't show up in a police car. My friends will think I'm a grass."

"I'll take him home," Henry said. "When he's finished his breakfast."

"Thanks, Professor." They fist bumped.

I gathered up the few things I had, but Gareth took my suitcase when I met him at the door.

"I have it," he said.

Outside, the sun was up, and it was at least fifty. That was unusual for this time of year.

"I appreciate the ride home," I said.

"You aren't worried about being a grass?" he asked. Then he laughed.

"No. I'm most grateful for the police at the moment. I don't mind riding with you."

He opened the car door and helped me inside.

"There's something else I wanted to ask you." He pulled out on the road.

"Is it about the case? I'm happy to help."

"No. It's more personal."

More personal?

"A date. Maybe dinner. Or lunch, if that makes you more comfortable," he said nervously.

"Uh. I . . ."

"It's okay to say no. I won't be offended."

"No, it's just a surprise. I think that would be nice," I said.

"Nice." He smiled. "Exactly."

He wanted to take me on a date.

When is the last time that happened?

I didn't want to think about it.

"Okay," I said. "Great. Just let me know when. Though I'm going to be very busy catching up with work for the next few days with classes starting. Maybe on the weekend, though." Did I sound desperate?

"That works for me," he said. "I'm off on Sunday. Maybe lunch?"

"Yes."

The rest of the trip, which took only a few minutes, we were silent. I think we were both nervous.

When we arrived at the apartment, he parked. "I'll take this up for you." He smiled.

"I can . . . okay, thanks."

But when we opened the door to the foyer, Laura and Becca were waiting for me.

"Finally," Becca said. "We've been so worried."

"Not *worried* worried," Laura said. "Carolyn kept us updated. But we're so glad you're home."

"Oh, hi, Detective," Becca said.

"He gave me a ride home," I said.

"That's sweet," Laura said.

He cleared his throat. "I'll just take this upstairs for you."

My new friends followed us up. I used the key to open the door. He set the bag inside, and then his walkie-talkie squawked.

"I need to go. See you, uh, soon," he said, and nearly ran away.

Laura and Becca followed me in.

"Shouldn't you two be at work?"

"Carolyn texted and wanted you to have a welcome party, which we were going to do anyway," Becca said.

"What's going on with you and the detective?" Laura asked. "I noticed the way he watched you when you were out at the hospital."

"He was there?"

"She doesn't know," Becca said.

"He carried you out of here and to the ambulance, which was just pulling up. Then he rode in it with you."

"And then at the hospital, he kept stopping by to check on you while you were asleep."

"I think he's sweet on you," Laura said.

"Right. So, I need to know what I'm facing when I go back to the office. What are the rumors?"

Laura shrugged. "Not really rumors. More truth. That you and Ellis are heroes and helped capture a couple on a murder spree."

"It wasn't really a spree," I said.

"Ellis's article was thoughtful and inciteful," Becca said. "We all knew he was a great writer, but you really brought it out in him."

"He's a talented kid," I said. But they weren't wrong. "By the way, thank you. I'm grateful that I didn't have to walk in here alone. I'm fine, but I wasn't sure."

"Hey, even if Carolyn hadn't called, we would have been waiting," Laura said. "We adore you."

They reached their arms around me and hugged me. There was something about it that made me laugh.

Ellis and I were the same in that we were orphans, but we'd found our people here.

"Okay, you two. Thanks. You know this is inappropriate. I'm your boss."

"And our friend. You're stuck with us."

That wasn't such a bad thing.

And I had a date.

Life in Dillynaidd was looking up. Well, as long as people weren't trying to kill me.

Acknowledgements

Tara Gavin, I'm so grateful for your continued support. I hope you know how amazing it is to have an editor who believes in me the way you do. And a big shout out to the whole Crooked Lane team. All of you help to make every book the best it can be, and please know your efforts are appreciated.

Jill Marsal, thank you for sticking with me through the highs and the lows. Having you in my corner is one of the best things that ever happened to me.

To the readers, thank you for the kind words and support through the years. I often say I write books I want to read, and I do. But you matter to me so much more than you will ever understand. Thank you.